THE WHISPER

AARON STARMER

SQUARE
FISH

FARRAR STRAUS GIROUX
NEW YORK

SQUARE
FISH

An Imprint of Macmillan
175 Fifth Avenue
New York, NY 10010
mackids.com

Square Fish and the Square Fish logo are trademarks of Macmillan and are used by
Farrar Straus Giroux Books for Young Readers under license from Macmillan.

Our books may be purchased in bulk for promotional, educational, or
business use. Please contact your local bookseller or the Macmillan Corporate
and Premium Sales Department at (800) 221-7945 ext. 5442 or by e-mail
at MacmillanSpecialMarkets@macmillan.com.

Library of Congress Cataloging-in-Publication Data

Starmer, Aaron, 1976–
    The whisper / Aaron Starmer.
      pages cm. — (The Riverman trilogy ; 2)
      Summary: Twelve-year-old Alistair continues his quest to find his
missing friend, Fiona, in Aquavania, a world where wishes can nearly come
true, but he learns that the Whisper, once a boy named Charlie from his
own world, has plans for Alistair and has used Fiona to try to get to him.
      ISBN 978-1-250-07336-5 (paperback)   ISBN 978-0-374-36312-3 (ebook)
      [1. Friendship—Fiction. 2. Fantasy.] I. Title.

PZ7.S7972Whi 2015
[Fic]—dc23
                                                          2014013168

Originally published in the United States by Farrar Straus
Giroux Books for Young Readers
First Square Fish Edition: 2016
Book designed by Elizabeth H. Clark
Square Fish logo designed by Filomena Tuosto

1 3 5 7 9 10 8 6 4 2

AR: 11.0 / LEXILE: 740L

For Toril & Tim

November 19, 1989

---•◆•---

A whisper is a monster with many mouths. It invites, it infests, it assures: I am not for all ears, I am just for you. There are whispers in the water, as strange as that may seem. But it's only strange to the ones who don't hear them. The ones who do hear them have a choice. They can ignore or they can follow.

On a rainy November night, Alistair Cleary chose to follow. The whispers came out of radiators. "We've waited so long for you," they said.

He followed them down to the basement of Fiona Loomis's house, where a boiler, tall and round, disappeared, revealing a cylinder of water. The water was unbroken, immune to gravity, suspended in the air.

Alistair reached out and touched it. His body tingled and then crossed over. What was once a basement became an entire world, a place smudged sick and gray. His eyes burned. Tornadoes of ash swirled around him, while in front of him a colorful river raged. With an arm over his face, he rushed toward the sound of the current.

This is how Alistair's tale began.

BUT FIRST, ANOTHER TALE

———— ◆ ————

IN A YEAR BEFORE YEARS

THIS TALE BEGINS WITH A GIRL AND A CREEK.

The girl's name was Una and she lived with a tribe called the Hotiki at the foot of some mountains that were perpetually clad in snow. The Hotiki could have passed for hunter-gatherers, but they were scavengers more than anything. They ate whatever they could dig up, or pull down, or find along the banks of a creek that trickled, cold and clear, by the caves they called home.

Una was an inquisitive girl who asked questions like *Where do the stars come from?* and *What happens to us when we die?* Her elders gave her answers, but none that satisfied. Answers led to more questions until the asking felt like throwing tiny stones into a bottomless pit.

Sometimes at night when her tribe was sleeping, Una would sneak off, hide in a jumble of boulders, and dream of what it would be like to run away, to live alone by her wits. She was not fully grown, but she was strong and knew how to make fire and how to spear fish. There was only one problem. Escape was impossible.

You are Hotiki. Hotiki is you. When you bleed, Hotiki bleeds. If Hotiki dies, you die.

That's what the elders always said, and it meant that no one lived alone in this world. To leave your tribe meant ceasing to exist. There was no reason to question that belief either. Only one person in Una's memory had ever left the Hotiki, a woman named Jaroon who had set off into the mountains after the birth of her first baby. No one ever saw her again.

The jumble of boulders was not far from the creek, and one of the reasons Una hid there was that when the moonlight cast shadows on the stone, she could imagine that the shadows were a tribe that she lorded over. She would wave her arms and the shadows would move. They were at her bidding.

Among the Hotiki, the only person at her bidding was her younger brother, Banar, and his loyalty was waning. Banar was a trickster and a master of animal calls, and while he still adored his sister, he had taken to taunting her. One night, when Una was conducting the shadows on the boulders, Banar climbed a nearby tree and pretended to be a raven. "Kaw, kaw, kaw," he squawked.

She ignored it.

"Ugly, ugly, ugly," her rascal of a brother said, though he croaked it like a bullfrog.

Una was particularly sensitive to such taunts, because she had eyes that bulged, a ghastly scar that ran from her left eye to her mouth, and arms so long that they hung down to her knees. So she scrambled up the boulders, spotted her brother lounging on a branch near the top of the tree, and hissed, "Get down, Banar."

He laughed in response and hooted, "Stupid, stupid, stupid."

Una's fury would not abate. This was her only time to be alone, and her brother was spoiling it. She slid down the boulders and crept over to the base of the tree.

"Get down, Banar," she growled as she jabbed at the bark with the heel of her hand.

"Stinky, stinky, stinky."

The earth was soft near the roots, and Una scooped up a handful of muck and pebbles. "Down. Now," she commanded.

Banar twisted up his face and stuck out his tongue, and Una flicked her wrist. Her aim had never been so perfect. The mud struck Banar square in the nose with a satisfying *splat*.

Una couldn't help but laugh. "I win," she cheered.

Banar harrumphed and reached to wipe his face. As he did, he lost his grip on the tree. A foot flew out, an arm pinwheeled in the open air, and Banar fell.

He landed in the shallow creek, his neck striking a rock. There was a snap and a crunch. Banar didn't even scream. Una rushed to help him, flailing her way through the knee-high water, but it was too late. He was dead, his body twisted and broken.

Una scooped him up in her arms and carried him back to the caves, where she collapsed. "What happened?" her mother asked when she found Una's body splayed across the ground, her wet arms draped across her dead brother.

"I do not know," Una whimpered. "I woke to a yell. I found Banar in the creek. There was nothing I could do. Nothing."

Una's mother stood motionless, but her father howled, yanked Una away, and shook his son's body, trying to rouse life. "Chaos spirits," he moaned. "Why do they always take the best ones? Cruel, cruel."

"Yes," Una whispered. "The best ones . . . chaos spirits. So cruel."

Una had never lied before. Among the Hotiki, truth was as essential as food, and no one ever doubted the words they shared. And yet Una couldn't bear to tell them the truth, that she had essentially killed her brother, a boy so attuned to the natural world, a child who many predicted would grow up to lead the tribe.

The next night they buried Banar in a deep grave, beneath a pile of wildflowers and animal pelts, which was their custom. They sang songs and spoke remembrances until they were too tired to carry on. As they all fell asleep next to a bonfire, Una slipped away and sought out the solitude of the boulders once again. It was here that she made a decision. Just like Jaroon before her, she would leave. The other options—to tell the truth or to keep lying—weren't options as far as she was concerned. Both brought too much shame.

So she followed the path of the creek upstream. Before that night, the farthest Una had traveled was a one-day journey from her home. She may have only been twelve winters old, but as far as she knew, no one in the Hotiki had ever traveled farther. There was never any reason. Food was plentiful near the caves. Life was livable. Una assumed if she were to travel any farther, she'd either reach the end of the world or she'd simply disappear.

For three sunsets she followed the creek, eating berries and taking shelter under rock outcroppings. Each stretch of the forest was barely different from the last. Yet on the fourth morning, there was a change. The creek tumbled over a small waterfall and into a deep round pool. Una knelt down next to the pool to take a sip when she noticed something glowing at the bottom. It glowed not like the stars or the sun, but like an animal that had strands of light covering its body instead of hair. The sight was intoxicating and it compelled Una to dive into the water so that she might examine things closer. Down she swam, her eyes fixed on the strange beacon, and when she was close enough to touch it, she reached out a hand.

Tingling spread through her body, and Una closed her eyes. Something tugged at her arm and sucked her deeper into the pool, and when she tried to open her eyes it was impossible. The water was pressing too hard against her face. The force pulling her was too strong and it surely meant to drown her. It wasn't ever going to let her go.

Until, of course, it did, and Una sprang up to the surface.

Her eyelids drew back, and she found that there was now water all around her, stretching to every horizon. A brilliant sun and a blue sky were above, but nothing else. No waterfall. No creek. No forest. It was as if she had been pulled through the bottom of the pool and ended up at the top of a place where only water existed.

She swam and she wondered, *Is this the edge of the world? Is this the last thing I will ever see? I wish I could at least see the stars one more time before I die.*

As soon as she had that last thought, waves leapt around her and slapped against the sky. What was blue became black, and stars sizzled into existence. The sky was now a night sky, shimmering and deep. Her wish had been granted.

I wish I could see Banar once more, Una thought.

From the water emerged hands, arms, shoulders, and a head, wet hair clinging to a face like dark algae on a rock. Una pushed the hair away and looked into the pair of amber eyes.

"Banar?"

"Yes."

"You've come back."

"You've created me."

Banar shivered in the water, his breaths rattling and short.

I wish we were in a warm cave, Una thought.

Another wish made and another wish granted. A mound of rocks emerged from the water and melded together until there was a hollowed-out shelter surrounding Una and Banar.

Una was a quick learner. She realized almost immediately that this was not the edge of the world. It was a place where her wishes could come true. So next she wished for fire. Flames leapt up from a pit in the ground. Meat? At the snap of her fingers.

"I'll bring you back to the Hotiki," Una said.

"You can't," Banar explained. "I live here. I can't live any-where else."

"Why not?" Una asked. "Where are we?"

"I don't know."

I wish I could go back to the Hotiki and take Banar with me.

Tingle. Pop. Gone.

Just like that, Una was transported back to the pool be-neath the waterfall. But she was alone. No Banar. So she swam down and once again touched the glow. Her body tin-gled, something tugged. She emerged in the cave next to the fire and Banar, who was still eating the meat that Una had wished into existence.

"There's no way I can take you home with me?" she asked.

"None," Banar replied. "*This* is my home."

"Will you wait here for me?" she asked.

"That's all I will do."

Una believed him and she wished herself back to the wa-terfall, where she decided to return to the Hotiki and tell them about what she had discovered. She had killed Banar but she had resurrected him as well. All could be forgiven.

However, during the journey back she began to question her plan. Did the Hotiki really need to know about this place? Yes, they all loved Banar, but the sad fact was that they loved him much more than they loved her. If she shared the place with them, would their wishes come true as well? Would those wishes make Una even less significant than she already was?

Selfishness, reassuring and warm, settled into her body, and when she arrived back at the caves, her parents embraced her. *They would have embraced Banar twice as tightly,* she told herself. Then she lied for a second time.

"I chased the chaos spirits into the forest," she said. "They captured me for seven sunsets. They told me that if I don't visit them again, then they will take us all."

As before, the tribe had no reason to doubt her, and they encouraged Una to do as the chaos spirits commanded. Not long after that, Una set off and followed the creek upstream for three sunsets until she reached the waterfall. She dove into the water and touched the glow. It transported her back to the world of Banar, to the world of fulfilled wishes. Una started to build.

She created landscapes of fields and forests, of valleys lined with caves. She created plants and creatures as wondrous as her imagination would allow. She spent many days summoning a world of her own, and the only person she shared it with was Banar. And when she was happy with her creations, when she felt that Banar had a suitable place in which to live, she wished herself to the waterfall again.

Three sunsets later, she was back at the caves, apologizing for being gone for so long, but the Hotiki didn't understand. "You have only been gone for six sunsets," her mother explained.

This was more than a surprise to Una. It was a revelation. It meant that no matter how long she spent in the other world, she would return to the waterfall at the exact moment after she had touched the glow.

Over the next ninety sunsets that she lived with the Hotiki, she spent ten times as many in the other world, a place she dubbed Mahaloo. In Mahaloo, her body didn't age and she had absolute power, so it was a preferable life in every way but one. Banar wasn't really Banar.

She began noticing it almost immediately, but she was good at denying it. *Death has changed him,* she thought. *He'll act like himself soon enough.*

Soon enough never came. Banar looked exactly like Banar. He sounded like him, could do all the animal calls and could taunt Una endlessly. And yet, he was different. He was an impression of Banar, not the real thing.

Eventually, Una lost count of the sunsets in Mahaloo, and she accepted that he would never act like her true brother. So she decided to try again. She brought forth another Banar. And then another. She resurrected him again, and again, and again, until she had a tribe that consisted of herself and 142,858 Banars. No matter how many times she tried, none of them were like the real Banar.

While Una didn't age in Mahaloo, all of her creations did, including the many Banars. The Banars started out exactly the same, but even after a short while, their personalities became distinct. They took on the traits of animals. They moved like animals, had eyes like animals. Their voices growled, or whinnied, or cooed. There was Banar the Wolf. Banar the

Snake. Banar the Beetle. They acted as faithful servants to Una, and she loved them all, for they were her creations. She was also ashamed of them, though, for they were living reminders of her failures.

I wish to give these Banars everlasting life. But I want to let them start over, to give them somewhere else to live, someone else to love.

All at once, 142,857 Banars disappeared, never to be seen again. One Banar remained, the first Banar she had created. The original impression.

Una started over too. She created a new tribe that consisted of people with names like Vinda and Hoo and Meck. She brought forth fifty-seven companions—every one of them a great hunter, cook, or magician—and she lorded over the new tribe. Life was pleasant, and Una had no reason to return to the Hotiki.

Time rumbled by in Mahaloo. There were births and deaths. Meck passed on, so did Hoo, then Vinda. But with two generations of descendants, the tribe had grown much larger. Banar still looked the same as the day she had given him everlasting life, and he still had pluck and vigor. Una, however, had grown weary. Sure, she had the body of a girl, but her mind was restless. She knew she couldn't go back to the Hotiki, because she wasn't sure she would even recognize that world anymore. And yet, she was tiring of the world she had created. It held no surprises, and though it could grant her so much, it could never take away her shame.

One night, she was alone in her cave and she whispered

into the darkness. "I wish I knew the point of this. I need to know why someone so guilty and sad has been given so much power."

An answer didn't arrive, but Banar did. He showed up in her cave not long after that. "Una," he said, his body dripping wet, "are you all right? Can I help you?"

He *could* help her. She realized that now. He could be whatever she needed him to be. "You love me, don't you, Banar?" she asked.

"More than anything."

"So if I asked you to do something for me, if I commanded you to do something, you would do it, right? No matter what it was?"

"You created me," he said. "You gave me everlasting life. I am here to serve you. Always."

Una placed a hand on Banar's shoulder and felt the dampness on his skin. "I don't need always anymore. I need you to end it."

Then Una lay down in her bed, and Banar, who was kind and sweet and loyal, but who could never be her real brother, shed a few tears. Because whenever Una asked him to do something, he was obliged to do it. Tucked behind his ear was a hollow bamboo reed. He pinched the reed between his fingers, and as he brought it to his mouth, he said, "I am sorry for not being what you wanted. I am sorry for doing all that you have asked."

Those would be the last words that Una would hear. The reed entered her ear and there was a slurping sound, like a mouth to cupped hands full of broth. Una tried to respond to Banar, to tell him it was okay, to say that she loved him for what he was, but no words came. She couldn't move a muscle. The only parts of her body that still worked were her eyes and her brain, and she watched helplessly as her creations left her.

All the color in Mahaloo began to drain away as liquid. The blue of the sky, the yellow of the fields, the green of the leaves. The liquid poured over the ground and merged into a river that sparkled and swirled with every shade of a prism. When all of Mahaloo's color had slipped into the river, the only things that remained were piles of ashes in the shapes of trees, rocks, animals, even in the shapes of the children and grandchildren of Vinda, Hoo, and Meck.

Am I just a pile of ash too? Una wondered.

An answer entered her head. She couldn't say where it originated. She could only say it was clear and true.

No. I am the water.

MUCH LATER

CHAPTER 1

WATER, LUMINOUS AND GAUDY, SLAPPED AGAINST LAND, AND
the boy named Alistair Cleary lay on the edge of the liquid
and the dirt where a river had coughed him out. He ached—
head and body. An oaky film of ash coated the roof of his
mouth. The sun pummeled his bare skin.

Alistair was twelve years old, a slight, bony kid with a
round nose and a birthmark on his chin and a curiosity that
sometimes lapsed into foolishness. Groaning, he stood, and
water licked his calves. He rolled his head, and his neck crack-
led like a campfire. Behind him, a river churned with color—it
was sherbet and gumballs, sunlight on an oil slick, and it cut
across a lifeless landscape of black and gray. Yet in front of
him it met an abrupt end. Weird.

There was no lake or ocean for the water to empty into,
but the river was disappearing, merging into the land like wet
paint becoming dry paint. It was transforming into a wide

field where waves of yellow grass billowed and flattened in conversation with the wind. Someone had even flipped a switch on the sky. Behind him, it was putrid and smoky. In front of him, it was bright, tinged with a healthy green. Water becoming earth, a sharp border between death and life—Alistair had never seen anything like it.

What is this place?

It was part of Aquavania, he knew at least that much. In fact, he knew more than he cared to know. He knew that he had touched some kind of liquid portal in his friend's basement and he had ended up in a windstorm of ash. He knew that to escape the storm, he had jumped into a brightly colored river and the river had carried him to this place. He knew there was no clear path home from here.

Send me home. Bring me home. There's no place like . . .

He wished over and over again to be transported back to his friend's basement. That's how it worked in Aquavania. At least that's how he *thought* it worked. You wished and your wish was granted. But it wasn't working, and the more he wished, the more he began to wonder if that was a blessing, if home was actually the best place for him to be at the moment. Because he also knew that back home they might call him something terrible.

Killer.

He started to cry. He took two steps into the field, but that was all his body could manage. He collapsed to his knees and surrendered to the tears. The guilt, the terror—they were invading his body, pirates looting his blood and oxygen. His hands were sore, bruised by the recoil of a gun, and he brought them to his face, drove their heels into the bony upper rims of his eye sockets.

This isn't real. I didn't do those things. I didn't shoot Kyle. Fiona isn't gone. Aquavania doesn't exist. I've been dreaming since that snowy night on the road two weeks ago, when I last saw Fiona. Two weeks of dreaming. Two weeks of fiction.

He slapped himself in the face. Hard. That's what people do in dreams to rouse reality. But he didn't wake up, because this was his reality now.

In the distance, movement. A band of men cut through the waves of grass. As they got closer, Alistair could make out their numbers. Six, walking shoulder to shoulder, spears held tight to the chests of the inner four, leather slings dangling from the hands of the outer two. Straggly-looking guys. They appeared to wear animal fur, but it was darker than any fur Alistair was aware of and it was flecked with sparkling white dots. Their hair was tied in long ponytails, and their skin was covered in streaks of mud and clay. War paint? They stopped about twenty yards from where the river ended, but they didn't poise their weapons. Water dripped off of Alistair's body. He was smart enough to stay quiet and still.

They're here to punish me for what I've done.

The tallest of the men took one step forward and leaned on his spear as if it were a staff. His bright blue eyes were ambiguous beacons. They were alive with curiosity. Or was it rage?

"Stand," the tall man said.

Alistair was in no position to object. He did as ordered.

"You swim?" the tall man asked.

Alistair was astounded that such an odd-looking person would speak English, or what seemed like English. Alistair could understand it, in any case.

"I . . . can swim," Alistair replied cautiously.

The tall man nodded. The other five remained stoic.

"This is your quest?" he asked. "Or you come to take our land?"

"I . . . I . . . am . . . not taking anything," Alistair stuttered. "I'm lost. I'm looking for someone. A girl."

The tall man nodded again and said, "She is here." Then he pounded his spear on the ground twice.

One of the others, a wrinkly and oafish character with scars on his cheeks, stepped forward and took a deep breath. His throat ballooned, all supple and bullfrogish. It was beyond strange. It was impossible.

"I don't know what—" Alistair started to say, but he shut his mouth as soon as the frog-throated man opened his. Because what filled that throat wasn't air. It was dragonflies.

Elegant insects, with wings veined in neon, streamed out from the man's gullet and toward Alistair's face. He struggled with two conflicting instincts. Swat? Or swoon? He couldn't choose either, though. Because once the dragonflies had swarmed around his head, his free will was gone.

Alistair was their captive.

*   *   *

To lose control of your body seems a horrible fate, but to Alistair it felt like a relief. His anxiety wafted away, and whatever fear he had of the men was replaced by a deep reverence. He stepped forward, marched, in fact—one, two, three—right into the band of strangers. They clustered around him, their weapons held casually but confidently. They showed no signs of fear, but they kept their distance as they ushered him in the direction of the high-hanging sun.

All logic told Alistair he should try to escape, but his brain was not beholden to logic. He walked with the men. He didn't question them. He didn't fight. The dragonflies, which orbited his head, had rendered him a lamb.

"We will not harm you, swimmer," the tall man said with a grave but respectful tone.

Perhaps it was the influence of the dragonflies, but Alistair believed this. Or perhaps it was something else that inspired his trust. Alistair wanted—or more accurately, he *needed*—to believe the other thing the man had said.

She is here.

They hiked at a steady pace, the sun wicking the moisture from Alistair's damp clothes. The field went on for at least a mile. No change. The yellow grass sashayed back and forth and tickled Alistair's bare arms. He was wearing jeans and a T-shirt and white socks with red stripes, his standard uniform from home. He wore no shoes, because he came here with no shoes. He was beginning to regret the fact. Luckily the earth was soft and free of stabby things.

Finally, a patch of trees appeared in the distance, the first sign that this world was not all pastures and tribesmen, and right before the trees, a perfectly round rock came into view. The rock was about twice Alistair's height and it rested in the field like a marble dropped from the heavens. The men approached the rock cautiously, keeping a buffer around it as they circled, but the dragonflies led Alistair straight to it.

There were images on the rock's surface. Bears, bulls, lions, and horses. Cave paintings—Alistair had seen similar ones in books. Only these didn't seem ancient. They looked fresh.

"We honor you and bid that you release the night," the tall man said. "Then we will feast."

A feast where I will see her? Alistair wanted to ask, but it was as if the dragonflies were speaking for him. "Yes, sir," he whispered instead.

The tall man pointed with his spear at the rock. The others followed suit, pointing if not with their spears, then with their fingers. Alistair waited for more instructions, but none arrived. So the dragonflies took the reins, guided him ever closer to the rock. The men let out deep, satisfied grunts. Alistair leaned in and examined the animal paintings.

They were shimmering. They were trembling. It was more than a symptom of the sunlight; it was as if tiny creatures lived in the pigment and were wiggling their way to the surface. Alistair looked back at his companions and saw that their weapons were poised. A bad omen. And yet it was irresistible. The paintings begged to be touched, like feathery scarves hanging in a costume store, like a freshly shaved head. Alistair reached out and placed his fingers on the rock and, as if startled from their sleep, the images jumped to attention and scampered from his hand.

Running, leaping, galloping, the silhouetted creatures circled the surface of the stone. They were more than paintings. These things were suddenly alive, and Alistair stood there transfixed. A lion tackled a horse and tore into its throat as the other horses scattered, only to be confronted by the bears. The bears stood on their hind legs, defending their corner of the stone with drawn claws and teeth. The bulls, swept up in the commotion, scuffed their hooves and prepared to charge, and when their charge began, there was no stopping it.

Alistair felt them before he saw them and tumbled to his back as the bulls leapt off the stone and emerged in the field, three-dimensional and fully grown. They weren't made of flesh, though. Their bodies had a solid black sheen, and their joints, horns, and eyes consisted of twinkling stars. It was as if they were carved from chunks of the cosmos. As the bulls plowed through the field, the dragonflies scattered. Finally in control of his movements, Alistair bolted, worried about what might leap out next.

The horses leapt next, followed by the lions, and finally the bears. Their bodies were also black and speckled with stars. None of the animals seemed particularly interested in Alistair as they fled the rock. Alistair's touch had lit a fire in them, and they seemed determined to burn, burn away.

The men were far more prepared than Alistair. They had spread their ranks and were now running among the bulls at speeds that didn't seem humanly possible. The two men with slings were twirling them so fast that blurry halos appeared over their heads, and when they snapped their wrists to deploy their weapons, disc-shaped stones rocketed out and struck a bull on the head with a one-two punch. *Thwack! Thwack!* The bull collapsed to the ground.

Before the lions or bears could reach the wounded prey, the four men with spears had it surrounded. The tall man lanced the bull's neck, and its body jerked for a second, then deflated. Blood, red and true, spilled out. It was a stunningly fast kill.

Ahead of them, the other bulls lifted their hooves. The confines of the rock couldn't hold them and neither could the confines of the ground. They dug those hooves into the air and took to the sky, where they charged right at the sun. The other animals streamed past the band of men and took to the sky as well, their dark and sparkling bodies amassing above like a murder of hulking crows. They roared and growled their way upward, speeding and then spreading, blacking out the green tinge until the sky was their bodies and their bodies were the sky. The sun faded and dimpled and transformed into a moon.

It was no longer daytime. Alistair had set free the night.

Nighttime back home meant damp, cool air. It meant solitary sets of headlights slicing through the black and illuminating the red reflectors on spinning bike wheels. It was almost endless in the winter, sixteen hours of darkness sometimes. Home for Alistair was Thessaly, a small town in northern New York, the sort of place where secrets mattered, where you held on to them because they defined you, or at least gave you something that you could call your own. The only time you shared your secrets was when you told them to the person you trusted the most. Or when you told them to the stars.

On a clear night back home, layers of stars trembled in the cold air, but it was nothing like what Alistair saw now. The sky in Aquavania pulsed and undulated. It had a heartbeat.

The men carried the dead bull by tying its legs to their spears and propping their spears on their shoulders. It didn't slow them. If anything, they moved faster now, and Alistair had to jog to keep up. Those dragonflies, those tiny shepherds, had flown away, yet he continued to follow the men anyway. If the men had intended to harm him, then they could have easily done it already. Alistair wasn't as strong or as fearsome as a bull. Even for a twelve-year-old boy—which is what he was, after all—he was considered timid.

At the edge of the forest, the group passed by an enormous blackened tree stump. It was even thicker than the sequoias Alistair had seen during a family trip out west, and though he wanted to examine it closer, the tall man advised against it.

"When that tree was mighty, evil lived up there," he said. "Do not put evil in your head."

Alistair nodded as the group moved into the forest, where the trees weren't nearly as big, but they were dense and dark. The twinkling of the bull's fur lit their way, and the moss that clung to nearly every stone and fallen trunk absorbed the light and glowed in earthy oranges and yellows. If this were a place on Earth, it would have qualified as one of the great natural wonders. It would have been swarming with shutter-bugs and scout troops. And yet Alistair and the small pack of men had it all to themselves, which perhaps wasn't a treat for them, but it was for Alistair. Sure, it was terrifying, but it was also unimaginably beautiful. He began to understand at least some of the appeal of Aquavania, the reason kids would keep coming back here, why they would stay rather than go home.

When they reached the bottom of a small hill, the sound of chattering voices greeted them.

"Is that her?" Alistair asked the tall man.

"You do not know the girl you seek?" the man replied.

"I do," Alistair said. "I . . . I'm confused. This is all new to me."

"You do not swim between realms?" the man said.

"I don't know what that means."

The men snickered. Such naïveté.

"What is your name?" the tall man asked.

"Alistair."

"I am Roha," the tall man said with a rumble in his voice. He pointed to the others, one by one, starting with the drag-onfly breather. "Dorgo, Haji, Mee, Utor, Koren."

The men bowed their heads slightly, and Roha spat on the ground, which Alistair read as *So there you have it*. Then Roha turned his attention to the hill and led the charge up a surface so powdery and soft that it was a wonder the men didn't sink in it. It spilled out behind them like sand, cascading with each footfall, and yet they climbed as if they were moving across flat and solid land. Alistair struggled and fumbled over the swells of dirt. It took him more than twice as long, but the group waited to greet him at the top.

"Mahaloo," Roha announced with his arms outstretched. The hill had been hiding a small valley. Caves nested in cliff walls below, and a group of villagers gathered outside the caves around a glowing hearth in the nook of the valley. Except for a solitary person seated on a stump, the villagers wore the same attire as the men: mud and cosmic fur. The stump-sitter was wearing something completely incongruous: a spacesuit.

"Fiona!" Alistair screamed. "Fiona Loomis!"

1989

⸻ ◆ ⸻

FIONA LOOMIS BACK HOME. A GIRL WITH SHARP EYES AND A knob in her nose, a girl who told stories that no person would ever believe, unless that person was Alistair. When she went missing, the police canvassed the neighborhood, asking people when they last saw her. Mrs. Carmine, who lived across the street from the Loomis family, told them that on the morning of Saturday, November 4, 1989, sometime around three a.m., she was having trouble sleeping, so she made herself a snack of potato chips and cottage cheese and sat next to her living room window to watch the snow.

"Fiona was standing in the street," Mrs. Carmine said. "All alone. Snow whippin' around her. Two, maybe three minutes she's there. Watching. Or thinking. Nowadays I don't know about these girls and what they think. All I know is she turned to go home."

But she didn't go home, for this was the last reported

sighting of Fiona Loomis. She ran away, or she was kid-napped; everyone was convinced of it. Everyone except Alistair. He feared it at first, and when the evidence became undeni-able, he knew it for sure. There was only one place she could have gone.

Through the portal in her basement. Through the cylinder of water behind the boiler, to another dimension, a land she visited often, a world from which she always returned, until, of course, the Riverman found her, and took her, and trapped her . . . in Aquavania.

CHAPTER 2

VISIONS OF FIONA—MEMORIES AND IMAGININGS—SIZZLED AND popped in Alistair's head like water in hot oil. His throat still vibrated from yelling her name as all eyes turned to him. The astronaut stood. Alistair took a step down the hill, then felt his feet slipping, his body being taken by a slow avalanche of silty earth. Members of the tribe rushed to intercept him.

"Do not attack!" Roha hollered. "He is a swimmer!"

Faces, both curious and apprehensive, looked down on him once he reached the bottom. One of those faces was his own, reflected in the dark glass mask of the astronaut's helmet.

A gloved hand rose. It pressed a button on the side of the helmet. The mask snapped back, and now there was a new face, young and wild and dimpled. "Who the hell is this Fiona?"

Devastating. There was indeed a girl inside the spacesuit,

but it was not the girl he had come to find. "She's . . . she's . . ." Alistair stuttered.

"A daydreamer?" the astronaut asked as she presented a gloved hand.

The tribe kept their distance, their hands at their sides or on their spears. The only person who spoke was the girl. Alistair let her help him up. "She's a friend," he said as he rose to his feet. "And I'm here to bring her home."

The girl smiled. "That's cute."

"What's cute?"

"You think you're going home."

Tribe members laughed as if it was the most spectacular joke, but Alistair didn't understand. "Of course I am," he said. "We're in Aquavania, right?"

"That's a name for it," the girl said.

"And Aquavania is made up of different worlds, created by the minds of kids, right?" This was something he had learned from Fiona. She had told him stories about worlds made of ice and robots, of clouds and jungles. Fantastic places, all born from the imagination.

"You got the basic gist of it," the girl told him.

"And the kids who created the worlds have ultimate power," Alistair went on. "They can invite you in and send you home with nothing more than a simple wish. I definitely didn't create this place, and I don't think Fiona did. So somehow I ended up in your world, right? Can't you wish me wherever I need to go?"

"I didn't hear 'pretty please,'" the girl said.

Alistair paused. He wasn't deaf to sarcasm, but he also wasn't taking any chances. "Um . . . then . . . Can you show me where Fiona is and then send us home? Pretty . . . please?"

The girl looked around for a moment. "Um . . . how about . . . no." She laughed, sharp and deep.

"What?"

"I'm messing with you," she said. "Jeez, you're such a doggie-paddler. And boy are you clueless about your . . . *situation*. I can't wish a damn thing because this world is as much mine as it is yours. I'm like you. I can swim, but I can't create."

"If this isn't your world, then whose is it?" Alistair asked.

The girl shrugged. "Some Neanderthal from way back. Beats me. Soul got sucked out like the rest of 'em, I guess." She placed her gloved fingers to her mouth and made a slurping sound like someone working on a stubborn milk shake.

"Who are you, then?"

"Well, since I didn't create this place, it means I'm not a daydreamer. And I wasn't created *in* this place, so I'm not a figment," the girl said. "Which makes me a swimmer. A swimmer is basically a wanderer, an adventurer, a nomad. And as swimmers go, I'm the best there is. Name is Polly Dobson. And you are?"

"Alistair Cleary."

"Nice to meet you." She didn't present a hand. Instead she turned to the tribe, raised her arms, and hollered, "Figments!

34

I thank you for finding me this swimmer, but now you must continue preparing the feast and give us our privacy. For we must discuss watery things!"

Tribe members nodded, whispered to one another, and turned away. There wasn't a single objection or word of dissent. They were fully under Polly's sway. "Pretty cool, right?" Polly said.

In a small clearing about two minutes' walk from the settlement, Polly placed her helmet down on a stone and sat on a tree trunk that was freshly fallen and still sprouting green leaves. Polly's hair, wavy but short, was the color of corn, and her skin was mottled, scarred by the sun. She looked more like a surfer than an astronaut.

Sitting on a stump across from her, Alistair asked, "Why do you wear a spacesuit?"

"You never know where you might end up," Polly said. "Besides, it impresses the figments. Lends an air of authority."

"So you're a visitor here too?"

"I wouldn't want to live here forever with these troglodytes, if that's what you mean," she said. "But they cook a mean barbecue. And this is *the* place to meet new swimmers."

"Is it like . . . an entryway?" Alistair asked.

"In a manner of speaking," Polly said. "So tell me. How did you get here?"

"You wouldn't believe it."

"You'd be surprised," Polly said. "Let me guess. There's some girl. Some Fiona Lupus."

"Loomis," Alistair replied, wincing as if Polly's mistake was a thorn scraping his skin.

"Whatever," Polly said. "She's a girl, that's what matters. And you're gaga for her. And you live in some podunk town where nothing bad happens. Until, of course, sweet li'l Fiona goes missing. Am I right so far?"

Jaw clenched, Alistair mumbled, "Go on."

"And you, all in love, go searching for her." Polly hopped down and poked the tip of her puffy gray boot in a puddle. "Then you discover a fountain behind her house or maybe a vase in her bedroom. Something that holds water."

"A boiler in her basement," Alistair admitted.

Polly pumped her gloved fists like she was at the horse races. "Oooo, a boiler! Extra spooky!" she cheered. "So I bet you hear a voice coming from that creepy boiler and you go to investigate and poof, it disappears and water is floating in the air and you touch the water and it transports you to another world. A world made of ash. Sound familiar?"

"Yes," Alistair whispered, but he might as well have yelled, *Holy crap, how did you know that?*

Polly winked. "And in this world of ash there's a river and it's all sparkly and rainbowish and you decide to dive in it, or maybe you fall in it because it's the only thing that's not crumbling all around you. And the river sweeps you along and brings you all the way to a field where you're surrounded by these cavemen, including one with dragonfly breath. Is that the gist of it?"

"You're . . . You're . . ."

"A genius?" Polly said. "Could be. But anyone would've figured that one out. It's basically every swimmer's story. We stumble in where we aren't supposed to be. And we doggie-paddle at first, but then we get the hang of it."

"Get the hang of what?"

"Living here. Traveling. Dealing with the figments."

Alistair knew the definition—creations of the imagination—but Polly's use of the word seemed odd. "Figments?" he asked. "You keep saying that. I don't know what you mean."

Polly pointed back toward the settlement. "Those cavemen. They're something that someone thought up a long time ago. They're not real. At least not like you and me. They're like action figures brought to life. Ideas of people, but not really people."

"What happened to the person who brought them to life?"

"Like I said . . ." Polly put a pinkie to her mouth and started to slurp. "Soul. Sucked away."

Alistair knew the answer to his next question, but he asked it anyway. "By who?"

Polly considered this as she looked back at that puddle. "Depends what name you use," she finally said. "There's Coco. Rawhead. There's Nøkken. The Whisper. Monstret. Bavbav.

I kind of like the Bugbear. Mánguang Anak. There's the Riverman. There's Lulu—"

"The Riverman?" Alistair asked. "The Whisper? Those are some of his names?"

Eyes up, eyebrows up, Polly responded, "Then you've heard of him?"

1981 to 1983

-◆-

ALISTAIR HAD NO FIRST MEMORY OF CHARLIE DWYER, NO
specific moment to revisit, to say this is where their relationship began. Charlie was there, always. Cross-legged in front
of the television, or standing at the front door, or pleading on
the telephone for Alistair to come over and play. He was
Alistair's neighbor and, by default, also his best friend. At
least for a time.

When they were four, they would sit in a sandbox together,
dig their bare toes in, and imagine that they were giants rul-
ing over some vast desert. Plastic action figures were the inhabitants of this desert, and the boys crushed them with
their feet, but not because they knew all that much about
death.

"I wanna see how far they bend," Alistair said once, and
Charlie wanted the same thing.

Sometimes they would try to dig to China.

When they were five, they learned to ride bikes together. Tottering up and down the driveway on training wheels, they'd encourage each other.

"You're getting it!"

"You're doing it!"

"We're the best in the world!"

Charlie's brother, Kyle, who was eleven at the time, didn't agree with the silly superlatives, but he did agree to help them. "Don't stop pedaling," he told them time and again. "You stop, you fall. It's that simple."

Alistair was the better cyclist of the two, but no one ever clued Charlie in on that fact. Not even Kyle, which was saying something.

When they were six, Alistair and Charlie presided over a funeral. Alistair's goldfish, found belly-up in his bowl, was buried in Alistair's backyard, and the boys wore ties and played music. Alistair's sister, Keri, watched through the window of the house, and even though she was already eight and knew that countless goldfish died every day, she cried a little bit and turned away from the glass, switched on the TV, and searched for cartoons.

Alistair *did* have a first memory of the Riverman, of the one who would call himself the Whisper. Of course, Alistair didn't realize what he was seeing, not back then. But revisiting that moment was like rewinding a mystery, going back over the evidence that may not have seemed like evidence in the first place.

It was June, a few weeks after the goldfish funeral, and the two boys were in Charlie's backyard. Long piles of cut grass spit out from the lawn mower looked like anacondas speckled yellow, due to all the dandelions. Alistair ran his fingers through the clippings and felt the dampness and smelled the greenness. The warm weather, the long days— summer had finally arrived in Thessaly.

Charlie sat next to Alistair. In one of Charlie's hands, there was a jar of rubber cement. Wedged in the crook of his other elbow and balancing on his forearm like a waiter's tray, there was a piece of limestone. In the middle of the stone, there was a potato bug, frozen by fear, by the sight of the boy.

"I'm making a fossil," Charlie announced.

Alistair examined the ill-fated bug. "Can we sell it to a museum?"

"Probably," Charlie responded as he lifted and tipped the jar of rubber cement. The goo fell slowly, like tree sap. When it finally hit the stone, it wrapped itself around the bug and enclosed it in a round shell, a bubble that would dry the color of root beer. Charlie set the stone in the yard where the sun could firm it up.

"How many do we have to make to get rich?" Alistair asked.

"A hundred," Charlie said definitively.

"That'll take a long time."

"I have a plan," Charlie said, handing Alistair the jar and

forging a path on hands and knees to the other side of the yard. It was there that a wasp crawled along the edge of a hole in the ground. It examined the dirt with its pincers and antennae, touched the grass, eventually decided there were more interesting places in the world, and took to the sky.

"There's a whole hive down there," Charlie said, pointing at the hole. "Dad ran over it with the mower. He's gonna have to use Raid. Unless . . ."

Alistair took this as his cue. He poised the open jar of rubber cement above the hole. Minus the small amount that Charlie had poured on the potato bug, the jar was full. "How many are in there, do you think?" Alistair asked.

"A hundred at least. Enough."

"And how do we get the hive out once it's covered?"

"Shovel."

It seemed like a good plan, and Alistair had visions of a papery hive the size of a watermelon, sheathed in rubber cement, wasps trapped on its surface or in the middle of flight, a real-life fossil created for the cost of craft supplies and displayed in a glass case at a natural history museum.

So Alistair tipped the jar.

As the rubber cement oozed into the hole, it disappeared from sight. Was it coating everything like glaze on a donut or was it soaking into the earth? The answer didn't come right away, but when it came, it came in force.

Wasps burst out of the hole like water from a broken pipe. In stories both boys would tell later, the wasps would number in the thousands, but in truth it was probably only thirty or so. Still, enough to cause some serious pain.

A wasp stung Alistair first, in the dead center of his wrist. Yelping, he dropped the jar of rubber cement. Another wasp lanced Charlie in the ankle, and as he reached to swat it, yet another one skewered the back of Charlie's neck.

"Run!"

Charlie's brother, Kyle, now twelve, had a clubhouse at the edge of the yard, near a swamp. The boys headed toward the clubhouse because that's the way they were facing. Kyle was inside with his friends, yakking loud enough that Alistair could hear them through the wooden door.

Charlie tried the handle. Locked. "Let us in!" he howled, batting the air around him.

"Password!" Kyle hollered.

"Abracadabra! Open Sesame!" Charlie responded.

"*Bzzzzz!* Wrong! Try again!"

The wasps were relentless, zeroing in on every untouched patch of skin. Targeted attacks. *Bam. Bam. Bam.*

"We're dying out here!" Charlie screamed.

"Nice knowing ya, then!" The harmony of laughter made it clear that all the boys inside found this very amusing.

"Water! Keri says they hate water!" Alistair yelled as he abandoned hope of the clubhouse and sprinted past it and into the swamp.

It was muck and puddles—nothing more than half a foot deep—but it would have to do. Alistair's sneaker sank, and the ground held on to it. He stumbled forward, and his foot came out droopy-socked and snagged a branch. There was no controlling his momentum now, and he flopped into the mud. Charlie followed. He launched his body in the air and landed next to Alistair.

Ten minutes later, stretched out on the picnic table next to each other, they endured the chill as Charlie's father sprayed them with a garden hose. Charlie's mother stood by with calamine lotion as muddy water spilled onto the patio. Their skin still throbbed from the stings.

"Don't worry," Charlie whispered. "I'll keep you safe. I'm *It*, you know."

"You're what?" Alistair asked.

"It."

"Like tag?"

"Sorta. I'm the one who gets to decide when things end."

Charlie's whisper was strong. It was reassuring. He reached over and grabbed Alistair's hand. They wrapped their fingers together and held them like that for a while.

CHAPTER 3

—————◆◆◆—————

ALISTAIR TRIED TO FOCUS ON POLLY'S EYES AS HE FOUGHT OFF the onslaught of memory. "Yes," he said. "I've heard of the Whisper. I've heard of the Riverman."

"I always preferred the name the Riverman," Polly said. "I mean, he leaves a river behind after he sucks out someone's soul, right? It's his mark, his signature. Very classy."

"You said he sucked . . . did that . . . to whoever created this world?"

"Yes."

"But there's no river. It ended way back there." Alistair pointed in the direction of the field where he had first met Roha and the others. "There's no ash either. I thought that when he took someone's soul, their world became ash."

"Yes and no," Polly said as she collected small stones from the ground. "How long's it been since you came through Fiona's portal?"

Alistair shrugged. The transition between day and night had been undeniably odd, but time seemed no different here than it did back home. He could feel his heartbeat counting off the seconds, could see the crawl of a millipede doling out the minutes. "I guess it's been a few hours," he said.

"And yet you've kept your cool." She laid the stones on a bare patch of dirt carefully, methodically. "Most doggie-paddlers are cuckoo-crazy for at least a day or two. *Where am I? How'd I get here? Why is that raccoon talking to me?* Stuff like that. Then there's you. You're here for a few hours and you see some lions made out of stars and a pack of Neanderthals and you hardly blink."

Alistair wouldn't have put it that way. He *was* on the edge of insanity. The reason he was hardly blinking was that he needed to keep his eyes wide open. He knew this was an unpredictable place. "I came here with some knowledge," Alistair told her.

"That's right," Polly said. "Fiona Looloo filled you in. And you're here to bring her home. Blah, blah, blah."

Alistair scowled. "Hey. Watch it. She's important. She's a . . . friend."

"They all are," Polly said, looking down at her handiwork. She had arranged the stones in a circle.

"What's that?" Alistair asked.

"That," Polly said, "is the answer to your question. About why the river dried up back there in the field."

"It's a circle."

"Okay, but it represents this . . . part of the universe.

Aquavania, as you call it. And Aquavania is made up of a bunch of worlds filled with figments, right? Dreamed up by a bunch of kids who traveled through their own special portals, right? Well, those kids are the daydreamers. Now let's pretend that each of these stones is one of their worlds. And let's pretend my finger is the Riverman."

Polly bent down and put an index finger on the biggest of the stones and proceeded to drag it to the center of the circle. It left a line in the dirt.

"When the Riverman takes a daydreamer's soul, their world drains into a river," she went on, pointing to the line in the dirt. "Sure, there's a pile of ash that's left behind, but that's like a footprint. Because the world doesn't actually disappear. The river takes it and deposits it here, in the center, where the Riverman has control over it."

She started dragging more stones to the center, leaving lines in the dirt like spokes on a wheel. She stacked each stone on top of the one before it. "So the Riverman takes the Neanderthal's soul. And he takes little Oric's soul and little Nusrat's. He takes your friend Fiona's soul. Whatever souls he can get. Then there's all this ash where their worlds once were, and all these rivers leading to where the worlds ended up, piled in the center. That's where the swimmers come in. Every swimmer is a kid who sneaks through someone else's portal."

"And on the other side of that portal is ash, where a daydreamer's world once was?" Alistair asked.

"Bingo!" Polly said as she put her finger in a dusty spot where one of the stones used to be. "So here you are in the

47

ash, and like every other swimmer, you have no choice but to swim a rainbow river. Every rainbow river leads to the same place, this first captured world, this entryway, as you called it. The figments call it Mahaloo." She moved her finger along the line of dirt and stopped at the bottom stone in the tower.

Alistair crouched down and examined the tower. "And the Riverman controls *all* of the captured worlds?"

"As much as he can," Polly said. "But there are tons of them. He's powerful, but not all-powerful. He can only know about a very small percentage of what's going on."

Alistair picked up the top stone and held it between his thumb and forefinger. "So Fiona's world still exists?"

"Probably."

"And maybe I can get to it?" Alistair asked. "Fiona told me how kids . . . I mean, daydreamers . . . could invite you over to their worlds."

"That's only true before the Riverman nabs 'em," Polly said. "Once their worlds are his, the Riverman is the only host, and he's not keen on invitations. You *can* travel between them, if you're clever. They're tangled together and there are secret ways in and out. But it's not like buying a train ticket and getting off at your chosen stop."

Alistair looked closely at the stone in his hand. "But if Fiona's world still exists, then she exists too?"

Polly sighed. "Hopefully . . . but she isn't gonna be easy to find. Fiona is a daydreamer. I've met plenty of swimmers and figments, but never seen a daydreamer around these parts. Honestly, I don't know what happens to them after the

Riverman is done with them. He gets their worlds, obviously, and all the figments in those worlds. And he gets their souls, which he sucks up with a fountain pen and hides away somewhere. That's as much as I know. As for their bodies? Well . . . they're not back home, obviously. So he's probably hiding them somewhere too."

Hmm, mmm! The sound of a throat clearing.

Roha had snuck up on them and was leaning against a tree, his hands folded together. Behind him, smoke billowed. "The feast begins," he said.

A rectangular pit of hot coals, about the size of a small in-ground pool, glowed orange and blue, except for the spot covered by the enormous bull made of sky and starlight. It seemed a primitive way to cook a meal, but then, so were the people cooking it. Surrounding the pit were the mud-caked families, happily trading stories and poking at the cosmic meat with charred sticks.

It didn't smell all that different from the backyard barbecues Alistair was accustomed to, but the conversation was poles apart. He caught snippets as he and Polly circled the crowd, looking for a seat.

"Blood! Heart blood! Must learn the spear. Ha! Gave himself a new face. Red cheeks! Blood . . ."

"Herd is restless. Restless sky . . ."

"She has been to the dreams, and they promised her this is a good place, a stay-forever place where . . ."

As far as Alistair knew, tribal people didn't speak English. "Why can I understand them?" he asked Polly.

"Same reason we can understand each other." Polly motioned to an open spot on the ground where they could settle in for a bit. "There aren't different languages here. You speak. The other person understands. It's that simple. Not everyone's a poet, obviously. We probably don't want to stick around past dinner. It's all farting and wrestling songs until dawn."

With the mention of wrestling songs, one of the burlier men grinned, stood, and stomped his feet. "I break your face, I break your nose, I break your face, I break your nose," he sang.

Polly rolled her eyes as she and Alistair sat on a bare patch of dirt near the pit of coals. "That's about as lyrically sophisticated as it gets around here."

The singer cut the song off midverse and glowered at her. When he saw Alistair, he snarled, "So who *is* this pup?"

Alistair tried to hide—dipping his head, curling a shoulder in front of his face—but Polly nudged his chin up so the singer could get a close look. "This is Alistair Cleary, and Alistair Cleary is like me. A god risen up from the waters! So don't you even think about messing with him or he will call in a storm and end every last one of you troglodytes."

Terror washed over the man's eyes. He bowed his head slightly and brought a trembling hand up to stroke his ragged beard. "I am sorry."

"Better be," Polly said as she stood, and the man puffed

up his chest as she walked toward him. "Chill out, square jaw. As long as you keep your cool, everything will be fine. We've got other business to attend to at the moment."

The man stepped back as Polly moved past him and approached a circle of women who were crouching and laying out ferns like they were setting a table. Polly used her foot to nudge one of the women on the shoulder, forcing her to turn and create an opening in the circle for Polly to step through.

Polly pointed down at each of them, as if doling out instructions. Her voice was hushed and there was no way for Alistair to hear the conversation, but the women nodded their responses with clear reluctance, and one of them even removed her leathery boots, which she handed over to Polly. With the boots strung over her shoulder, Polly flashed them a thumbs-up, hopped out of the circle, and returned to Alistair's side.

"What was that?" he asked.

She tossed him the boots. "Got you something to protect your tootsies. And I told them that they've offended us and that they should slice off some meat at the rib and wrap it in some fern. We're taking our meal to go."

Back at the clearing, Alistair and Polly sat on rocks, ferns in their laps like paper plates, as they ate the sparkling rib meat.

"It's good," Alistair said. An understatement. He'd been

famished, and even though a piece of meat resembling the night sky wouldn't seem appetizing, it was that and more. It was possibly the most delicious thing he had ever tasted.

"Whoever created this world liked to eat, that's for sure," Polly said.

"How did you first come to Aquavania?" Alistair asked.

Polly took a bite, and as she chewed she said, "You don't wanna hear that story."

"Sure I do."

"Like I told you, pretty much the same tale as yours." She took another bite, a bigger one this time, big enough to fill up her cheeks.

"Have you been here a long time?" Alistair asked.

She shrugged and drummed her fingers on the dome of her helmet, which sat on the rock next to her, a shining marvel of technology in a primeval forest.

"Where's your home in the Solid World?" he asked. The Solid World was a term he'd heard Fiona use. It meant the real world, the world we already know, but he wasn't sure if everyone in Aquavania used the same terminology, so he amended his question. "What I mean is, where are you from originally?"

Polly pointed to her cheeks. The message was clear: *Mouth full, can't talk.*

"I'm from a place called Thessaly," Alistair went on. "I live there with my mom, my dad, and my sister, Keri. Fiona lived up the street from me."

Polly flashed him a lazy thumbs-up, but Alistair wasn't

really expecting a response. Talking about home made home seem closer. He may have only been in Aquavania for a few hours, but he felt as if he'd been away for eons.

"Down the street there was a kid named Charlie Dwyer. Have you ever known anyone named Charlie Dwyer?" he asked.

It may have sounded like a simple question, but it was many questions wrapped in one. Did Polly know the sad truth that Alistair had only recently discovered? Did she know that his former best friend lived a double life—one in the Solid World and one in Aquavania? She had said that the River-man went by many names. Did she know that one of those names was Charlie Dwyer?

Polly shook her head and swallowed. "Charlie Dwyer? Hmmm. Sounds like a guy who plays baseball," she said.

Alistair wrinkled his nose. "Only if it's a video game."

"So he's your pal?" Polly asked.

"Not really," Alistair said. "Or not anymore. Wasn't sure if you'd heard of him, is all."

"He's famous?"

"I don't know," Alistair said. "He had an older brother. A guy named Kyle."

"Had?" Polly asked. "Kyle died?"

"I don't know," Alistair said. "Forget I even mentioned it."

"You're homesick," Polly said as she took another bite. "It'll fade."

God, I hope not, Alistair thought. He wanted such a virulent strain of homesickness that it would compel him to do the impossible, to find Fiona and bring her back and straighten out all the bent things in his life.

"Are you sure there isn't a way—"

A *whoosh* cut off Alistair's voice as a curved, sharpened stick flipped through the air and lodged itself in the soft ground at their feet. Alistair jerked his head around. A woman from the settlement was standing about twenty yards away, her face twitching with anger.

"Not good." Polly hopped up, snatched her space helmet.

The woman's feet were bare. Alistair was wearing her boots. "I thought you were friendly with them," he said.

"Pfff. Friends are friendly, and no one is friends with a god," Polly replied as she tucked the helmet under her arm.

"If she thinks you're a god, then why is she throwing things at us?"

"Well, you always gotta have a few atheists. Let's move!" And with that, Polly was off running.

Alistair paused for a moment to see if the woman would simply chase after Polly and leave him alone.

"Monster! Demon!" howled the woman, her eyes fixed on Alistair.

That settled that. So Alistair started running too, following in Polly's path. They kept to the woods, hurdling stones and ducking under branches. Considering she was wearing a spacesuit, Polly was incredibly nimble, and Alistair struggled to keep up. Luckily, he was fast enough to outrun the woman, but only barely.

This neck of the forest was even more brilliant than the

rest. Everything was *more*. The butterflies and mushrooms were more plentiful, more colorful. Ferns and orchids were more luscious and fragrant. Tree bark was more gnarled and branches more twisted. It was a storybook forest.

Within a few minutes, they reached a pond, its surface adorned with lily pads. Polly stood along the edge, waiting for Alistair. The sounds of the woman—her footfalls cracking sticks, her grunts and snarls of frustration—were getting louder, and Alistair held his hands up behind his head to shield it from projectiles. It threw off his balance and he wasn't sure how far he could run like that. He desperately hoped that Polly had a plan.

"Jump in," Polly ordered as soon as Alistair reached her.

The water was about twenty yards in diameter and appeared to be no more than four or five feet deep. An old-fashioned swimming hole—fine for a dip on a hot summer day, but for protection from a homicidal cavewoman?

"Are you crazy?" Alistair asked.

"Far from it," Polly said, and she took a shallow dive from a rotten log on the banks.

The woman tromped toward them, now within thirty or forty yards. "Monster!" she screamed again.

Polly's head surfaced in the center of the pond, her hair darker now and smoothed against the sides of her face. She resembled a seal, until she pulled her helmet up from the water, dumped it out, and snapped it into place on her shoulders. She kept the mask open so that she could speak. "If you don't think you're a strong enough swimmer, then grab my ankle. I'm watertight in this thing and I can pull you where you need to go. Even if you think you can keep up, you better jump in, because this gal will catch you and she will kill you. I guarantee it."

As Polly snapped her mask down, Alistair crouched on a rock and swept some fingers across the water. It was normal water—wet, chilly, nothing to indicate it would protect them. "I don't know," he said.

"Demon!" the cavewoman screamed again, but this time a stone accompanied the scream and it hit Alistair below the ear, sending him headfirst into the water.

His body somersaulted below the surface. He opened his mouth to gasp for air, and water filled his throat. His chest lurched and forced some of the water back out. Stones rained down on him. It was too murky to see bubbles or beams of light, so the direction of the impacts was the only thing that told him which way was up.

A hand grabbed his wrist. It felt like a small hand, but it tugged with such a violent force that it might as well have been the jaws of a sea creature. It pulled him down farther until the murkiness became blackness and the stones thrown by the cavewoman merely tapped Alistair, if they hit him at all.

Down they went. Alistair's lungs were straining, but not much, or not nearly enough considering he'd been underwater for at least a minute. The pressure should have been overwhelming too, but his eardrums felt normal, as if his body was built for this.

The hand let go of his wrist for a moment, but before the panic of abandonment could seize his chest, a foot was in Alistair's face. The rubber of a moon-boot grazed Alistair's cheek. He wrapped both hands around it and let it pull him.

Deeper, deeper, deeper.

CHAPTER 4

THEY FELL FROM THE SKY. ONE MOMENT THEY WERE IN THE pond, and the next they were in a cloud, plummeting alongside drops of rain. Alistair held Polly's ankle even tighter, but he wasn't sure how long he could maintain his grip. She had straightened her body into a missile, head pointed downward as gravity piled on the momentum.

"We're gonna die!" Alistair screamed, but with the hiss of the wind and with the space helmet covering Polly's head, it would have been difficult for her to hear him. He had the choice of letting go, of course, but then what was he going to do? Flap his arms like wings to stay aloft?

They had entered a new world. As they escaped the wispy haze of the clouds, they faced an expanse of red. Whether it was earth or liquid was hard to say. Red. That was the only sure thing. Even the rain around them was red, lashing

Alistair's face and washing pink lenses over his irises. He closed his eyes and clenched his teeth.

Standing atop the high dive at the high school's pool when he was eight years old, Alistair had done the same thing. Blind, molars grinding, he had stood there enduring the chants of "Do it! Do it! Do it!" coming from Charlie and the chorus of third graders standing shoulder-deep in the shallow end. He had leaned forward and let his body fall and he had hit the water sideways, taking the impact in the ribs. He might as well have been hitting the ground.

What Alistair hit in the world of red wasn't the ground, but it wasn't exactly liquid either. It was like porridge and it swallowed him whole. *Flurrrrrp!* was the sound it made as his body entered it. It didn't hurt, though. The substance hugged Alistair with a chilly quiver and worked its way between his fingers until they finally slipped from Polly's ankle and Alistair was alone.

He didn't dare open his eyes. The stuff was oozing into his nostrils. He tried to swim to the surface, but it was of no use. He couldn't move his body in any direction. The fear of suffocation was even worse than the fear of falling. At least falling had a visceral thrill. Suffocation was torture, pure and simple.

As spasms of panic rippled through Alistair's torso, the sludge started to quake. Then, all at once, it opened up beneath him. There was a slurp and a tug from below, and he couldn't fight it. Like a loosened clog through a drain, he was sucked through some sort of tube. His shoulders rubbed against its edges.

For at least a minute the tube carried him along, twisting back and forth as if it were a digestive tract. And like a digestive tract, it expelled him, shot his body out into a dimly lit chamber. His body fell, landed on a slightly taut net that stretched across the length of the chamber, and bounced twice—once high and once low. When his body settled, its weight was too much to anchor Alistair in place, and he rolled down the net to the valley at its center, where he crashed into Polly.

She patted him on the cheek, as if to say, *Sorry, kid,* then she nudged him away, onto his back.

From below came a cacophony of doors opening and feet shuffling, followed by an eruption of rousing cheers.

"New blood! New blood! New blood!"

Above, torches mounted on walls exploded to life, painting the surroundings in a fresh and fiery light. The walls were made from all shapes and sizes of stone, immaculate masonry, with granite and marble clinging together. The ceiling was covered in giant fleshy tubes, swaying like squid tentacles, a couple dripping red sludge.

"New blood! New blood! New blood!"

Alistair and Polly flipped over onto their stomachs. A fist-pumping crowd of hundreds dressed in tunics and leather surrounded a large pedestal, which stood directly below the net. At first, it seemed like the pedestal was growing or moving up to meet them, but it was soon clear that ropes tied to the corners of the net were spooling out from dark holes in the walls and lowering Alistair and Polly.

"New blood! New blood! New blood!"

They came to rest on the cold, flat surface of the pedestal, which the net, like a woven tablecloth, now draped over. Polly jumped to her feet immediately and began wiping the remaining red sludge from her spacesuit. As he pushed himself up, Alistair could feel the chants, the vibrations from the rowdy crowd. The mob was at least twenty feet below, but that did little to allay his fears. They were a pack of hyenas at the base of a tree. Even if they couldn't find their way up, Alistair would probably, eventually, have to go down.

"New blood! New blood! New blood!"

A curved balcony jutted out from the wall, mounted only a few feet higher than the pedestal. Over the middle of the balcony hung a swing fashioned from rusty chains and a giant tortoiseshell. On the swing sat a boy.

"Silence!" the boy bellowed, the tremor of his voice giving the swing a wee push.

Like that, the crowd cut out. Their roar became whispers and attention settled on the boy.

"Thank you, my lovelies," he told the people. "I understand your excitement. It has been a while since we've had visitors. And now we have two! Most promising. But we must be gracious hosts. Rabble-rousing is sure to frighten them."

The boy had tight curls in his hair and a swarthy complexion. He wore scale mail on his chest and steel armor on his legs. Above him hung a curtain of looped ropes that resembled a line of nooses. Each rope was painted a different color—maroon, turquoise, beige, purple with neon green stripes—and they stretched up into the jumble of fleshy tubes above. A small sword with a ruby-encrusted handle rested in the boy's lap. If Alistair had to guess, he would have said the boy was six years old.

Polly pressed the button on the side of her helmet and the mask snapped open. "Good afternoon, your highness," she said to the boy.

The boy leaned forward, his shoulders pressing against the swing chains. "Is that . . . ?"

"Polly, your highness. In the flesh and"—she wiped her spacesuit off again—"blood."

A look of amazement cloaked his face. "Of all that is holy, a girl who keeps her word."

Polly shrugged. "I said I'd be back."

"And you said you'd bring another swimmer."

With open hands, Polly motioned to Alistair. "I'm sorry," Alistair said. "I'm a little confused. Where are we exactly?"

A haggard woman shouted an answer from the crowd. "You're in the realm of Lord Hadrian! And if you know what's good for you, you'll not be acting a fool, you gilled—"

"Hush, figment!" Hadrian commanded from his swing. "The boy is obviously new here. We shall learn about him before we determine the level of his foolishness." He turned to Alistair. "So who are you, boy?"

"My name is Alistair Cleary."

"Do you swim?"

"I . . . guess so."

"And has Polly told you why you are in this realm?"

"No, sir." The honorific came out without a thought. Lord Hadrian looked like a six-year-old, but because of his regal demeanor, he quite clearly demanded the respect of someone much older.

"Sir?" Hadrian sniped. "Not 'your highness'? Not 'Lord Hadrian'?"

"I'm sorry . . . your highness, I didn't—"

Hadrian winked and let loose a little giggle. "It's fine," he said. "It's nice, actually. Reminds me of my days as a knight. I am not immune to nostalgia, young Mr. Cleary."

"Okay . . . sir."

Hadrian scratched his chin. "So Polly did not inform you of your predicament? Most interesting."

The masses responded in kind. "Oooooooo!"

"It's hardly a *predicament*," Polly explained. "It's an opportunity. Besides, when did I have time to tell him? No matter how I get here, I always end up in that disgusting sea of coagulated blood. Not the sort of welcome that inspires rational conversation."

Alistair looked down at the beads of red still dripping off his body. "That was . . . ?"

"It wasn't cherry Jell-O," Polly answered, and then she turned back to Hadrian. "Simple fact is this: the kid was about to be clobbered by a cavewoman. He owes me his life."

Hadrian's eyes narrowed. "Is this true, Master Cleary?"

Alistair looked at Polly. Clad in the spacesuit, she still cut the figure of a wise and experienced explorer. "Yes, your highness . . . sir."

Hadrian nodded. "Fair enough. So I am the owner of this debt?"

Polly wiped her hands together and then whisked them apart. "Free and clear. All yours."

In the crowd, devilish grins sprouted, accompanied by guttural, satisfied hums. The reaction was not lost on Alistair. "What exactly . . . is my . . . *predicament*?" he asked.

Before Hadrian could answer, Polly pointed up to the hanging ropes and said, "You don't need me around for this. I'd just like to conclude our business and be on my way."

Hadrian shrugged and said, "A deal is a deal. I'm still un-sure why you'd want access to the Ambit of Ciphers, but I've given up trying to figure out people like you. If you survive, come back and regale us with your saga. We'd all be curious to know what sort of madness *He* has unleashed in there."

From the crowd came nods and hushed proclamations of "She's crazy, she is."

"Wait a second," Alistair said. "You're not staying here with me?"

Polly crinkled up her nose, tipped her head, and replied, "No. I'm sorry. You seem like a good kid, but I'm not cut out to be some guide. I'm like you. Looking for someone. I can't let anything get in the way of that. So . . . so good luck, Alistair Cleary."

She'd obviously had enough of his pleading eyes. She turned away from Alistair and pointed again at the ropes.

Hadrian nodded, reached up, grabbed a silver-and-gold-colored rope, and tugged it. Gears clattered, and one of the tubes hanging from the ceiling shot down like a frog's tongue and enveloped Polly. There was a *voom* and a *slurp* and then bye-bye, Polly, the proverbial fly snatched off the leaf.

Hadrian released the rope, and the tube retracted and took its place among the others, gently swaying in the open air above. The force of the tug had added momentum to Hadrian's swing, and it creakily swept over the chamber, almost reaching as far as Alistair's pedestal. Hadrian pumped his feet to keep it going as the crowd whooped and whistled.

Alistair asked again, "What exactly is my predicament?"

Rather than addressing Alistair, Hadrian shouted his answer to the masses. "The quest this young swimmer has accepted, my lovelies, is the bravest one of all. He is to kill the fearsome Mandrake!"

Cheers. Applause. A thunder of happiness.

1988

WINTER BACK HOME, ALMOST TWO YEARS BEFORE.

Alistair was ten, nearly eleven, and he had begged Charlie to go sledding with him in a state forest that was connected to their neighborhood by tangled strings of trails. He promised an adventure the likes of which no boy had ever known. Charlie wasn't a big fan of physical activity, or cold weather in general, so he scoffed at such a notion, but then agreed anyway, because that's what best friends do.

It was a two-mile hike to the hill Alistair wanted to conquer, a steep and rugged swath of dirt that locals called Wheelbender on account of all the bike tires it had claimed. The boys didn't bother telling their parents, because parents generally advise against such endeavors. Instead, they made up stories about building snow forts and slipped out of their houses dressed in down coats, snow pants, and mittens. They left their hats behind. As Kyle had often told them, hats were for girls.

A brutal winter had left a solid two-foot base of hardpack, and a storm the night before had topped it with a powdery fourteen inches. A lack of snowshoes made the hike difficult, but these were ideal conditions. Their sleds kicked up wings and tails of white, and the ride down Wheelbender was fast and smooth. Even Charlie, usually so hangdog and sluggish, didn't pause after the first run. He simply raced back up the hill and went again, and again, and again. Adrenaline was their lunch, and they had no complaints about the icicles on their sideburns or the biting wind that painted their ears pink. It was a perfect day.

Until Charlie wiped out.

On what was to be one of their last runs, his sled hit a rock and he lost control, started to spin, stuck his leg out to stop, and smashed his ankle into a tree stump.

"Gahhh!" he howled.

Alistair rushed over to find his friend writhing, facedown on the sled, biting at its red plastic edge.

"Can you stand?" Alistair asked.

"I . . . don't know."

"Can you at least move it?"

Charlie rolled up the fabric of his snow pants. Blood had yet to answer the call. The skin of his ankle was still pale—no swelling to speak of—but when Alistair poked it with his mitten, Charlie winced.

"I'm pretty sure it's broken," Charlie said.

The sun was sneaking behind the trees and was halfway down to the horizon. It would be dark in about two hours.

Snow wasn't falling, but the wind was picking up and blowing it into drifts. Alistair rolled down Charlie's pant leg and made a promise.

"I'll do whatever it takes to get you home."

Over an hour later, Alistair was starting to find his rhythm—taking four steps, pausing for a breath, then four more steps, pausing, and so on. Two thin towropes that were once attached to the fronts of their sleds were now fashioned into a crude harness that Alistair wore around his chest. Charlie, cross-legged on the nesting sleds, held the other ends of the ropes like he was holding reins. Charlie was the driver, Alistair was the dog. Whenever the reins were less than taut, Charlie gave them a flick and cried, "Yah! *Vámonos!*"

They had gone only a half mile—barely a quarter of the way back—and Alistair was already exhausted. The temperatures were in the teens, but the work was so hard that it was beckoning sweat. Alistair's coat was off, tied around his waist. Everything with a zipper was unzipped. The ventilation helped at first, but when the sweat finally arrived and began to chill the inside of Alistair's clothes, the choice was between freezing and dehydrating. For the moment, freezing seemed preferable, so he reached down, scooped up a handful of snow, and filled his mouth. It melted on contact, sending cold, earthy liquid down his sandy throat.

"Did you check to see if it was yellow?" Charlie laughed. Awfully chipper for a boy with a broken ankle.

"How about not talking for a bit?" Alistair asked.

"Jeez. I'm only trying to keep your spirits up."

"My spirits are fine. Awesome. The greatest. It's freezing out and it's almost dark and I'm yanking your fat butt through the woods because you can't sled worth diarrhea."

Charlie drove the heels of his mittens into the snow, putting on the brakes. "You knew I hated sledding. But you insisted."

Alistair pulled harder. He wasn't going to be slowed down. Not now, not so late in the day. "I didn't insist," he said.

Because snow was working its way up his coat sleeves, Charlie relented, lifted his mittens, and said, "Let's think about it. Who would you rather be at this moment? Me, defeated by a tree stump, soon to be a laughingstock, or you, playing sled dog for a few hours, but soon to be the hero?"

Alistair didn't have an answer.

"You're not wearing the shirt I gave you," Charlie said. "That's a shame. Because I'm wearing the one you gave me." Charlie was referring to a swap the two had made a few months before. A shirt for a shirt, a symbol of solidarity.

"No," Alistair said softly. "Sorry." He put his coat back on and forged ahead.

One more hour and still one more mile to go. The sun had set, but luckily there was a bit of moonlight sneaking through the pines. Alistair had about ten paces of visibility, so he kept to his four-pace cycle. It hadn't gotten any easier, but the rhythm of the slog was now pulsing through his body.

Step, step, step, step, stop. Step, step, step, step, stop.

The two weren't talking. Words only led to arguments, and arguments weren't getting them home. Charlie was humming, though, the only music he cared about, the sound tracks to video games. The boops and beeps might have been grating when played through television speakers, but when done a cappella, they were exponentially worse. Alistair's solution was to use snotty tissues from his pocket as earplugs and let the rhythm of his steps worm into his brain instead.

Step, step, step, step, stop. Step, step—

But he was losing the rhythm. Darker thoughts were more powerful and rushed in uninvited.

I could leave Charlie here. There's snow forecast for to-night. He would freeze. I would never have to deal with him again.

Alistair hated that his brain couldn't defend itself against such swill, but he also had to accept that it was honest swill. He didn't really like Charlie, not anymore. He was having trouble remembering the last time that he had.

Another hour, another half mile. Clouds smothered the moon and the darkness was pudding-thick. Alistair ached all over, except for his toes. His toes had been in pain—plenty of it—an hour earlier, but not anymore, and that wasn't a good sign. Frostbite comes after the numb, or so Alistair had heard, and while he was confident he would survive the trek, he wasn't sure all of his appendages would. He pictured himself sitting next to the fireplace in his living room, pulling off his boots and socks and watching blackened nubs of flesh and bone fall to the floor.

I could leave him here.

I could abandon him.

No more Charlie in my life.

No more Charlie.

Alistair stopped for a moment and looked back at Charlie's dark shape, bent like a chubby *Z* in the sled, his mittens balled up and clinging to the towropes like they were a beloved blanket. It was hard to tell if his eyes were open.

There was anger trying to claw from Alistair's chest, but it was buried in regret—for not wearing thicker socks, for all his decisions that day—mainly for not telling his parents where he was going. If Alistair had told them, they surely would have dispatched a search party. As it was, the wind had blown snow over the boys' original tracks, and there were too many trails to go down, too many houses in the neighborhood to call and ask *Have you seen the guys?*

No one would find them anytime soon. So Alistair turned back and faced the darkness.

Step. Stop. Step. Stop. Step . . . I could leave him here.

They reached the tiny parking lot at the trailhead about an hour later. Temperatures had dropped close to zero. Breaths not only condensed, they crystallized in the air. The sweating had ceased, and Alistair's underclothes were crusty with ice. He still couldn't feel his toes, but that was no longer a concern. After two miles in four hours, pulling more than a hundred pounds over drifts of snow, he had almost made it home. All he cared about now was a hot drink and a warm bed.

The lot was haphazardly plowed, and even though there were patches of snow and ice, there were also bare stretches of pavement, and Alistair wasn't sure he could pull the sled over them. It didn't matter really. Once they hit the road, pulling the sled would be too difficult, and there was only a few hundred yards to go along the road.

"I might have to leave you here for a few minutes," Alistair said. "I can run back to your house and have your mom drive over to get you. Probably the fastest way."

Charlie opened his eyes and sat up. He yawned as he considered the plan, then he swung his legs over the edge of the sled and planted his heels on the ground. "Why don't I just walk?" he asked.

Alistair peeled the harness off and dropped it in the snow. Thin bruises and chafing on his shoulders roared to life, and he massaged them as he pointed out the obvious. "Um . . . what about your ankle?"

Charlie shrugged. "My ankle? Well, about that. Honestly, back there, I was pretty sure it was broken. But I wasn't *totally* sure. Now I'm pretty sure it's okay."

That's when Charlie pushed himself up and stood. Just like that, no problem at all. There wasn't a lean or a wobble—

nothing to indicate an injury—and Alistair, still wallowing in guilty thoughts, tried to put together a sentence. "But—"

"But," Charlie said, "it's a good thing you're such a great friend. My ankle would have been pretty sore if I had walked that entire way." Charlie patted Alistair on the back and smiled, but it wasn't a malicious smile. It was grateful.

"You're . . . okay?" Alistair was too shocked and too tired to deploy the fire building up in his lungs.

Charlie winked. "I think we'll both be feeling it tomorrow. But you should come over in the morning. We'll play Nintendo, and my mom will make wings and milk shakes for lunch. Beats being stuck out in the cold."

The closest house to the lot had a bay window, and Alistair could see some kids clearing dessert plates from the dining room table. Somewhere in the distance, a dog barked and two other dogs barked their replies, and the sound ricocheted off the gusts of cold, cold air. Chimneys coughed smoke.

"I hate you," Alistair said.

This coaxed a smile too, and before he turned to walk home on his own two legs supported by his own two sturdy ankles, Charlie said, "No you don't. If you hated me, you would have left me back there. You're a great friend. The best. I'll never forget what you did for me."

CHAPTER 5

IT WAS TRUE. THERE WAS NO FORGETTING WHAT ALISTAIR HAD done for Charlie. The memory was still too fresh, too real, and shame, an all-too-frequent visitor, sat on the pedestal next to Alistair, reminding him of Charlie's betrayal and mocking him about Polly's betrayal. Why, after so long and so much, hadn't Alistair smartened up? Why did he keep letting people trick him?

Hadrian swooped up and down, clearly relishing his perch, and he said, "There are three things you must know about the Mandrake. First, he is a liar. He will try to deceive you by making you think he is weak. He is not weak. He is a most vicious creature, almost as vicious as his master."

Alistair didn't have to ask, but he asked anyway. "Who's his master? Is it the Riverman?"

"Ah, the Riverman," Hadrian said. "Been ages since I've heard that name used. We've grown more accustomed to calling him the Whisper. But yes, you are correct. He is master of the Mandrake. This was a peaceable kingdom once, but the Whisper loathes harmony. So he gave us the Mandrake, and therefore we have been forced to take shelter beneath the ground."

Behind the crowd there was a pair of wooden doors. Did those doors lead to an entire underground city? Did all of these people live beneath that sea of blood?

"The second thing you must know about the Mandrake is this," Hadrian went on. "He does not always look like a monster. Sometimes he takes on different forms. Small ones. Deceptively innocuous ones. But there is always one way to recognize him. There is a blue mark, in the shape of a horseshoe, hidden behind his left ear. If you see that blue mark, then you kill. You do not hesitate. You do not doubt. You kill."

"How do you . . . ?" Alistair couldn't bring himself to say *kill*. Aquavania may not have been like home, but it wasn't like a video game either. These figments appeared to have flesh. There was something unmistakably alive behind their eyes.

"Fair question," Hadrian said. "For that brings us to the third thing. We do not know how to kill the Mandrake. All we know is that the sea of blood protects us from him. He will not enter it. Beyond that, we do not know what the Mandrake's weaknesses are."

"And I'm supposed to know what his weaknesses are?" Alistair asked. "I've been here for barely a day, and you're expecting me to—"

"You are a swimmer!" Hadrian barked. "And being a swimmer comes with responsibilities!"

"Aren't you a swimmer?" Alistair asked. It was a guess, but an educated one. Figments seemed to look up to swimmers, or at least treat them differently. With a crowd of figments at his bidding, Hadrian certainly fit that bill. Fiona had told Alistair stories about how the kids who traveled from the Solid World to Aquavania never aged, at least not physically. Hadrian might have looked like a six-year-old, but that obviously wasn't the age of his heart and his mind.

"Once upon a time, you could have called me a swimmer," Hadrian said. "But now I am simply Lord Hadrian, protector of these beautiful people. We count on swimmers like you to help us."

"And what do I get if I help you?"

"Honor. Esteem. And your choice of tubes."

Before that tube had jolted down from the ceiling and snatched Polly away, Hadrian had mentioned a place called the Ambit of Ciphers. The name meant nothing to Alistair. "Would one of the tubes take me home?" he asked.

"Unlikely," Hadrian said. "But there are many ways from this world to other worlds. I'd venture to guess that Polly brought you here through a passage to Mahaloo. Many of the tubes can bring you to worlds like Mahaloo. But they won't bring you home. That's simply nonsensical."

"Is there a tube that will bring me to Fiona Loomis?"

"I don't know who that is."

"What about the Riv . . . the Whisper? Does one lead to him?"

The crowd laughed. Either the answer to Alistair's question was obvious or it was ridiculous. Probably a bit of both.

"You don't seem nearly up to that task," Hadrian chuckled. "But that's neither here nor there. You have to deal with his Mandrake first."

"And what if I refuse?" Alistair asked as he climbed to his feet.

Hadrian smiled and dragged his heels on the ground to slow himself down. When the swing was almost at a standstill, Hadrian reached up and stroked the loop of one of the hanging ropes. This loop was red, and when Hadrian pulled it, exerting only a small bit of pressure, one of the tubes from the ceiling descended a few feet. There was a whirring sound, and inside the tube there were spinning teeth shaped like the blades of a blender.

"Like all the others who have refused, you will become one with the sea," Hadrian said.

All at once, fists shot up and the crowd belted out their favorite chant.

"New blood! New blood! New blood!"

Hadrian showed no interest in questions or objections. He simply tossed him the sword with the ruby-encrusted handle, which Alistair didn't attempt to catch. When Alistair bent over and picked the sword up from the net, Hadrian yanked at a yellow rope, and a tube shot down from the ceiling and vacuumed Alistair away. Liquid rushed all around him as he snaked through the darkness, up and down, twisting and looping as if riding a waterslide. It might have even been fun, had it not carried the paralyzing prospect of certain death.

Eventually the tube spat Alistair out and he landed buttfirst on a dirt road. Before he had a chance to even knock the dust from his clothes, the tube retracted into the sky and disappeared. No maps, no further instructions, no idea where he was. Only a mission to find and kill the Mandrake.

The dirt road wound through a field of wildflowers. In both directions it looked the same: pleasant, bucolic. There were patches of apple and cherry trees, mossy stone walls, and rough signs hewn from wood.

THIS WAY TO THE HUTCH read a crooked sign staked along the side of the road. With nothing else to guide him, Alistair was forced to follow. The air was full of birdsong and the gentle *chee* of insects, and as he walked toward whatever or whoever the Hutch was, Alistair let the tip of the sword drag in the dirt.

This was the second weapon he had held in as many days. The first one was a gun, with a cold handle and a trigger that fell too easily. In the dark of the clubhouse behind the Dwyer home, Alistair had shot Kyle Dwyer in the stomach. Accidentally, he had to keep reminding himself. Guns weren't made for shaky hands like his.

The handle of the sword bore the perfect curves to fit Alistair's grip, but his hands were even shakier now. He wanted nothing more than to drop the thing or, better yet, toss it in a lake where it could vanish, become rusted over and useless. He wanted to stay alive, but not at the expense of someone else's life. And yet he held on, because he also wanted to see Fiona. He needed to see Fiona, wherever she was.

The road led to a village, but not one like the primitive settlement in Mahaloo and not one like Thessaly, not one like home. It was made up of a grassy square surrounded by a series of stone huts with thatched roofs. A large wooden platform, like a stage on stilts, sat in the center of the square.

Alistair wouldn't have necessarily called the village pretty, but it felt like a warm and welcoming place to visit. There was what appeared to be a blacksmith's shop, with an anvil and a rack of iron tools, and what had to be a bakery, with a large open fireplace near the back, and what was clearly a house of worship, with stools for the parishioners and a pulpit for whoever delivered the sermons. It seemed lived-in, this place, but perhaps not lived in for quite a while.

The ivy and weeds had grown cocky, clinging to surfaces and sprouting from patches of ground where they had no right to be. The structures themselves appeared stable enough, relatively free of pests and rot, but they were also lonely. This village was completely empty; not a single person roamed about.

Alistair made his way to the platform so he could examine it closely. A ladder led the twenty feet or so to the top, and with the hilt of the sword tucked under his arm, Alistair climbed rung by rung. Expecting to find something significant, he was disappointed to discover that the platform was merely a platform, a bare, flat rectangle of wooden slats. The view was lovely, but unenlightening. Below and around him was the village. Beyond the village, it was nothing but rolling fields and the dirt road.

Alistair headed back to the ladder, but as he crouched to prepare his descent, a deep voice gave him pause.

"Oh dear, please do not hurry off." A red hummingbird, wings aflutter, hovered in front of his face.

"That . . . wasn't . . . you?" Alistair asked.

"Who else would it be?" the hummingbird replied.

The sane response for Alistair would have been *Hummingbirds can't talk*, but sanity seemed to have no place in Aquavania. Animals were made of the night sky, so why couldn't they talk? Alistair stood up and squeezed the handle of the sword.

He does not always look like a monster, Hadrian had said. *Sometimes he takes on different forms. Small ones. Deceptively innocuous ones.*

"Who are you?" Alistair asked.

"I am Potoweet, noble defender of our fair Hutch," the hummingbird said. "I do not surrender. I do not hide underground. I was first and I shall be last. Who might you be?"

"Alistair. Alistair Cleary."

It was strange enough that the bird was speaking, but his deep voice was even stranger. One would think a

hummingbird's pitch would be unbearably high, but Potoweet spoke like a wise and distinguished gentleman.

"Ah," Potoweet said. "You are another fool sent to his destruction. Hadrian's cruelty and desperation know no limit."

As he hovered, Potoweet kept his eyes locked on Alistair's.
Each time Alistair tilted his head, Potoweet mirrored the
movement with his body, making it impossible for Alistair to
see whether he had the blue mark behind his ear, or if he
even had ears. *Do birds have ears?*

"I am looking for the—"

"Mandrake?" Potoweet asked. "And you want to know if I
am he?"

Alistair didn't respond.

"Allow me to land on your sword and you may examine my
body," Potoweet went on. "You will see I have nothing to hide."

Alistair began to raise the sword, but then thought better
of it. "That sounds like a trick. I'm not a fool."

"Evidence suggests otherwise," Potoweet said. "You serve
Lord Hadrian."

"I serve myself," Alistair retorted. "All I want is to find
my friend Fiona and go home."

"And if you dispatch the Mandrake, Hadrian promised to
grant you these things?"

"Not . . . really."

"Then you are a fool."

Back home in Thessaly, when Alistair was seven, he had
watched Kyle, then thirteen, shoot a robin out of a tree with
a BB rifle. The bird had fallen into the mud at the edge of

the swamp, where Kyle fetched the dead body and held it up by a tail feather. Alistair had winced and looked away, and Kyle had said, "Don't get all weepy over a stupid bird. Do you cry over your chicken nuggets?"

Alistair took a step away from Potoweet and readied his sword. "What if I sliced you in half? Then who'd be the fool?"

"Still you, of course," Potoweet said. "Even if you had the speed to strike me, which I am sure you do not, then you will have killed your one ally."

"Or I will have killed the Mandrake," Alistair said.

Potoweet rolled his minuscule eyes and then zagged through the air with the speed and precision of an insect. Alistair could barely fix a gaze on him, let alone a sword. The bird finally stopped when he was right next to Alistair's ear.

"Let me tell you a story," Potoweet said.

POTOWEET'S STORY

LONG AGO THERE WAS A BOY NAMED ORIC WHO LIVED NEAR THE ocean, and one night he came upon a floating orb of liquid and he touched it and was spirited to another land, a magical realm made exclusively of water, a place where all of his dreams could come true. In this realm, he created a hummingbird and dubbed it Potoweet. That hummingbird was I, but I was not like other hummingbirds, for I was given the power to speak and I possessed knowledge of the magical realm. I knew not where this knowledge originated, only that it was born into me. I shared the knowledge with Oric. I became his friend and guide.

Within the magical realm, Oric created a village that he called the Hutch, and beyond the Hutch, he created fields and stone walls, a dirt road along which to come and go. He populated the Hutch with friendly and happy souls who attempted, but sometimes failed, to lead virtuous lives. Oric adored playing pretend, and every afternoon he staged theatrical performances on a raised platform in the middle of the Hutch. The people cherished the performances and they bestowed endless praise upon Oric.

Oric, however, soon grew discontented. He had dark feelings within him, resentment toward his loyal creations. He knew better than to let such feelings be known and risk the loss of their adoration, so he constructed an underground fortress, a stone palace where he could be alone on occasion. He hid the fortress beneath a sea of blood, so that the people of the Hutch would keep their distance. Of course, *I* knew of this fortress, for Oric shared all of his secrets with me.

"Before I created the Hutch, back in the world where I was born, there was a sea beast that died among the rocks in a cove," Oric confided to me one evening. "It had many legs, slick and twisty appendages that when sliced open were hollow inside, like a bone without its marrow, like tunnels that connect faraway places. This beast has haunted me and haunts me still, for I imagine it is the sort of monster that steals people away from their slumber. If one is haunted, then one must be master of that which haunts him, and so I would like to have a similar beast in this fortress for me to command as I wish."

Thus and therefore a giant mass of hollow tentacles was born upon the ceiling of the fortress, and Oric gave himself control of the tentacles by way of a series of ropes. Pull a rope and a tentacle would stretch to unimaginable lengths and snatch up animals and people from far away. Now, as I've made clear, Oric was a god and had the power to smite using nothing but a simple wish, but it was a power he had always wielded judiciously. He believed in gracing his creations with a certain amount of free will. The tentacles, however, brought out a sinister side in him.

If someone in the Hutch angered him or annoyed him, whether by word, action, or simple gesture, then Oric would retreat underground. He would use the tentacles to capture that person and to bring them to the fortress and set them upon a pedestal. Whilst reclining in a tortoiseshell swing above the pedestal and disguising himself in a red cloak and a mask made of goat horns, Oric would play the part of a wraith.

"You have been wicked," he would say, or, "You have been selfish," and the people would grovel, weep, and beg forgiveness, which Oric would grant them, but only on the condition that they alter their ways. Upon their agreement, he would once again deploy the tentacles and transfer the people back aboveground, where they would regale the others with stories of the horn-faced monster that they soon titled . . . the Mandrake.

Yes indeed, yes indeed, and once this fictitious Mandrake was introduced, a curious and fortuitous change occurred. As long as Oric's creations feared the monster, then their lives strained closer toward virtue, and Oric could safely exercise his dark feelings without anyone surrendering their love for him. The Hutch was more peaceful than it had ever been. I, as you might surmise, was wary of the arrangement, but I had no right to object. "Someday the dark feelings will abate,"

Oric assured me, "and we will have no need for the Mandrake."

Sadly, the opposite occurred. His feelings became darker and darker still, and soon playing the part of the Mandrake did not suffice for Oric. He had the urge to destroy what he had created, to rain Armageddon down upon everyone and everything.

"I wish I could purge these thoughts from my head," he cried one night whilst he and I were alone in the fortress. "I wish I could put an end to this evil inside of me."

A voice arrived in his head and remarked, "I can give you that."

"Please do, please do," Oric whimpered in reply.

A creature both featureless and nameless and made entirely of nothingness instantly appeared in the fortress, wielding a pen constructed of bamboo. It placed the pen into Oric's ear and placed its mouth upon the pen and began to suck.

That is when my mind went blank. For how long it was blank, I may never know, but when my mind returned, it arrived with the knowledge that while the creature was gone, so too was Oric. Vanished, disappeared, like the stars with the dawn.

I, of course, mourned the loss of my master, but I knew that I must carry on. I returned to the surface through a small tunnel I burrowed with my beak, and I told the people of the Hutch that Oric was no more.

"What about the Mandrake?" they asked.

Knowing that the Mandrake was the one thing that kept order in the Hutch, I lied. I told them that the Mandrake lived on, but they need not fear him so long as they were good and honest people. And they *were* good and honest people and remained as such for a long time.

For reasons I've never fully understood, I possess the gift of everlasting life, but nobody else in the Hutch shared this gift, and so generations lived and died, on and on for many years, until Oric was completely forgotten to all but me, and the Mandrake was all that was remembered from the days of old.

Until one morning, someone we had never seen before, a boy clad in scale mail, arrived in the Hutch. "Who are you?" the villagers asked. "And where do you come from?"

"I am Hadrian," the boy replied. "I come from a place very different from this. Will you host me as I pass through on my journey?"

Though they had never had a visitor, they were a kind people and they agreed to help Hadrian, yet they told him that he must act honorably or else he would face the wrath of the Mandrake.

"This Mandrake frightens you?" Hadrian asked.

"Most thoroughly," they replied.

"What if one were to hunt down and destroy this Mandrake?" Hadrian asked.

"We would be forever grateful," they told him. "We would be indebted to you, for you would have saved us."

"Where does he dwell?" Hadrian asked.

"Beneath the sea of blood," they told him, pointing in the distance to the red liquid they so carefully avoided.

"Then I will swim to the bottom and find him," Hadrian said.

This thrilled the people, but it worried me, for I knew that Hadrian might gain access to the fortress, where he would find nothing except for the ropes and the tentacles. So I burrowed down to the fortress once again and waited for him. It was not without some guilt that I prayed for Hadrian to drown and no longer pose as an impediment, but alas, Hadrian was a skilled swimmer and a determined and wily boy, and he reached the fortress mere moments after I arrived.

"It is a hoax," I regretfully admitted.

"To keep them docile?" Hadrian asked.

"Indeed," I said, and I proceeded to tell Hadrian about the tentacles and how they operated.

Hadrian was understandably intrigued. "So a dead Mandrake is of no use?" he asked.

"No, it is not."

"I see," Hadrian said, and it was then that I recognized the lust for power in his eyes, and it was also then that Hadrian climbed onto the swing, seized the ropes, and commanded the tentacles to capture the blacksmith and the baker from the Hutch. Only he did not simply scare these men. He bade that the tentacles suffocate their lungs and place their dead bodies upon the pedestal.

"What are you doing?" I shouted.

Sneering, Hadrian leapt to the pedestal and produced a quill from within his underclothes. He began piercing the men's dead bodies with the quill. "I am giving them their Mandrake," Hadrian said.

"Oric was kind to them," I pleaded. "He never hurt them. This is not the proper way!"

Hadrian laughed and climbed back upon the swing. He pulled the ropes and made the tentacles transport the bodies to the wooden platform in the middle of the Hutch, and when the people awoke to discover this horror in the morning, they were understandably upset.

"Who did this?" they cried.

Bloodied and dirty, Hadrian appeared before them and said, "The Mandrake. I fought him. I could not defeat him. Yet I uncovered his identity, and now that I know his true nature, he means to destroy us all."

"His identity?" they asked. "His true nature?"

"The Mandrake has lived among you for many years. He takes different forms, and one of them is that of a hummingbird. I believe you call him Potoweet."

The small holes on the bodies matched the width of my beak. The culprit seemed clear. Enraged, a mob set out to destroy me, but I was too quick and my small size made it easy for me to hide. One would think I would have tried to explain, but I was always viewed differently in the Hutch. Everlasting life has a way of breeding suspicion and contempt.

"You are not safe here anymore," Hadrian told the villagers. "The Mandrake is too fast, too clever, but I know of a place where we can be protected from him."

He led the people to the blood sea, and while they were hesitant at first, they saw that the sanguine waters did not harm Hadrian, so they trusted their faith and they followed him below the surface. They lived there, within Oric's secret fortress, for years, trusting in and serving Hadrian whilst fearing the Mandrake. To keep me out, he blocked my tunnels with stone. I am not the type of bird suited to swimming, so unless one of those tubes snatches me up and carries me there, I will never be able to enter that fortress again. And Hadrian will have those people forever under his spell. Occasionally, to show his commitment to their safety, he dispatches a noble hero to fight the Mandrake, and that noble hero almost always meets an ignoble end.

As will you, Mr. Cleary.

CHAPTER 6

THE FLUTTER OF THE BIRD'S WINGS ADDED DENSITY TO THE air. Potoweet's story was a convincing one, but Alistair knew that *convincing* doesn't always mean *true*. He switched the sword to his left hand for a moment, wiped the sweat off his right palm, and switched it back.

"Why am I supposed to believe this?" he asked.

"You are not *supposed* to believe anything," Potoweet said. "You have the choice to believe. As you had the choice to believe Hadrian. He is an adept manipulator, you do understand? He has usurped other worlds and will usurp more. His power grows so long as he has his loyal figments to protect him and wishful swimmers like you under his thumb. There is only one problem that remains. Me."

Potoweet pivoted his body in the air and gave Alistair a full view of it. Sure enough, in the place where an ear might be, there was a blue mark in the shape of a horseshoe.

"You . . . you . . . are . . ." Alistair started to raise his sword.

"Precisely what you feared?" Potoweet asked. "I have no doubt that Hadrian told you about my embellishment. He hopes that you kill me. For if you kill me, then no one will ever know the truth again. I possess the true story, and it is in veracity that the real power lies, young man."

"He sent others to fight the Mandrake, though," Alistair said. "What happened to them?"

"They learned the truth from me," Potoweet said. "So they attempted to swim back down to the fortress, only to be suffocated or eviscerated by one of the tentacles. Hadrian has modified those horrid appendages. Some are used for transportation. They stretch as far as gateways to other worlds. Some are used for spying. Should you see one poke out of the sky, be mindful. It is watching. Finally, some are used for murder. All are at his command."

"So I'm doomed," Alistair said as he raised his sword. "And no matter what you are, my best bet is still to kill you. Because then Hadrian will let me go where I want. He let Polly go where she wanted."

"Oh joy!" Potoweet cheered. "You've met Polly. A rambunctious but resourceful girl. I am so glad she soldiers on."

"You know her?"

"Indubitably," Potoweet said. "Hadrian sent her to vanquish me once. She actually came the closest. She managed to capture me in her tight fist. She might have squeezed the life out of me, but I slipped away at the last moment."

"Aha!" Alistair retorted. "But in your story you said that you had everlasting life."

Potoweet twittered as if clucking his tongue. "Dear boy, dear boy, dear boy. This is where you are mistaken. Everlasting life is not the same as immortality. I will not die of old age or disease, but should someone choose to kill me, then I will cease to exist. The same goes for you. And for Hadrian and Polly. Creatures like us do not age, but that does not mean we are invincible. We are similar to rocks. We can sit for lifetimes unchanged, but a hammer can still render us into dust."

The platform was about two stories off the ground. A fall from it wouldn't necessarily kill Alistair, but it would certainly hurt him. He took a few steps away from the edge, and Potoweet moved with him. "How did Polly manage to get away from Hadrian?" Alistair asked. "If all the others died, what did she do to survive?"

"That I do not know," Potoweet said. "A bargain, I suspect. That young lady is a schemer of the highest order."

As Potoweet jagged through the air effortlessly, things started to come into focus for Alistair. Mahaloo, the women who spoke to Polly near the bonfire, the borrowed boots, the chase—was it all a setup? The way those people could move through the forest was remarkable, and that crazed woman should have easily caught Alistair. And yet she didn't, because maybe she wasn't meant to. Polly was a schemer, and a schemer could have easily rigged the whole thing, created a charade to gain Alistair's trust, to lure him into Hadrian's net, where he could be used as a bargaining chip.

"What's the Ambit of Ciphers?" Alistair asked.

Potoweet paused. "Please do not say that this is where our Polly now resides."

Alistair nodded.

"Oh my goodness," Potoweet said. "I have heard tell of this place. It is a realm of vengeful and jealous things. Frightening, frightening things."

"The boy named Oric you told me about," Alistair said. "Could he be there?"

Potoweet's head wiggled back and forth as fast as his wings flapped, and Alistair couldn't tell if this was a forceful denial or just a hummingbird's gesture of uncertainty. "The inhabitants of the Ambit of Ciphers are creations, and Oric was not a creation. He was a creator. Something else happened to Oric. He is somewhere else."

"I'm not so sure," Alistair said. "Polly said she was looking for someone, just like I'm looking for someone, and the Ambit of Ciphers is the place she chose to look. It's where I plan to look as well."

"Unwise, but you seem to have little interest in wisdom," Potoweet said as he zipped back and forth in the air like a UFO in some old science-fiction movie. There was no way Alistair could catch him or strike him with his sword, no way to shut him up. He was far too quick.

"I'm going back to Hadrian," Alistair said, "and I'm going to make a deal. That is the wise thing to do."

"That is the risky thing to do," Potoweet said.

"Well, you haven't provided any other solution," Alistair said.

"True enough," Potoweet said. "But I will provide you with the following advice. Never think that you are anything more than what you are . . . or anything less."

It hardly felt like advice to Alistair, but still he said, "Thank you."

Potoweet responded, "You are most welcome. For now I bid you good luck. And Godspeed."

The flutter was there and then it wasn't, and within seconds the bird was nothing but a speck, retreating into the distance. Alistair was alone again. He sat down cross-legged on the platform. He looked up into the sky.

1984

———◆———

FIONA LOOMIS, BACK HOME, SEVEN YEARS OLD, IN A SWIMSUIT, her hair even blacker when drenched in water. It was blazing hot, and Keri had set up a Slip'N Slide in the yard, and while she was in the house fetching watermelon, Alistair and Fiona traded turns.

"I want a Slip'N Slide that's a mile long!" Alistair hollered as he ran, jumped, and skidded over the wet yellow plastic.

"I can make one a million miles long!" Fiona hollered back as she followed in his wake—leaping, sliding, almost kicking Alistair, who had to roll out of her way.

They lay there for a moment—Alistair in the grass, Fiona on the plastic—and they looked up at the clouds. Not puffy clouds, wispy ones, the shape of cotton pulled thin. There were no puppies or dragons to imagine, but they were nice clouds all the same. Inside, a phone rang, and seconds later

Keri was at the window, watermelon juice running down the front of her swimsuit.

"Fiona," she called out. "That was your mom. She says it's time to come home."

"Tell her I want to stay," Fiona replied, not looking away from the clouds.

"Already hung up," Keri replied as she dabbed her chin with the shoulder strap of her swimsuit. "You can call her and tell her yourself."

Fiona harrumphed, rolled over, and looked at Alistair. "If you could do magic, what magic would you do?"

"I don't know," he said. "Fly, I guess."

She rolled back over and looked at the sky. "Flying gets old. Trust me. Freezing time. That's the best magic. Know what I mean? Stop everything so you can keep doing what you want. You don't ever have to go home if you can freeze time."

It was a good point. Alistair could see the appeal of freezing time, of continuing to play, of cherishing a sun that never sets. And yet, he didn't want that now. He wanted to go inside.

He stood up and wiped grass from his legs. "Later, gator," he said.

"Where are you going?" she asked.

"Inside. Don't you have to go home?"

Her eyes narrowed. "I'm freezing time. I don't have to go anywhere."

"I have to pee," Alistair admitted, his hand fidgeting, clawing at his thigh.

"Pee on a tree," she said. "Time is frozen. No one will see you."

"Later, gator," Alistair said again, because even if time was frozen, he was not settling for a tree. He waved over his shoulder as he waddled to the house.

A little bit later, with a slice of watermelon in hand, Alistair joined Keri at the window that looked out into the backyard. Fiona rolled off the Slip'N Slide, stood, and walked across the grass, water streaming from her hair like heavy rain out of a gutter.

"She lay there for, like, five minutes," Keri said. "Looking up. Not even moving."

"She's weird," Alistair said as he took a bite of the watermelon.

"You can say that again."

He swallowed. "She's weird."

Keri chuckled. "Mom and Dad don't hang out with her parents anymore," she said. "Why do you still hang out with her?"

Alistair shrugged in response. "Because she comes over."

By that point, Fiona was gone, beyond their yard and line of sight. Keri turned away from the window. "There's a mouse in the attic that plays the violin," she said. "If you find it and kill it, I'll let you have my allowance."

CHAPTER 7

———•◦•———

"I'LL MAKE A DEAL WITH YOU, HADRIAN!" ALISTAIR CRIED INTO the cloudless sky. The sky was a hard blue. No cracks, nothing to indicate that it didn't go on forever. Still, Alistair suspected there were edges to it; if not roofs and walls, then boundaries of some sort. "Whatever Polly promised you," he yelled, "I'll give you the same! I need to find someone. I need to go home!"

No response. A breeze, lilac-tinged and confident, caused his arm hairs to echo the dance of the grass. Birdsong skipped back and forth, calls and responses. Time did its thing.

The view of the Hutch from the platform sparked Alistair's imagination. He tried to picture it bustling with men, women, and children, the same ones who swarmed the pedestal in the underground fortress and chanted "New blood! New blood!" Could they really be the descendants of peaceful and friendly folks? Could they have been so easily corrupted by lies and fear? How could he know for sure, and why should he even care, because what was there to do, really?

He was stuck. Potoweet was right. He was a fool, and this was a fool's errand.

He closed his eyes. It had all come at him so fast. Ever since he touched that floating cylinder of water in Fiona's basement, ever since the ash swirled around him and he plunged into the rainbow river, ever since he washed up in Mahaloo and met Polly and ran and swam and floundered in Hadrian's net, ever since he came face-to-face with a story-telling hummingbird, there had been no time to think things over. Now he had time, nothing but it.

The urge to cry returned, because Fiona had told him something else. No matter how long Alistair stayed in Aqua-vania, not a second would pass back home. Back home, time was frozen, and Kyle was lying dead, or dying, with a bullet wound to his stomach. Yes, it was an accident, but Alistair couldn't kid himself any longer. That bullet was meant for someone. It was meant for Charlie, to stop him from . . . being who he was, from . . . being whatever it was he had become.

The longer Alistair stayed in Aquavania, the longer he would have to worry about what might have happened to Kyle, about what was going to happen to Kyle. The longer he stayed in Aquavania, the longer that wound stayed fresh and open, a reminder of all of Alistair's mistakes.

He threw the sword to the side, and it clanged against the platform and slid off the edge. "No no no no no . . ." he mumbled, balling up his fists and pressing them against his eyes.

His blood couldn't keep up with his heart. His hands went numb. He tried to pull in a deep breath, but instead of air, something solid entered his mouth.

Good God!

It squirmed and wiggled, tickling his uvula. Rather than hack or gag, Alistair gulped, and that something became lodged in his windpipe. It cut off all of his oxygen. Choking, he fell to his back, and his eyes turned to the sky long enough to see a tentacle descending to scoop him up and suck him away.

"New blood! New blood! New blood!"

The chant built into a crescendo as the tentacle spat Alistair onto the net, back in the underground fortress where Hadrian reigned. The trip through the fleshy tube took about a minute, but Alistair still hadn't dislodged the blockage in his throat. As the net lowered him onto the pedestal, he pounded his own back, trying to knock loose the clog.

"Don't go so hard on yourself," Hadrian said, chuckling as he rocked on his swing. "You surrendered faster than most, but that doesn't make you a coward."

The crowd snickered as Alistair—now on his knees, doubled over—winced and continued to strike himself between the shoulder blades. It was useless. With his arm twisted the way it was, he couldn't produce adequate force.

"So you'd like an arrangement similar to the one I made with Polly?" Hadrian went on. "I suspect you have no idea what that entails?"

Alistair couldn't have responded if he wanted to. His eyes watered; his head was a squeezed lemon. He placed his hands down and arched his back, tried to turn himself into a cat coughing out a hairball.

"I exercised trust and compassion with Polly," Hadrian continued. "You must understand that I am the only known swimmer who controls a gateway to the Ambit of Ciphers, and Polly desperately wanted to travel there. So she paid her passage by delivering us ten swimmers to fight the Mandrake. The first nine were unsuccessful. You, young sir, are number ten. Would you like to agree to the same bargain?"

His chest heaving, Alistair tried to cough, but all that came out was a throaty rattle. The crowd responded with a fresh chant of "New blood! New blood! New blood!"

"What ails you, boy?" Hadrian said, planting his feet and stopping the swing. "Did you eat something foul up there in the Hutch? Please do not regurgitate on our pedestal. We've only just had it cleaned."

This is it, Alistair thought. *I'm going to die right here, choke to death without ever fighting back, without ever knowing squat about Fiona's fate.* It felt like more than a punishment. It felt like being ridiculed. With his last bit of strength, Alistair rose to his feet and, instead of coughing, he tried to swallow. He tipped his head back.

"Here's the difference between you and Polly," Hadrian remarked. "She had wit and spark. She knew that making a deal means jousting with words. You, on the other hand, are a complete and absolute bore. Better suited to the froth of the sea."

Hadrian reached up to grab the red rope, the one that dispatched the toothed tentacle.

"New blood! New blood! New blood!" went the crowd.

And Alistair, head still tipped back, neck straight, opened his mouth. Out flew a bird.

Potoweet shot up from the boy's throat like a cork from a champagne bottle. As soon as he reached the height of Hadrian's eyes, Potoweet stopped midair and hovered, wings blurring. Alistair gasped for breath as his body finally surfaced from the depths of suffocation.

"Greetings, Hadrian," Potoweet said.

"Oh. Sweet. Merciful. Heavens," Hadrian replied.

"And so it is that we find ourselves entangled once again," Potoweet said.

The crowd fell silent. The only sound was Alistair's thick breaths. *Haw, huh. Haw, huh. Hawwww, huhhhh.* Until Hadrian screamed.

"Mandrake!"

That's when Potoweet unfolded and expanded. His wings fanned. His feathers flared. His body ballooned, and his legs sprouted. His beak twisted until it wasn't a beak anymore. It was a horn, and floating in the air there was now a creature both beautiful and terrible, a monster with a face like a bird's face, but with that horn instead of a beak, and with a mouth like a serpent's mouth that curled up around the sides of his head. He had wings like a peacock's wings, a body like a man's body, but with two muscular and furry legs that were part equine, part lupine. This was the Mandrake, and he advertised his delight with a mad shriek.

Panic. The crowd began to scream and push and trample and clog the exit with their flailing bodies. The Mandrake wasted no time. He lunged through the air at Hadrian, and Hadrian tried to dodge but wasn't fast enough. The Mandrake's twisted horn pierced the scale mail that protected Hadrian's body and sank into the boy's chest.

"You . . . worthless . . . bucket . . . of pus," Hadrian coughed, and Alistair couldn't tell if he was talking to him or to the Mandrake, for Hadrian's eyes fell closed and his body started to convulse.

The Mandrake roared again and kicked at the balcony with his powerful legs. The balcony crumbled, raining stones on the raging crowd, and with a still-writhing Hadrian skewered to his horn, the Mandrake flew up and across the room, over the pedestal and then down toward the teeming masses below. A blast of arctic air erupted from the Mandrake's mouth, freezing and leveling each and every body it hit.

"Stop!" Alistair screamed. "Please stop! You shouldn't be doing this!"

The Mandrake responded with a cackle. "I was designed to do this!"

The room flashed from sweltering to frigid in an instant. The exit was still clogged with people and would remain clogged, because the Mandrake released another blast of cold air from his mouth and it froze the bodies in place.

"The red rope!" came a terrified scream from below. "Pull the red one! It'll pulverize the beast!"

Hadrian's empty swing rocked back and forth in the open air, its tortoiseshell seat coming close to the pedestal. In Alistair's sixth-grade gym class, there had been a track and field day when he had registered a long jump of eight feet, which was considered not bad for a twelve-year-old. The shell appeared to reach within eight feet of the pedestal at the apex of its sway, and since it was only going to lose momentum, it was now or never. Alistair took a few steps back. He started to run.

As he reached the end of the pedestal, his foot snagged a bunched-up section of net. He stumbled, and what was a planned leap became an impromptu fall.

"Waaaaa!" Alistair screamed, his voice joining the chorus of cries from the frenzied villagers below. Down he went into clouds of frosty air. Whatever broke his fall was likely to be person or stone, so when he struck a meaty and feathery wing, he was relieved, but only for a split second.

The wing flapped up and Alistair slid down onto the Mandrake's back. It was an enormous back, rife with rib and muscle, and Alistair was astounded that this was the same beast as Potoweet. Balancing would be impossible without a firm grip, so Alistair reached forward and grabbed at the feathers on the Mandrake's head.

The Mandrake roared again, tipped its head back, and flew upward, out of the billows of cold air and toward the hanging garden of tentacles. Alistair held on like it was a bucking bronco, but his sweaty hand was already slipping, and when the Mandrake took a sharp turn, Hadrian's impaled body spun like a propeller and his foot hit Alistair in the face. Alistair lost his grip.

He grabbed at the air as he fell again, and the first thing his hands found were the dangling colored ropes.

Yank, yank, yank, yank.

He snatched and swung from rope to rope like he was on a jungle gym. Tentacles came rocketing down from the ceiling, snapping at the air, striking the pedestal, striking one another, becoming intertwined.

Yank, yank, yank, yank.

More tentacles, ricocheting off one another—the hollow ones pilfering the frozen bodies of figments, the ones equipped with blades chopping things to bits, all of them zipping past the Mandrake, who dipped and dodged as he flew.

Yank, yank, yank, yank.

The walls took a pounding, the screams got even louder, and the ceiling began to crack and let in the chunky, viscous sea. Red liquid began to rain down on them.

Through a torrent of blood and a tangle of tentacles came the awful visage of the Mandrake. The beast was tilted sideways, weaving through the air past the many obstacles, his eyes locked on Alistair. As the blood doused the Mandrake's body, the creature howled in pain but kept moving.

Alistair was holding on to one rope, and there was one final rope in front of him. Since everything was drenched in blood, everything looked red. He had no idea what pulling this final rope would do, but pulling this final rope was all he could do.

Yank.

As a blast of cold air struck Alistair's legs, a tentacle grabbed at his head, and with the ceiling caving in and blood pouring down, Alistair slipped away into the dark.

Up and over and around he went as the bays of agony faded and the only noise was the sluice of his body through the tube. It reminded him of a babbling brook, but it was the opposite of relaxing. Because next came a jolt and a crash as the tube busted through a flimsy layer of ice and spat Alistair out onto cold ground.

He was now in a dark cavern where the air was frosty but ripe, and standing in front of him was a penguin.

"Greetings and salutations," the penguin said.

November 19, 1989

His shirt was wet from the rain. Also the blood. Kyle Dwyer, Charlie's older brother, lay in the grass, bleeding from the stomach. The autumn sky cursed and spat.

Charlie crouched down and waved his bare hands in the air above Kyle's wound. They were mangled hands, casualties of a fireworks accident. The left one had a thumb, pinkie, and ring finger; the right one had only a thumb and pinkie. Yet Charlie moved them with grace—slowly, confidently. The movements seemed practiced, a ritual of sorts. Charlie had done this before. To Alistair, that much was clear.

But what was he doing exactly? Kyle writhed and the blood kept coming, while Charlie swept his hands over and under each other like he was casting a spell. It didn't appear to be helping.

Alistair couldn't bear to witness this anymore. Yes, Alistair had shot the gun. Yes, he had caused Kyle's wound. But rather than help, he chose to run away. He said that it was to call 911, but that wasn't the only motive. That moment—that image—had potential. To stick. To stay. To never leave. Like the final page of a tragic book.

Because this appeared to be the end of Kyle's tale.

SO LET'S
START ANOTHER

IN ANOTHER YEAR
BEFORE YEARS

———◆———

THIS TALE CONCERNS A BOY AND HIS STORIES.

Stories, fictional ones at least, were unknown to those people who lived at the foot of those snowy mountains, in those caves next to that creek. There were no storytellers in that tribe called the Hotiki—that is, until the one named Cabal was born.

Cabal was born during a rainy season, and when the next rainy season arrived, he was already speaking. Six rainy seasons later, he was telling long and complex yarns that kept the Hotiki enthralled well into the night. He told them about how the stars were enchanted beings. He spoke of faraway places where the forests and fields were awash with flowers and the snows never came.

"Where do you learn such wondrous things?" the elders asked, for they only knew of things they had witnessed with their own eyes and ears. They observed. They shared knowledge. They didn't invent like Cabal.

"I am not sure," Cabal admitted. "Like the rain, sometimes stories fall on me."

It was as acceptable an explanation as any, and the elders actually didn't care where his stories came from, so long as Cabal kept telling them.

One night, Cabal told the story of a girl and her brother. The girl had long arms and big round eyes and a scar on her cheek. Her brother was a mischievous boy who happened to be a shape-shifter, a person who could transform into any creature alive. While playing near a pond one day, the girl dared her brother to take on the form of a frog and to hop across the water on the tops of lily pads. Never one to resist a dare, the boy dove into the water and emerged transformed, entirely slick and green. But before he had a chance to even hop once, a turtle surfaced and gobbled the frog-boy up.

The girl was terrified and filled with sadness. Also guilt, plenty of guilt. She feared that her tribe would accuse her of murder, so she devised another solution to her predicament. She journeyed into the woods and rounded up animals.

"You must pretend to be my brother," she told the animals. "And I will let you live among us and eat our food. But only one of you at a time. If the tribe becomes suspicious, then I will replace you."

Because humans always had the best food, the animals agreed. A wolf was the first one to accompany the girl back to her tribe. Since the girl's brother was a known shape-shifter and spent most of his time in the form of animals, the tribe had no reason to doubt that the wolf was the child they all knew. And they all lived in harmony for quite a while. Until one morning the wolf could not control himself and he stole a baby from a bed of hay and ate the baby in the woods.

"You wicked beast," the girl told the wolf as he slinked away into the brush. "You are no longer my brother."

The tribe never suspected the wolf. They thought he was simply the precocious, but peaceful, shape-shifting boy. Instead they blamed the missing baby on the wrath of their creators.

"The creators give and so they must take," the elders pronounced.

The girl, determined to continue with her charade, replaced the wolf with a bear. Life with the bear was nice. Good. He was part of the tribe and all was well. Until, as anyone could guess, the bear gave in to temptation, his insatiable hunger for old ladies. One foggy night, the bear stole the girl's grandmother from her slumber and devoured her in the woods.

"You wicked beast," the girl told the bear. "You are no longer my brother."

Like the wolf, the tribe did not suspect the bear. They laid blame upon the creators. And the girl replaced the bear with a lion. The arrangement worked once again, until it didn't. The beast's appetite won out. This time the tribe's greatest hunter was the meal.

It kept on like this for a while. The girl refused to tell the truth about her brother, she continued to replace the animals, and people kept getting swallowed up in the forest. Soon, the only ones left in the tribe were the girl and that turtle, the one that had originally eaten her brother. Due to a steady diet of frogs, the turtle had grown to the size of a mammoth.

"Do you plan to eat me and end this tribe?" the girl asked the turtle.

"No," the turtle told her. "I plan to protect you. To keep you alive so that you will grow very old and realize how foolish and selfish you have been."

Sure enough, that's just what the turtle did. He kept the girl from harm, lending her his shell when she needed protection, catching extra frogs and fish so that she would always have food. And she lived a long, healthy life.

When they were both quite old, the turtle asked her if she regretted what she did.

The girl, now an old woman, replied, "No. Because I lived much longer than I would have without your help. Lying was the smartest thing I ever did."

This angered the turtle so much that he finally revealed the truth to her. "All of these years and you haven't learned one thing!" The turtle then transformed into an old man and stood in front of her.

"Brother?" the old woman asked.

The old man nodded. "The same," he said. "That day at the pond, I did not become a frog. I became a turtle. And you became a liar."

This was not the end of Cabal's story, but it was all the

tribe would hear, for Cabal stopped the tale when Hela, who was their oldest member, began to weep.

"Do not worry, Hela," Cabal said. "It's only a tale. This girl did not exist."

"But she did," Hela cried. "The girl you described was Una, with her long arms and big eyes and scar on her cheek. And the boy? He was Banar."

"Who is Una?" Cabal asked. "Who is Banar?"

"I am the only one old enough to remember," Hela said. "When I was a girl, there was a boy named Banar who impersonated animals. The chaos spirits drowned him in the creek one night. Not long after that, they took his sister, Una. We never saw her again."

The rest of the Hotiki gasped at this. "I know nothing of these people," Cabal said.

"Of course you don't," Hela said. "No one does. Because we chose not to speak of them, for fear that the chaos spirits would come after us all."

"I believe you're seeing something in my tale that is not there," Cabal said.

Hela stood up and pointed a finger at Cabal. "I believe your tale comes from an evil place. I believe you know not what fills your head. I believe you are possessed by the chaos spirits and have no place in the Hotiki."

Since Hela was the eldest in the tribe, she was trusted to be the wisest. The rest of the Hotiki agreed with her when she said that Cabal might be dangerous. Even Cabal's parents thought it best when the tribe decided to isolate him for two rainy seasons.

"We will not speak to Cabal," Hela decreed. "He will not speak to us. We will bring him food, but that is all. He will live alone in the smallest of our caves. And if after two rainy seasons we are safe from the chaos spirits, then we will let him live with us once more. But he must not tell such tales ever again."

There was no arguing with Hela, and Cabal accepted his fate. He set out to live in the small cave. It was a cramped and dank place. Water dripped from the stalactites and onto Cabal's head when he tried to sleep. It kept him awake for hours. In the past, when he couldn't sleep, he would make up stories, but he tried to wean himself of that habit now.

I must think of only things I know, he told himself. *I must not let the stories in.*

There was no stopping them, however. The stories rushed in at an alarming rate, piling up in his head. Soon there was no room for them and they started replacing his memories. By the end of the second rainy season, Cabal hardly had any memories left. His head was only stories.

Hela came to him one morning and said, "You have been noble and brave to live alone for all these days and nights. The Hotiki have been safe. Would you like to rejoin us now?"

With an innocent smile, Cabal said, "Yes. But first I'd like to finish that story."

MUCH LATER

CHAPTER 8

————◆————

BROKEN ICICLES AS THICK AS TREE TRUNKS COVERED THE
floor of the cavern. Cracked and splintered bones lay scattered throughout. A penguin stood a few feet from Alistair,
his black wings crossed like arms across his white chest. The
penguin winked and smiled, and Alistair scooted away on
his butt and the heels of his hands. "It's okay," the penguin
whispered. "Forget your worries."

*Forget your worries? Easy enough for him to say. He isn't
sitting where I'm sitting.*

The penguin clearly hadn't just witnessed a monster attack hundreds of people. The penguin clearly wasn't covered
in blood. Sitting on the frosty ground, Alistair examined
himself—his clothes and their rusty, earthy sheen. He paid
particular attention to his hands. Yes, they were bloody too.

"It's confusing, I know," the penguin said. "New places.

New creatures. Takes some adjustment. I can help with that. My name is Baxter. My game is hospitality."

The penguin bowed low, his beak almost touching the ground, but the gesture didn't impress Alistair. He wasn't about to be burned by a bird once again. "Stay back," he said.

Baxter nodded respectfully, held his ground. "I take it that your visit is an unplanned one?"

On the walls of the cavern there were little lights, not much different from Christmas lights. Only a handful were lit. They spelled out a message:

HE WON.

A few raggedy, emaciated polar bears hovered overhead, in the upper reaches of the cavern, aided by propellers that sprouted from their backs. The propellers were flesh and bone, as much a part of the bears as their chapped noses, as their yellow teeth, as their crescent-shaped claws that grew like terrible black flames from their dangling feet. Their eyelids were low, and their eyes were glassy and pink. They didn't seem to notice Alistair, and he had never seen anything like them.

Yet he had heard of something like them. Exactly like them. "Your name is Baxter?" Alistair asked.

"Yes."

"Baxter the penguin?"

"Yes. Would you prefer another name?" Baxter replied. "I'm open to suggestions."

In the middle of the cavern, there was a throne made of ice. It was cracked and empty, but Alistair imagined a girl with a fur-lined parka perched on it. "Who created you?" he asked.

The tip of Baxter's beak dipped and his voice became somber and respectful. "You are looking at the first and most loyal friend to Chua Ling, a creator of great wit and generosity."

Chua Ling. She was Fiona's friend. Fiona had told Alistair stories about her. "You're serious?" he asked.

Baxter put a wing to his heart. "I don't kid about Chua."

Chua had gone missing almost a year before Fiona. It was her disappearance that had set off a chain of events that led Fiona to tell Alistair about Aquavania. If it weren't for Chua Ling's insistence on stopping the Riverman, Alistair would have been at home, asleep in bed, instead of stuck sitting on the ice talking to a penguin. Of all the corners of Aquavania he could have ended up in, Alistair had landed in one of the few he had heard about. It was either a fabulous stroke of luck or another elaborate trick.

"If you were really created by Chua Ling, then tell me, what was her favorite snack?" Alistair asked.

The question sparked Baxter's eyes, and with a flick of a foot, the penguin sent himself sliding across the ground as if he were wearing skates. It was impossible to avoid the bones, and as Baxter plowed through them, femurs and vertebrae clattered together like wind chimes. Eventually, his curving path led him to the throne of ice, behind which he ducked down for a moment. When he reappeared, he was carrying a bowl filled with potato chip crumbs.

"Salt and vinegar were her absolute favorite," Baxter said. "But for guests, she served barbecue. More of a crowd-pleaser."

A simple answer of *potato chips* would have sufficed, so

Baxter's thoroughness was impressive, but Alistair wasn't completely satisfied. The best liars are thorough. "What did Chua say when she was excited?" Alistair asked.

"Hot chocolate!"

"And who did she love?"

"Her mom. Her dad. Her sister. Werner Schroeder . . . and me."

The bird was right on all counts, and Alistair only had two more questions.

"Do you know Fiona?"

"Of course."

"Then what's her last name?"

Baxter put the tip of his wing to his chin and thought on it until the best answer he could give was a squint and a "Haven't the faintest clue."

It was a trick question. If Baxter had known Fiona's last name, or had given a false one, then he wouldn't be Baxter, because Fiona had never told anyone in Aquavania her last name. The only person in Aquavania who knew her last name was the Riverman, the Whisper . . . Charlie.

Charlie. He might never have learned that Fiona visited Aquavania. But Alistair had scribbled her secret on a bathroom stall. Stupid. Charlie had read it and had figured out how to find Fiona in Aquavania, how to exploit what she needed and capture her. Sure, it was another of Alistair's numerous mistakes, but the fact that it was a mistake didn't make it feel any less shameful.

"You realize I have to be cautious?" he told Baxter. "I have to be sure you are who you say you are."

"You're frightened?" Baxter asked.

"Aren't you?"

Baxter shrugged. "Worst possible thing has already happened to me: I lost Chua. What else is there to be frightened about?"

"You don't even know who I am," Alistair said. "That doesn't frighten you?"

Another shrug. "You're in trouble. Doesn't take much to see that. People don't usually crash through our floor covered with blood and asking a bazillion questions. You need help, and I'm here to help. Besides, you know Chua. Are you her friend?"

Alistair shook his head. "I only know Fiona."

"I see," Baxter said. "How is good ol' Fiona?"

"You don't know?"

The split in Baxter's beak twisted up in embarrassment. "Since Chua's been gone, I haven't talked to anyone. It's been pretty much me and the bears. Not all of them have survived, as you can see. Lean times here."

The remaining bears continued to fly in lazy circles near the top of the cavern. That's when Alistair realized that there was no sunlight, starlight, or firelight in there. Except for the dim message on the wall, the only illumination came from the bears' patchy fur. They were like glow-in-the-dark toys that were almost out of juice. Watching them made Alistair sad and dizzy, so he turned back to Baxter. "Do you even know where you are?" he asked.

"I'm . . . where I've always been?" Baxter asked.

Alistair sighed. He was used to being the ignorant one in Aquavania. Now, met with this penguin's pleading eyes, he was the one who had to explain. "The Riverman took Fiona," he said.

Baxter took a breath, closed his eyes, and nodded.

"Just like he took Chua," Alistair went on. "And when he took them, he took their worlds too. You are where you've always been, but you're also somewhere new. Your world has moved. Floated into other hands. The Riverman has your world now. And around here, they call him the Whisper."

Baxter opened his eyes. A tear slipped out. "It's been so hard without her."

"I know."

"I'll admit I felt it," Baxter said, shuffling closer to Alistair as his voice gradually crumbled. "It's been more than her absence. Things have been . . . different. Things have been . . . off."

Alistair didn't realize what was happening until he found himself stroking Baxter's head. The penguin was hugging Alistair's shoulder and burying his face in Alistair's armpit. "I'm sorry," Alistair told him.

"I tried to ignore the difference," Baxter cried. "All I cared about was getting Chua back."

"I know, I know," Alistair said. "I care about the same thing."

Baxter pulled his head out from the pit and looked up at Alistair. "You do?"

"That's why I'm here. To find Fiona . . . to find both of them."

The words slipped out and there was no taking them back, especially since they made the penguin's webbed feet wiggle with excitement. Alistair could only nod with a feigned confidence that he hoped would convince Baxter he wasn't in over his head. That he hoped would convince himself.

Over the next few hours, Alistair told Baxter his story. He didn't mention Charlie Dwyer, because he didn't want Baxter to think he could be friends with such a . . . person. But he talked about everything else he knew about Aquavania and the Whisper. He told him about Mahaloo, Polly Dobson and the Ambit of Ciphers, about Hadrian, the Hutch and Potoweet, about the Mandrake.

"I'm not like that," Baxter said. "I am penguin through and through."

"I know," Alistair said.

"Where do you think this Mandrake came from?"

"Hadrian said the Whisper is his master."

"And why does he make him do horrible things?"

Alistair pretended to think this over for a moment, but he knew the answer immediately. "For fun."

"I don't understand," Baxter said. "What's so fun about destruction?"

Even if he could explain, Alistair didn't have the time or energy to explain. Instead, he patted Baxter on the head and said, "I don't really understand either."

"The girl named Polly," Baxter said. "I may have heard of her."

"Really? How?"

"Saw her name written in the snow once. *Polly Dobson Will Have Her Revenge*, it read."

"Where?"

As if to return the favor, Baxter patted Alistair on the back and said, "It's been covered in snow many times since, so you can't read it. But I'll show you the place. Interesting, to say the least. Come with me."

The penguin led him across the cavern, and Alistair did his best to maintain his balance as the thin soles of his leather boots shuffled on the icy ground. He fell twice, landing on his butt and his shoulder, and snapping bones— not his own, thankfully—as he struck the ground. It hurt, but Baxter was always there to offer him a wing up and some words of encouragement. Alistair had trusted Polly. He had trusted Potoweet. And now he was trusting Baxter. There was an earnestness to the penguin. Kindness. At least that's how it seemed to Alistair. Or was he being a fool once again?

When they reached the edge of the cavern, Baxter pointed to a wall with a vertical crack in it, an opening barely wider than Alistair's chest. "That's the way."

"To where?" Alistair asked.

"You'll see," Baxter said as he slipped his body through the crack and disappeared into the darkness.

"Baxter?" Alistair said.

"It's not far," came Baxter's faint voice. "Suck in your gut. Forget your worries."

It was the second time he'd used that phrase: *Forget your worries.* Easier said than done. Back in the cavern, the polar bears continued their orbit, the throne remained empty, the bones still scattered, and the message lit in dim lights:

He won.

There was something else Fiona had told him about Chua's world. The dim lights cataloged the feelings and events that occurred in that cavern. They changed with the mood of the room. Once the Whisper captured Chua, the lights must have frozen on this final message of victory.

He won? Really? Not yet, he hasn't.

Alistair sucked in his gut and wedged his body into the crack in the wall.

1989

Alistair and Fiona walked along the slush-covered road away from Thessaly's library. Fiona had just shown Alistair a newspaper story about Chua Ling. It frightened him, but not only because it was about a girl who was missing. It was because Chua was a girl who lived all the way across the country, and yet Fiona said she used to see her all the time. In Aquavania, of course.

Fiona blamed the Riverman for Chua's disappearance, but Alistair didn't believe in the Riverman. Not then, at least. What he believed in then was the tangible, the *real*. Maybe someone was out there stealing children, but it couldn't possibly be a monster from another land. If anything, it was someone Fiona knew.

Alistair and Fiona walked in silence, passing a gas station with a convenience store lit by fluorescent lights. A man sat on a parked motorcycle near the gas pumps and sipped a fountain drink through a straw. As they passed him, the man tossed the cup to the ground, the plastic top popped off, and red liquid spilled over the pavement and mixed with the gravel and mush.

Fiona snorted her disapproval, but she was too far from the man for him to hear. "My sister, Maria, dated a guy who rode a motorcycle once," she told Alistair. "He smelled like oil."

"My sister, Keri, doesn't date anyone," Alistair replied.

"That's because she's in eighth grade," Fiona said. It was a somewhat valid point, but there were plenty of people who were dating in middle school. Sixth graders, seventh graders. Even a few fifth graders.

"Maybe it's that she doesn't have a crush on anyone," Alistair said.

"Maybe," Fiona said. "You know, choosing a guy is more than choosing a guy. At least that's what Maria tells me. She says it's opening an interesting-looking door. It's buying a ticket somewhere that promises sun and thunderstorms and food you've never tried. But you never really know where that place is."

Alistair wanted to say *Isn't that true of most choices?* but he remained quiet. He kept walking. They weren't dating, at least not technically. But still.

Fiona had chosen him.

CHAPTER 9

⊶◆⊷

THE WARMTH OF THE MEMORY FOUGHT OFF THE CHILL IN Alistair's bones as frigid rock brushed against his chest and back. He held his hands up and slid sideways through the dark passage.

"A little farther, a little farther . . ." Baxter's voice faded into nothingness, and once again, Alistair felt like a fool.

Why do I always follow? Why do I let others determine my fate? As soon as I get to the other end, then I'm making the decisions.

The other end was a long way off. Baxter must have had a poor sense of distance or time—probably both—because the passage went on and on until Alistair wasn't sure he could keep going, and yet he knew he couldn't turn back.

"Baxter!" he shouted. "Are you there?"

The response was muffled and unintelligible, and Alistair began to panic. The tight space felt even tighter, the darkness even darker. "Please," he pleaded. "Where are we going, Baxter?"

Nothing.

Alistair closed his eyes. *Baxter is good. Baxter is Fiona's friend.*

Fiona. His focus turned to Fiona. It had been about two weeks since he'd last seen her, since she'd told him that Charlie was the Riverman, since she'd said that Alistair was "so much better here," kissed him on the lips, and then left for Aquavania one final time. Not even fifteen days—not very long—but already he was forgetting what she looked like. Memories were hitting him without warning, but he couldn't summon the ones he wanted. He couldn't will her face back into his head. Her dark hair. Her crooked nose. Her eyes. *What color were they exactly? Green? Amber? Almost gray?*

If there was any hope of answering such questions, then maybe it lay at the end of the passage. *Baxter is good, Baxter is Fiona's friend,* he told himself again. He opened his eyes and pressed on.

Light. First barely a flicker, but soon it was illuminating every vein and bump on the surrounding stone. He quickened his pace. The air lost its staleness. There was an opening ahead.

At the other side of the passageway, where there was sun, wind, and earth, mountains dominated the skyline. There was no way to avoid them—immense, jagged, and capped with pink snow. They must have been miles high, perhaps higher than the Himalayas, the tallest of mountains. Well, the

133

tallest in the Solid World, that is. Perhaps in Aquavania they were considered puny. Alistair had given up trying to understand the space and time of this place. All he wanted to know was how to get from point A to point F.

A frozen lake had the potential to hold some clues. It sat at the foot of the mountains, and Baxter stood along the edge of it with his wings outstretched. Alistair followed the path of three-toed footprints through the pink snow.

"It was written on the lake," the penguin said. "I never saw who wrote it, but I've seen others come and go. From one hut to the next. They have little interest in chatting. Busy as bees and often strangely dressed."

Scattered over the surface of the lake were a series of ice-fishing huts. They were all of similar construction—corrugated aluminum, shingles, knotty scraps of plywood. They were actually the least foreign things Alistair had come across in Aquavania. The lakes and ponds near Thessaly were dotted with similar makeshift shelters every winter. Alistair's dad never built one, but occasionally he'd join a buddy with a thermos of something hot and they'd spend a Sunday bundled up and listening to football on the radio, catching mostly nothing. Alistair and Keri had even joined him once, but they both found it to be a cold and boring affair.

"What are you telling me?" Alistair asked Baxter.

"Back when Chua was around," Baxter explained, "these were fishing huts. Go inside, drop a hook in the hole, and seconds later you would pull up a big Swedish fish."

"Like the candy?" Alistair asked.

Baxter shrugged. "Like the Swedish type of fish, I guess. Red. Flat. Sweet."

Alistair nodded. "Yep. Go on."

"Well," Baxter said, "ever since the . . . Whisper . . . got Chua, I haven't gone in the huts. I don't particularly like the feeling I get around them. But I see strangers sometimes, coming out of one and going into another."

"They're gateways?" Alistair asked.

"I suppose they could be. There were originally ten of them, but it seems someone's added one recently. Though that's hardly the oddest thing I've seen around here."

"You said the people were strangely dressed?" Alistair asked. "How so?"

Baxter shrugged. "Hats, costumes, accoutrements of all varieties. Like I said, these weren't chatty sorts. They came and went. That's all."

Baxter's count was correct—there were eleven huts. Eleven doors, in other words, each possibly leading to a different world. "Should I look inside?" Alistair asked.

"Do they say 'Look before you leap'?" Baxter asked.

"Who?"

"People."

"They do."

"Well, there you are, then."

I'm making the decisions, Alistair had told himself earlier. Had he known his decisions would involve eleven different choices, he might have been a bit more careful with his proclamations. "Any other suggestions?" Alistair asked.

Baxter thought about it for a moment and then replied, "Whenever Chua would leave Aquavania and go back to the Solid World, she'd tell me and the polar bears to 'be smart, be safe . . . and try not to eat one another.'"

Alistair smiled and Baxter smiled back. "Well, I guess the smart and safe thing to do is to check them all out first," Alistair said.

So that's what he did. One by one he opened the doors to the huts and stepped inside. The interiors were almost identical. On the floor of each, there was a perfectly round hole in the ice, an entrance into the frigid water. There were walls, a few wooden seats, some fishing poles. There was only one significant difference. In each hut, a hook was mounted above the hole, and on each hook hung a different object. They were as follows.

Hut One: A leather saddle.

Hut Two: A paintbrush.

Hut Three: An empty backpack.

Hut Four: A spyglass.

Hut Five: A rubber flipper.

Hut Six: A white glove.

Hut Seven: A nylon harness.

Hut Eight: A baseball bat.

Hut Nine: An arrow.

Hut Ten: A locked diary.

Hut Eleven: A hunk of dried meat.

Of all the objects, the white glove was the most intriguing.

Alistair went back to it a second time and felt the fabric. It was smooth and cool. He brought it out and showed it to Baxter. It shimmered when held in the sunlight.

"Polly Dobson wore a spacesuit," Alistair said. "The material of this glove is kinda like the stuff that suit was made of. Have you ever seen anyone in a spacesuit coming from this hut?"

Baxter looked at the ground. "Not that I remember," he said. "But that's not to say it didn't happen. I don't spend much time here. Like I said, the ones who come and go aren't exactly sparkling conversationalists."

Without warning, the door to Hut Seven—the one that contained the harness—opened, and a boy dressed in a thick down coat stepped out onto the frozen lake. Water dripped off his body. He wore boots with spikes on the bottom that made a crunching sound when he walked.

"Hey there!" Alistair shouted, and he started across the ice toward the boy. The boy appeared disinterested as he moved quickly toward Hut Four—the one that housed the spyglass. He opened the door and slipped inside without saying a word. When Alistair reached the hut, there was an audible splash, and when he opened the door, the boy was gone.

Baxter cocked his head and offered a look of *See what I mean?*

"I could follow that kid," Alistair said. "Or I could see if the hut with this glove leads me to where Polly came from. Maybe someone there can tell me about the Ambit of Ciphers.

Polly was going to the Ambit of Ciphers because she was looking for someone too. That place may be where the captured kids are hidden."

"You can also stay here," Baxter said. "I'd be thrilled if you found Chua and Fiona, but from what you've told me, it's dangerous out there. So if you feel safer here . . ."

Staying put wasn't an option, and besides, it didn't seem any safer than leaving. It was cold here. The polar bears were starving, probably desperate to eat anything or anyone. Strange people passed between the huts, and there was no telling if the Whisper would send something like the Mandrake to destroy them all. There was no telling anything. The best Alistair could do was make an educated guess.

He headed back to the hut where he'd found the glove. "I appreciate the offer," he told Baxter, "but the sooner I find them, the sooner things will be back to normal. I'm going in this one."

His own decision, clear and definitive. This was what he should have been doing all along.

"You told me how you got here," Baxter said. "But tell me this: what did Fiona do? You know, after Chua was taken?"

Alistair placed a hand on Baxter's shoulder and said, "She, Rodrigo, Boaz, and Jenny, they tried so hard to stop the Whisper. Rodrigo and Boaz . . . they were captured too. Jenny chose to hide. Then there's a big chunk of time where I don't know exactly what Fiona was doing. Twelve years, actually. But I can assure you of this: she did everything in her power to get Chua back, to get back every captured kid. And when she'd exhausted every option, she wrote books about them."

"Books?"

Alistair nodded. "She wrote down their stories and buried them in Aquavania. She wanted to make sure the kids weren't forgotten. Maybe someday people will dig up the book about Chua and then they'll know how great your creator was. Sorry, *is*. How great your creator *is*."

"You think so?"

"I do."

"And you can find them? Both of them?" Baxter asked.

I really don't know, Alistair was tempted to say. *I've been trying to make you feel better, but I'm grasping at straws. Finding Fiona is going to be hard enough. Chua too? I really don't know.*

Instead, Alistair said, "Yes." And he handed the glove to Baxter and opened the door to Hut Six.

Stepping into the hut, he didn't gauge the consequences of what he was about to do. He simply did it. He hopped, landed feetfirst in the center of the hole, and plunged into the icy water.

CHAPTER 10

———— ◆ ————

ALISTAIR'S WORLD WENT BLACK. THE SHOCK OF THE COLD
knocked his guts up into his throat. There were no visions,
no dreams. Black. Utter, complete. Yet he didn't lose conscious-
ness. His mind simply lost its way. He jerked and wiggled,
clueless as to whether he had entered the water one second
ago or one minute ago. When the cold somehow got colder, he
began to struggle for breath. He moved his arms, trying to
swim, but the water felt thin. Nonexistent.

It was dead silent, and Alistair was weightless. A blast of
warmth hit his body, and something pulled at him. Nothing
touched him, and yet he moved like metal to a magnet. He
thrashed his arms and legs again. There was nothing to grab,
to dig his heels into. He couldn't fight against the pull, and
he was too scared to open his eyes or mouth, even though he
desperately needed to breathe.

The warmth got warmer, and suddenly there was

sound—the flit of something mechanical. There was also light. It announced itself in orange through the skin of his closed eyelids. His arms and legs regained their weight. Gravity reintroduced itself, and Alistair fell onto something hard. It was like he had flopped onto a table. Another sound—another flit—and he felt, if not normal, then safer.

He took a chance. He took a breath. Oxygen spread its glorious wings in his lungs, and he opened his eyes and faced the light. It wasn't sunlight, however. It was tinted. It was harsh. As everything came into focus, small yellow circles materialized above him, like faraway planets. It took a few moments to realize that they were actually faint reflections on curved glass. He was lying on his back on a small metallic countertop. Surrounding him was a clear domed shell, and surrounding the shell was a room where all four walls were covered in round yellow lights and square white buttons. No doors. Nothing but buttons and lights.

A boy and a girl stood in a corner. After they whispered to each other, they approached.

"Yep, human," the boy said. "Looks like one, anyways." His voice was muted a bit by the glass, but the words were clear. He was dressed in a green jumpsuit with white racing stripes down the sides. He had a round belly and an Afro like a broccoli floret.

"Vital signs are good," the girl said. Her voice was forceful, but her body was small. "A real firecracker" is what Alistair's dad might have called her. Her green jumpsuit was similar to the boy's, but snugger, and instead of racing stripes, it had a white curlicue design down the sides. She held a tiny typewriter in the palm of her hand. It was like something out of a dollhouse, but somehow she managed to type on it and it managed to spit out a dangling, unbroken stream of paper covered in illegible little words.

They both had glasses perched above their foreheads and they both wore gloves. White gloves, exactly like the one from the fishing hut.

The girl pulled her glasses down over her eyes. Red and white spirals spun where the lenses should have been. They seemed designed to hypnotize, so Alistair turned his head. "Skeleton is consistent," she said to the boy. "Femurs. Humeri. Everything fits."

"Good to know," the boy said.

"But I'm getting strange brain readings," the girl confirmed. "There's more to this guy than matching bones."

"Where . . . am . . . I . . . ?" Alistair grumbled.

"We'll get to that, buddy," the boy said as he pressed some of the buttons on the walls and the walls chirped in response. "First we have a question or two for you."

The girl pushed the glasses back to the top of her head and continued to type on the typewriter. "More to analyze," she said. "More to discover."

Alistair pressed his hands against the domed shell. It was warm. In fact, the entire chamber was so warm that his clothes had already dried, but the shell didn't budge. He was still trapped. "Why do you have me in here?" he asked.

The boy didn't turn away from his task. "Hold your horses, we're getting there," he said, and he continued to press buttons, seemingly at random.

"You find a magic lamp and you rub it and a genie pops out," the girl said, still typing away.

"Excuse me?"

The girl flashed Alistair a condescending smile. "Pretend you find a magic lamp with a genie inside."

"I'm not sure how that's relevant."

"It's beyond relevant," the girl said.

"Okaaay," Alistair replied, wishing he did actually have a magic lamp that would shut these two up and release him from this strange glass cage.

"Good," the girl replied. "So you have this magic lamp and this genie grants you three wishes. He says that one wish will come true. One wish will not come true. And one wish will backfire. It will cause the opposite to happen. Only you don't know what will happen with each wish. So what are your three wishes?"

"Um . . . what?"

This time it was the boy who gave a smile, only it was a slightly less condescending one. "She talks fast, I know. Even I miss half of what she says, and we're basically cell mates."

She rolled her eyes.

"But really, it's simple," the boy went on. "You have three wishes. One wish happens exactly as you wish it. Wish for a duck and you get a duck. One wish happens in the inverse. Wish to be rich and you end up poor. And the other wish?

Nothing. Nada. Doesn't do a thing. You wish for a go-cart and you get zilch. The catch is, you don't know what's going to happen with each wish, and you have to wish them all at once. So what are your three wishes?"

"This is the important question you have for me?" Alistair asked. He could feel his strength returning, so he tried pushing on the glass again. It didn't budge an inch.

"The question," the girl replied, "is beyond important."

"Yes, I get it," Alistair said, though obviously he didn't. Not in the slightest. Still, he had to ask, "If I answer, does it mean you'll let me out of here?"

The boy and girl looked at each other and offered the same response: "Depends on your answer."

Ridiculous. How could anything depend on an answer to a question like that? Alistair wanted to scream at his captors, but he was in no position to do anything other than think. He brought a hand to his mouth and pinched lightly at his lower lip. He considered the options.

There's got to be a trick answer.

He inspected the room, hoping to spot a clue, but the room wasn't anything but a bare floor, a bare ceiling, and the walls full of those yellow lights and the white buttons the boy kept pressing. The girl still typed away on the minuscule typewriter. Paper streamed out like film from a reel. Neither of them looked at Alistair now. They seemed satisfied to let him puzzle through things.

A thought, an answer. It hit him before he could consider

all the angles. "I'd wish the same wish three times," Alistair said. "That way . . ."

He clammed up.

Stupid. That just cancels it all out. Then what's the point of wishing in the first place?

"Is that your answer?" the boy asked.

"No," Alistair said. "I'm thinking out loud."

"Try to think out quiet, please," the girl said.

The comment didn't sting so much as it annoyed. What did these two expect? Alistair had no idea where he was, or who they were, and yet they were deciding his fate with a stupid riddle. He closed his eyes and put his hands over his ears, trying to block them out of his world. Then he paged through thoughts and emotions—his greatest desires, his greatest fears, the things he was ambivalent about. Surely there was a way to figure out the answer they wanted.

What if one of my wishes is to flip all my wishes? Like the good wish becomes the bad wish . . . but if that's the good wish, then . . . no, no, that's doesn't make any sense.

What if I wish three wishes where the good and bad are equally appealing, where the opposite is just as good as . . . but how is that possible? That would take a lot of . . .

It wasn't coming together. He sat there for an eternity going through scenarios in his head, but each one was either too confusing or didn't accomplish anything. There had to be a way to tie it all up in a perfect little bow, but he wasn't seeing it. He tried to remember famous riddles. What were the ones the Sphinx told? What was the one about the two doors and the liar and the truth-teller? Were there famous fairy-tale riddles? He tried to focus, to be clever, but he didn't feel particularly clever. Curious, definitely. Clever, no.

Exasperated, he finally said, "I don't want any wishes." He opened his eyes and rapped his knuckles on the glass like he was knocking on a door. "I'd rather have nothing than try to figure this stupid riddle out."

The girl typed frantically on the typewriter, then let out a resigned grunt. The boy smiled, nodded, and pressed another button. The glass dome retracted and disappeared into the countertop.

Alistair was free.

1988

—————◆◆—————

THE VIDEO GAME WAS SIMPLE IN CONCEPT. YOU WERE AN astronaut stranded on an unexplored planet. You had to collect various objects that you would then use to rebuild your ship. When your ship was complete, you could fly home. There were alien baddies in your way, obviously, and you could choose to shoot them from a distance with a ray gun or slice them at close range with your deadlier laser whip.

What was simple in concept was nearly impossible in execution. Except when Charlie was at the helm. Barely eleven years old, he was a prodigy at video games. Games that would take most people weeks to get the hang of, he'd master in a day or two.

Alistair watched as Charlie's thumbs raced over a controller, which made the astronaut jump, juke, and slide. Charlie had bought the game on the morning of its release, and forty-eight hours later he was on the final level. As far as Charlie was concerned, spring break wasn't complete until he'd beaten at least four or five games.

It had been over two months since that snowy day in the woods, since Charlie's strange betrayal. Alistair hadn't suffered any frostbite, but his toes now tingled whenever they got a bit chilly. He had told himself over and over that it was the last straw, that he and Charlie couldn't be friends again after that. And Alistair tried—diligently, relentlessly—to avoid Charlie, but with each passing day, he found himself wondering if maybe his memory of that afternoon was wrong, tainted by fatigue and confusion.

At school, Charlie had told everyone that Alistair had saved, if not his life, then at least his hands and feet from frostbite. There were girls who looked at Alistair differently now, boys who picked him earlier for gym class teams. He suddenly had more "school friends," kids he'd hang out with at lunch and study hall, not the types who would come over after class, but friends just the same. Not everything from the incident turned out to be a negative.

And so it was that by February, the two boys were hanging out again. It started in the cafeteria. Alistair was sitting alone at one of the long tables, waiting for a school friend like Trevor Weeks or Mike Cooney to join him, when Charlie sidled up and presented him with a package of miniature donuts.

"They're the ones with the powdered sugar," Charlie said. "Your favorites, right?"

Alistair knew this was Charlie's way of apologizing, but he decided not to acknowledge it with anything more than a nod. That was enough for Charlie, who smiled and sat and started pointing at girls and yapping about which ones had reached their "womanhood."

By March, things were back to normal. Charlie would invite Alistair over for TV or video games, and whenever he didn't have other plans, which was most of the time, Alistair would go. They never mentioned the day in the woods. After a little while, Alistair stopped even thinking about it. When spring break arrived, it meant that days would be filled with video games and nights would be occupied by sleepovers. Spring break was hardly spring in Thessaly. The snow usually lasted until the beginning of April, but it was wet snow, not the sort of stuff that made for fun romping.

Alistair was sleeping over at Charlie's when they played the game with the astronaut. Alistair had ceded his turns to Charlie because Alistair was, quite frankly, pretty lousy. He couldn't even clear the first level, while Charlie easily swept through all seven levels and seemed to be having no trouble with the final one.

"I'm designing a game," Charlie said as he played puppet master to the astronaut, making him zap and whip hordes of aliens.

"Like on a computer?" Alistair asked.

"Not yet. Maybe someday," Charlie said. Charlie was good with computers, knew a bit of programming, but programming a game wasn't exactly easy.

"So where are you designing it?" Alistair asked.

"Um . . ." Charlie tapped a couple of buttons and made the

astronaut leap over a pool of lava. "I guess you could say I'm designing it in my own little world."

Alistair could relate. He often made up stories in his head. "What's the game about?" he asked. "What's the goal?"

Charlie kept his eyes locked on the screen. "Well, it's about chaos," he said. "Imagine there are all these different levels. Like an underwater one. One full of castles. One in the jungle. And once upon a time they were peaceful places. But there's nothing interesting about peaceful, is there?"

"I guess not," Alistair said.

"Peace is boring," Charlie said. "And so in my game, there's a different monster that sneaks into each world. Starts ripping the places apart."

"And the hero's job is to stop the monsters?" Alistair asked.

Charlie guided the astronaut through a tunnel where the final piece of the spaceship was guarded by a giant alien that belched clouds of acid. "No way, nohow," he said. "Because there's an awesome twist in my game. The hero isn't the one who stops the monsters. The hero is the one who designs them."

The alien on-screen oozed slime. The astronaut pummeled it with the whip, and slime splatted on the walls of the tunnel. "So what's the object of your game?" Alistair asked.

"Hmmm . . . I haven't really figured that out yet. For now, it's all about the chaos."

"It's interesting," Alistair said. "I guess there aren't any other games out there where the bad guy is the hero."

On the screen, the giant alien screeched and melted into

a puddle of slime, which the astronaut skipped over to retrieve the final piece of the spaceship. Charlie turned to Alistair and said, "The one who designs the monsters isn't the bad guy."

"But don't the monsters hurt people?"

The astronaut climbed into his now-completed spaceship.

"The monsters do what monsters are designed to do," Charlie said. "But you need monsters, don't you? Someone has to create the beautiful things. And someone has to be in charge of the monsters. It doesn't mean that the monster master is the bad guy. Actually, it's probably harder to deal with monsters than it is with beautiful things, because the monsters will be hated. And hunted. Forever. So a game where you design monsters might be the hardest game of all. You're already setting yourself up to lose."

The spaceship flew into the stars, and the final credits for the video game scrolled down the screen. "I guess I see your point," Alistair said. "Do you have a title?"

"Well," Charlie replied, setting down the controller, "the most powerful monsters are the ones that don't even seem like monsters. They're the little things, the soft things that sneak in and haunt you."

"Ghosts?" Alistair asked. "That might be a good title."

Charlie shook his head. "Whispers."

CHAPTER 11

———————◆———————

ALISTAIR SAT UP, CHARLIE'S SOFT VOICE STITCHED LIKE THIN threads into his brain. His legs dangled off the edge of the counter, and blood rushed down to his feet. All the yellow lights in the room had changed. They were now green.

The boy approached him with a hand outstretched. "So you're a swimmer?"

Alistair kept his hand at his side. "Where am I?"

"You mean you didn't come here on purpose?" the girl asked.

"So you're not *much* of a swimmer," the boy added, pulling his hand back.

"I was in Chua Ling's world and I jumped into a hole in a frozen lake," Alistair told them.

"Ah," the girl said, finally pocketing the typewriter while tearing the paper like a receipt from a cash register and dropping it on the ground. "And you didn't wear a spacesuit? Foolish of you."

"How was I supposed to know where I was going?" Alistair asked.

The boy whistled like he'd seen a pretty woman. "Oh, li'l doggie-paddler. How long has it been since you were on the solid side of things?"

Alistair didn't have a watch, so he had to guess. "About a day."

The girl flinched. Her face spoke volumes. This might have been the craziest thing she'd ever heard.

"*One* day?" the boy said. "One day and you're already here? Hot damn!"

"I didn't plan it that way," Alistair explained. "It kinda happened. Where am I, anyhow? Whose world is this?"

The boy ignored the question, simply shook his head in disbelief and asked the girl, "How far in was Ivan Marinovich when he came to visit?"

The girl pulled the typewriter out of her pocket and tapped away. "Two years," she said. "And that was unprecedented. This is . . ."

"Un-stinkin'-believable?" the boy asked.

The girl pointed at the paper on the floor. "And yet, he seems legit. Don't ask me to explain it, because I can't. But this doggie-paddler is about as puppy as they come."

"I'm not a doggie-paddler. My name is Alistair. I'm looking for Fiona Loomis. And . . . Chua Ling . . . I guess."

"Two ladies?" the boy asked. "Aw shucks. Your name shouldn't be Alistair. It should be Romeo. But I'm sorry to say we don't know your Juliets."

"What about someone named Polly Dobson?"

"Well, that's a name we haven't heard in a while," the boy said.

"You know her?" Alistair asked.

"*Of* her," the girl said. "Bit of a loose cannon by all reports. Friend of yours?"

Alistair grumbled. "Not at all. I'm trying to find her, though. She might know where Fiona and Chua are."

"Interesting," the girl said, her eyes narrowing. "We can't help you in that department, sadly. Polly Dobson likes to keep moving, as we understand it."

"Can you at least let me know what's going on?" Alistair asked. "Who you are? Where I am?"

Smiling, the girl said, "That we can do. I'm Dot. This guy is Chip. We're both swimmers. You're in Quadrant 43, where we study figments, assist other swimmers, and, how shall I say this? Where we . . . *put an end* to ciphers."

Ciphers. There was that word again. But before Alistair could ask another question, Chip pressed another button. All the walls and the ceiling began to split, retract, and fold like venetian blinds pulled open. In seconds, the small room was gone, and they were in the middle of an enormous space with arched marble ceilings, stone pillars, and a tile floor. It resembled a natural history museum. Motionless creatures were floating or standing in menacing poses, or trapped in elaborate display cases. Oddities abounded.

"Our lives' work," Dot said. "For your safety, for your study, for your entertainment."

It was, quite simply, breathtaking. Alistair's mind shifted from *Where the heck am I?* to *What . . . in the hell . . . is that?* He hopped down from the counter and walked past Dot and Chip and straight to what appeared to be a sea creature, but it wasn't like any fish, whale, or dolphin he had ever seen. It was perfectly round and covered in bulging eyeballs, spikes, and little translucent fins. It was all body and it was all face.

"The Orbilisk," Chip said, approaching Alistair from behind. "That cipher was nabbed by a swimmer named Joslyn, who found it terrorizing a world of merpeople. It sees in three hundred and sixty degrees and has venomous spikes. A mean piece of work."

Alistair could have stared at the Orbilisk and its awful elegance for hours, but the room was brimming with things as strange or stranger. He moved on to the next one, a short, troll-like creature who was the centerpiece of a glassed-in display. The troll had blue skin and wore nothing but a loincloth. He was frozen in place on one foot, head tipped back, arms out wide, performing a joyous dance. In the background, lightning bolts made of foil pummeled a small model of a mud hut village.

"That's Rimtillious the Rascal," Dot said. "He could redirect the weather and cause all sorts of trouble. A swimmer named Malik caught him, stuffed him in a sack, and we took care of the rest."

"Other kids caught these things?" Alistair asked.

Chip nodded. "And that ain't the half of it. We're in the cipher business, chief. We research these things, figure out their weaknesses. Some are susceptible to fire, others to things like saliva. Some are big. Some are small. Some change shape. We get the cold hard facts and then we employ bounty hunters. So yes, kids catch these things. But that's because we send them to catch these things."

Alistair proceeded to the next creature, and the next, and the next. There was Yabbo DeGobbo, a disgusting blob with big veiny lips and flatulence that caused earthquakes. There was the Horgon, a furry, star-shaped monster that apparently suffocated people in their sleep. There was Tiki-Tiki, who looked like a giant parrot with metallic feathers. According to Chip, when this bird laughed, it caused figments' brains to explode. All of the creatures were frozen in place, stuffed like hunting trophies.

As Alistair gazed at a giant eight-armed wizard known as Spidrex the Great, he finally broke down. He placed a hand over his face as his chest convulsed, but there was no hiding the tears.

"Come on, ace," Chip said. "Get a grip. They're harmless. Most have been out of commission for years."

"This is what we do," Dot added. "Our purpose. And we're good at it."

"It's not that," Alistair said, coughing. "It's . . . I saw one of these. It attacked a whole bunch of people. It drove a horn through a boy's stomach."

"You haven't even been here one day," Dot said, "and you've already escaped a cipher? I don't believe it."

"They called it the . . . the Mandrake."

Chip couldn't contain himself. He shouted, "The Mandrake! You saw the brother-trucking Mandrake? This is colossal! This is huge!"

"There were these tubes . . . and this blood . . . and he was freezing people . . . and I keep messing up . . . and it's always my fault . . ." Alistair's voice dissolved into nothing but a sad whimper.

"I don't know if you realize what you're telling us," Chip said. "The Mandrake is pretty much the nastiest of the nasties. Kids have been trying to bag that bugger for ages. Jeez Louise. Last I heard, this wiseass named Hadrian was sacrificing swimmers to the thing."

"Hadrian was there," Alistair whispered. "The Mandrake . . . ran him through."

Dot crossed herself like a good Catholic. "Well, good riddance to bad rubbish. I never liked that megalomaniacal twit."

Alistair didn't like him either, but he suddenly found himself on the defensive, the strength slowly returning to his voice. "But he was a kid," he said. "A swimmer like us, right? He must have had friends and family back home. If the Mandrake killed him, then what happens? What about them?"

Dot shrugged and said, "Then they probably found him dead in a lake, or maybe the bathtub, next to whatever portal brought him here."

Chip wagged a finger. "We don't know that. How could we know that?"

"That's what the data suggest," Dot replied. "You see, once a swimmer gets here, there's pretty much no way to leave, except . . ." Dot ran her finger across her neck, like she was slitting her own throat.

Chip turned away from Dot, a look of mild disgust on his face. "All of us swimmers are trying to get home," he explained. "We haven't found a way yet, but it doesn't mean there *isn't* a way. Unfortunately, some have croaked. We don't know what happens to ones who croak, because once they croak, well, we don't see 'em anymore."

Wiping his eyes, Alistair peered across the room at one of the more fearsome ciphers, a scaly man with the head of a Tyrannosaurus rex. "And do the ciphers . . . Are they the ones who . . . cause the swimmers to croak?" he asked.

"Mostly," Dot answered. "Though maniacs like Hadrian have contributed to the carnage. That's why we're not going to lose any sleep over his demise."

There must have been over two hundred ciphers in the room, an impressive collection. They may have been out of commission, but they certainly still looked fearsome. "If these things are so awful, then why are you sending kids to hunt them?" Alistair asked.

"Two reasons," Dot said. "First, these ciphers are slaughtering figments, and even though they're nothing but figments, they don't deserve to be slaughtered. And second, the more we know about the ciphers, the more we know about *Him*. The closer we get to *Him*."

Alistair didn't need her to say who the *Him* was, and Chip and Dot looked at Alistair slightly cockeyed, because his face must have told them something.

"What is it?" Dot asked.

No. He couldn't tell them. He wasn't ready. He could barely trust Baxter. How could he trust these two? "Nothing," Alistair said. "I was thinking about the riddle. What was the right answer?"

Chip chuckled. "Wouldn't you like to know?"

"It was a test," Dot said. "Figments answer one way. Ciphers answer another. Swimmers . . . well, we could tell you were a swimmer."

"Is there a *right* answer?"

Chip chuckled again, but neither he nor Dot said anything.

In place of an answer, a siren went off, bleating like an angry goat. Immediately, Dot grabbed Alistair by the wrist and led him back toward the counter. She was powerful, and he was tired. Even if he had had the strength to fight, he wasn't sure he'd have been able to wrest himself free. "Where are you taking me?" he asked.

"This isn't about you," Dot said.

As they neared the counter, the walls started to form around them. Almost instantly, they were back in the small room filled with the buttons and lights. The buttons were still white. The lights were once again yellow.

"Pulling up a picture," Chip said as he started tapping buttons.

Dot let go of Alistair's arm. It didn't matter, though, because there was nowhere for him to go now. The space was completely enclosed.

"Analyzing," Dot said as she pulled out her tiny typewriter.

On the countertop where Alistair had rested minutes before, a projected image appeared. It was slightly blurry, but it showed stars and the vast nothingness of outer space. In the middle of the frame was a floating body, arms and legs stretched out like an *X*.

"Latching on," Chip said, pressing more buttons. "Drawing it in."

The image of the body got bigger, as if it were moving closer to them, and as it got bigger, it pulled its hands to its face and its knees to its chest, making itself into a ball.

"Opening the hatch," Chip said, fingers leaping from button to button. Then a sound—a mechanical flit.

"He's angry," Dot said as skinny loops of paper piled up at her feet. "Plenty angry."

The image disappeared from the counter, and the counter opened up in the middle, like a pair of church doors. A man—now more than an image, now flesh and blood—floated up and out of the opening. The opening snapped shut, became a counter again, and the man, still curled up, fell down onto its surface. Another flit, and the glass shell shot up and around the new captive.

"Human as well, at least by the looks of him," Chip remarked.

"Vital signs are perfect," Dot said, typing away. "Blood is pump, pump, pumping."

Alistair moved closer to the glass to get a better look. "Who is he?"

"Oh, we get swimmers like you all the time," Dot said. "Though they're always younger than this guy. And most are smart enough to wear spacesuits. It's dangerous to be out there for more than a minute or two. You were lucky we pulled you in when we did. So is this character."

The man was still curled in a ball, but his feet were fidgeting. He wore jeans, sneakers, and a slightly dirty T-shirt. He rolled over onto his back, but his hands still covered his face.

"So he's another swimmer?" Alistair asked.

"Not necessarily," Chip said, still at the buttons. "Sometimes a cipher will sneak through, or someone will drop one through a gateway for us, like it's some cipher laundry chute."

Alistair took another step closer because he recognized the jeans the man was wearing. They were plain old blue jeans, but he was familiar with the stains, the rips. He took yet another step closer, and the man must have heard him, because he turned his head toward Alistair and pulled his hands away from his face.

Alistair stopped. He stared into the man's eyes.

"Kyle?" Alistair asked.

1987

KYLE DWYER BACK HOME. HE WAS CHARLIE'S OLDER BROTHER, but that wasn't obvious to the casual observer. Charlie's face was chubby; Kyle's was close to gaunt. Charlie shuffled; Kyle sauntered. While Charlie was at home playing video games, Kyle was out "playing the field." They weren't buddies, probably never had been. If you said a bad word about Charlie, Kyle would defend him, because that's what an older brother does. Otherwise, they steered clear of each other.

Kyle was arrested once. It was a sunny autumn afternoon, the beginning of fifth grade for Alistair. He and Keri had just come home from school, and their father met them at the front door and presented them with a pair of rakes. Grumbling, they took to the front yard, where they clawed at the mess of leaves. A police cruiser carrying two officers glided past. Lights weren't blaring. There was no emergency.

Ten minutes later, the cruiser was heading the other way

and it stopped in front of Alistair's house because a pair of plastic trash cans had rolled into the road. The officer on the passenger side got out to move the cans, and Kyle's face was framed in the backseat window. Kyle smiled and held up his hands. Cuffs decorated his wrists.

"Can you say *jailbird*?" Keri whispered as she rested her rake against a tree.

The officer tossed the cans into the Colters' yard next door, and Kyle blew on the window, fogging up the glass. Using a finger, he wrote out a message that Alistair read as:

TUO EM KAERB

"Is that, like, written in Russian or something?" Alistair asked as the officer climbed back into the cruiser and they pulled away.

Keri cracked up. "No. That's, like, written in Moron. He wrote the letters backward, but not the words."

Alistair furrowed his brow. With the car gone, he'd already forgotten the exact letters, so it would be tough to solve. Keri grabbed her rake and used the handle to lightly poke him in the ribs. "'Break me out,'" she said.

"Oh . . ."

"So you gonna do it?"

"I assume . . . it's a joke?"

"You think?" she said with a laugh.

"I wonder what he did."

Keri attacked the leaves with the rake and looked up quizzically. "Sold black-market babies. Spied for the Commies. Squeezed the Charmin. Could be anything."

"A butterfly knife," Charlie told Alistair over the phone later that evening. "They found it in his locker after school."

"How'd they know it was there?" Alistair asked.

"Anonymous tip."

"Is he going to jail?"

Charlie huffed. "Probably not even juvie. He's only sixteen, and this is his first offense. I think the police wanted to scare him. He's suspended for two weeks, though."

"Man," Alistair said. "What are your parents doing?"

"Freaking," Charlie said. "Dad mentioned something about kicking him out."

"You think they would?"

"Naw. It's a bluff. Mom wouldn't let it happen."

"So what are they gonna do to him?"

Charlie adopted a deep voice, an impression of his father. *"Gonna teach him right from wrong. How to be a civil member of society."*

Alistair knew that Kyle wasn't a perfect guy, but Kyle had always been nice to him. "Why do you think he had the knife?" he asked.

With a strangely joyful laugh, Charlie said, "For stabbing, of course."

CHAPTER 12

HANDS PRESSED AGAINST THE GLASS, FINGERS STAINED WITH tobacco, nails filled with gunk. Sunken eyes, a mole on his cheek, a crooked incisor. This was Kyle. The same one from the police car, from the neighborhood, from all that came before. To Alistair, there was no doubt.

"Is that you, Cleary?" Kyle asked.

Chip, who had been frantically pressing buttons, paused and asked, "You know each other?"

Alistair's gaze didn't budge from Kyle's face. "Yes, it's me," Alistair said. "Are you okay?"

"I'm . . ." Kyle's voice faded as he pulled up his shirt and revealed a bloody wound in his stomach.

"Vital signs are *perfect*," Dot said again, making sure there was no confusion about it. She typed away.

"BS!" Alistair snapped. "He's clearly injured. You have to get him out of there. You have to help him."

"How do you know this guy?" Chip asked.

"He's from home," Alistair said. "He's a . . . friend."

"That's right," Kyle said with a gurgling chuckle. "Discountin' the fact that the kid shot me, we're good buds. From way back in Thessaly."

"How'd you get here?" Alistair asked as he placed his hand on the glass.

Kyle rubbed his face with his dirty fingers. "There was, like, a fishbowl and . . . rain . . . and it's a bit of a blur, honestly."

Dot consulted her stream of paper and said, "It's hard to tell if he's lying or not." She pulled the swirling glasses back down over her eyes. "But this skeleton? Definitely not primate."

"What the hell can a stupid typewriter and glasses tell you?" Alistair asked. "He's a friend. He's in trouble. That's all you need to know."

Dot ignored Alistair. "So, Kyle, if that really is your name," she said, pushing her glasses back up to her brow, "I have a question for you. Let's pretend you have this magic lamp and there's a genie inside. The genie grants you three wishes. He says that one wish will come true. One wish will not come true. And one wish will backfire. It will cause the opposite to happen. Only you don't know what will happen with each wish. So what are your three wishes?"

Alistair threw up his hands. "Are you kidding me?"

"We know, buddy," Chip said. "It's a bit weird, but it's necessary."

"A bit weird?" Alistair said. "It's plain stupid. Kyle, say you don't want to make a wish. That's how I answered, and they let me out."

Dot shot Alistair a disapproving look. "If he says that, then we'll definitely know he's a cipher."

"What? You make no sense." Alistair put his hands back on the glass and tried to shake it open. Impossible.

"Don't sweat it, little guy," Kyle said. "I got this. I've even heard this riddle before. My three wishes would be . . ."

He put up a thumb. "Numero uno: I'd wish for infinite wishes."

He put up an index finger. "Second wish: I'd wish that I'd never met the genie."

He put up his middle finger and lowered the thumb and the index. "Wish the third: I'd wish you'd all stick this where the sun don't shine."

Then he laughed, hard.

If anything was going to seal it for Alistair, a vulgar joke was it. "That's definitely Kyle," he said. "You have to let him out."

It also sealed it for Dot and Chip. "Cipher?" Dot asked.

Chip sighed and confirmed. "Cipher."

All the yellow lights in the room shifted over to red. Chip pressed some buttons. Water began to fill Kyle's chamber, pooling up around him like a bath being drawn.

"What's going on, little guy?" Kyle asked Alistair.

"They're trying to drown you," Alistair cried as he sprinted over to the wall and slapped his hand against every button he could.

Chip and Dot didn't bother to stop him. Water kept coming. "Sorry, guy," Chip said. "Press all you want, but if you don't know the combos, you aren't gonna do a thing. It's like playing a piano. You can't hit random keys and get Beethoven."

The water was up to Kyle's chin when he said, "Okay, you can shut off the taps. Point taken. You don't appreciate gettin' flipped the bird."

"You're insane!" Alistair yelled at Chip and Dot.

"He's a cipher," Dot said calmly.

"He's a friend!"

"He's a cipher," Chip echoed.

As the water slipped over his face, Kyle began to fight. He swung his fists and feet wildly. Alistair ran back to the glass shell. The chamber was soon full, and Kyle was flailing under the water, his arms and legs slowed by the liquid. Alistair pounded on the glass. It didn't give at all. "Let him out!" Alistair cried. "Let him out! Let him out! Let him out!"

"He's trying to fool you," Dot said.

"He may look like the guy you know, but he's not that guy," Chip added. "Trust us."

"Let him out! Please! Just let him out!"

"He's a monster. Sent to trick. Sent to destroy," Dot said.

With the chamber now full, Kyle's eyes rolled back. His body went limp, floated to the top, and pressed against the glass. The blood from the wound in his stomach swayed red ribbons through the water.

"Let him out. Let him out. Let him out . . ." Alistair's voice faded as his fists slowed down and finally stopped. He spread his palms across the glass and positioned them so he was almost cupping Kyle's lifeless face.

More typing and button-pushing, lights shifting to green, then the counter opened again and the water and Kyle's body slipped away. Even more button-pushing and the walls and ceiling folded up and Alistair, Chip, and Dot were back among the collection of ciphers. At a far end of the gallery, Kyle's body ascended from a hole in the floor. A stick shot up and mounted him in place, his body frozen in a manic pose—fingers curled, joints bent, like he was about to pounce. He was now part of the collection.

The instinct to run was strong. This place was poison. These kids were heartless. And Alistair had a chance. He spotted a door, not far past where they'd mounted Kyle.

"Don't bother, ace," Chip said, placing a firm hand on Alistair's shoulder. "You wouldn't know how to open it, anyway."

Dot passed Alistair her glasses. "Put them on."

"I don't follow orders from murderers," Alistair replied.

"Put them on," Dot repeated. "And then you can apologize to us."

"Put 'em on, buddy," Chip said, in a much kinder tone. "You'll want to see this."

The glasses were warm and hummed as if a little motor

was running inside them, but the lenses looked normal. It was only when Dot had worn them that the red and white spirals had appeared.

"What the heck am I supposed to see?" Alistair asked.

"Proof that we're not murderers," Dot said. Then she snatched the glasses back, flicked her wrist to open the frames, and slipped them over Alistair's face.

Everything became black or glowed an electric purple. A purple skull, with dark eye sockets and slightly crooked teeth, hovered in front of Alistair. "See what we mean?" the skull said in Dot's voice.

The punch of surprise knocked Alistair back a few steps. Two purple human skeletons with two purple skulls stood in front of him, presenting their hands in a gesture of peace. "Spooky, right?" said a skeleton in Chip's voice.

Alistair raised his own hand in front of his face and, sure enough, there was no flesh to see, only purple glowing bones. "X-ray?"

"Specs," the skeletal Chip said. "That's right. X-ray specs. Finest you'll ever wear."

"Look around," the skeletal Dot said.

This was an order Alistair was happy to follow. For years, ever since he saw them advertised in the back of a magazine, he'd wanted a pair of these things. Even after Keri had told him they were "as fake as the tooth fairy," he'd harbored hopes that someday science would catch up with his desires.

Though he was unlikely to admit it, back home, he would've

wanted them to see through clothes, and he would've used them for more scandalous purposes. Here in Quadrant 43, they saw through flesh, and all he had were ciphers to look at. Mounted in the displays were glowing skeletons. There were the bones of a dog, maybe a hippo, possibly a sloth, and numerous other animals of various shapes and sizes. When Alistair lowered the glasses to the tip of his nose and peered over the rims, the same ciphers—those misshapen and terrifying monsters—populated the room, but when he pushed the glasses back up, it was animal bones that lurked inside of the flesh.

"That doesn't make any sense," he said. "The bones don't match."

"The mark of a cipher. Dem bones, dem bones gonna defy the laws of biology," Chip sang.

"Now look at Kyle," Dot said.

Lowering the glasses again to get his bearings, Alistair located his friend, taking notice of his hair, his eyes, his build, which was the build of an eighteen-year-old guy—skinny but basically normal. Pushing the X-ray specs back over his eyes revealed bones that were also normal. Only they were normal for a bird.

"No," Alistair said.

"Yes indeedy," Chip said.

"A penguin," Dot added. "Small one too. A rockhopper I'm guessing."

"No, no, no." Alistair took the glasses off and thrust them at Dot, who happily took them back.

"A strange bit of voodoo," Chip said, "but the Whisper works in mysterious ways."

The air came out of Alistair all at once. "I need to sit down," he said.

To open the door at the back of the gallery, Chip had to enter a code. To enter the code, he had to spin a rotary dial mounted on the wall, exactly like the type found on older telephones. He must have done it countless times, because he dialed so fast that Alistair couldn't tell what the code was.

Through the door, Chip and Dot led Alistair down a passageway with a ceiling of glass. Starlight and the glow of distant planets provided the only illumination, but it was enough to light their way to another door where Chip dialed in another code and granted them passage into a dimly lit room outfitted with leather sofas, wooden coffee tables, and walls that doubled as movie screens.

Alistair immediately flopped down on a sofa and closed his eyes.

"I guess I don't have to say, 'Go on, make yourself at home,'" Dot remarked.

Alistair didn't bother responding. His body was melting into the cushions.

"You should obviously sleep," Dot went on. "But first we need to clear a few things up. Where exactly were you trying to get when you arrived here? And where exactly did you think you were going to find Polly Dobson?"

"The Ambit of Ciphers," Alistair said with a yawn. "She has a missing friend too, and that's where she's looking. So that's where I'm going. Give me a few hours, and I'll be on my way. As long as you can point me in the right direction."

Dot clucked her tongue in disapproval. "A long time ago, Chip and I teamed up and decided we were going to find our way home. We heard of the Ambit of Ciphers. We heard that if you battled through it, you would reach the Whisper and maybe even all the souls and people he captured. But were we ready? Could we handle it?"

"Short answer: no," Chip said.

"Long answer: heck no," Dot said. "We searched everywhere for the Ambit of Ciphers, but when we came upon this space station, we realized our time was better spent here."

"This is a space station?"

"Of course," Chip said. "Brought to life by some brainy daydreamer. The kid was a real sciency type, obsessed with studying and analyzing."

"Before the Whisper stole the kid's soul and world," Dot added, "this daydreamer made all sorts of gadgets that monitored the emotions, thoughts, and health of figments."

"You mean that room?" Alistair asked. "The buttons? The typewriter?"

"Yep, and the X-ray glasses, everything," Dot said. "And we've learned to use them and apply them to swimmers and ciphers."

"Kyle was not a cipher," Alistair said. "Couldn't you see that? He was a person. Not a monster."

"But you saw his bones," Dot said. "Clearly a penguin."

"That's ridiculous," Alistair said, and yet he couldn't deny the strange coincidence. It's not often that you meet a penguin and a man with penguin bones on the very same day.

"It's ridiculous to a mind that didn't come up with it," Dot said. "Just like that typewriter is ridiculous, or the glasses are ridiculous."

"Or this racing stripe," Chip added. He peeled the racing stripe off his green pants like it was a strip of masking tape and he crumpled it into a ball that he threw against the ground. It bounced back faster than it was thrown and ricocheted around the room, painting the air with little streaks of lightning before hitting his pants and reattaching itself as a stripe.

"Exactly," Dot said. "The daydreamer who created this world had a different mind from yours. Our personal imaginations are—how should I say this?—personal. We can only use the materials we have. And the Whisper does the same thing. Which raises the question: He made this cipher, this Kyle. You said you knew Kyle from home. How does the Whisper know who you know?"

"You know more about the Whisper than you wanna say, don't you?" Chip asked.

Of course he did, but Alistair was so fed up with the strangeness, with the violence, with everything in Aquavania, that exhausted anger split him open and he yelled his response. "Maybe I do! But what do you know? Really? If you're so smart, why haven't you stopped him yet?"

Dot tugged down on the fabric of her jumpsuit, flattening a few wrinkles. Her calm demeanor still in place, she turned toward the door and responded, "That's perhaps the question we should be asking you. But you're cranky and tired. I think it's best if you sleep on things."

CHAPTER 13

———◆———◆———

ALISTAIR'S DREAMS WEREN'T DREAMS AT ALL. THEY WERE memories. Soft and lilting visions and sounds from happier times. Alistair saw his parents unloading the car at a beach house they had rented when Alistair was barely five years old. He saw Keri dancing at a ballet recital, her face twisted in a grimace as she performed pirouettes. He saw Fiona Loomis on her bicycle, riding up and down the street, her dark hair fanning out behind her like a crow's wing.

Alistair watched snippets of his life, pleasant things, hopeful moments. For the longest stretch, he was back in the Skylark, a restaurant where he and Fiona went to dinner once. He was watching her smile, and eat, and laugh. Beautiful. He had never told her that, but it was true. She was beautiful, and not because she looked like she should be famous. It was how she cared about things. The tilt of her head. The way she brushed away her bangs. Her deep stare that told Alistair she was listening. And feeling.

Waking from these memories was jarring. It took Alistair more than a few moments to figure out where he was. To say he was disappointed would be an understatement. Each bit of realization slapped on another layer of dread.

I'm on a sofa . . . in a lounge . . . down the hall from a monster gallery . . . which is part of a space station . . . that is floating through Quadrant 43 . . . one of the many worlds in Aquavania. Damn it!

"There you are."

Alistair rolled over onto his side and looked across the room. Chip was sitting on another sofa. He cradled a thick leather-bound book. On the walls, four black-and-white movies played. Cowboys and Indians. A heroic dog. Gangsters. Teenagers in love.

"How long was I asleep?"

"More than a few hours," Chip said. "I couldn't sleep, so I thought I'd come and watch a few movies. Maybe powwow with you if you were awake."

"I am now," Alistair said, rubbing his eyes. He did feel well rested. Hardly calm, but certainly well rested.

"Did you enjoy your memories?" Chip asked.

"What's that?"

Chip looked up and sighed. "I wish I still had those. Thing is, when you first get to Aquavania, you don't dream. This place is already like a dream, right? So instead you get to look at memories when you sleep. Sometimes when you're awake too. Memories will smack you like gusts of wind."

Alistair nodded, because that was exactly what had been happening to him. Memories as vivid as the present seemed to be hiding around every corner in Aquavania.

"It passes," Chip told him. "Your brain changes. The memories stop coming. First during the day, then at night. Soon you only sleep. And it's black. And it's nothing."

"I prefer nightmares," Alistair said.

"Come again?"

"Really," Alistair said as he sat up. "When you wake up from a nightmare, it's a relief. You know that your real life is better than all that scary stuff. Give me nightmares or nothing over nice memories and dreams."

"You're not happy with how life is going for you?" Chip asked.

Alistair might have laughed if it weren't so sad. "I'm trapped in some alternate dimension, full of monsters and crazy people, and I'm looking for my friend, and I promised some penguin that I'd find his friend, and I'm basically guessing about where they might be, and my best friend, he's . . . well, let's say life could be better."

Chip laughed for the both of them. "When you put it that way . . ." He stood and walked over to the coffee table next to Alistair. He set the book down.

"Stories?" Alistair asked.

"A map," he said. "Actually, a collection of maps. An atlas. If it were one map, it'd be as big as this space station."

Alistair flipped the cover open and read the title and inscription:

THE CAPTURED REALMS OF AQUAVANIA

Without the tireless work of countless swimmers, this book would not exist. Remember their sacrifices and use this wisely. Pay heed to warnings. Whenever possible, record your discoveries.

He turned to the first page. It was a map labeled MAHALOO (THE ENTRYWAY).

On the edge of the page there were numerous candy-colored rivers, feeding into a ring of fields that formed a grassy border around everything else. In one of the fields there was a rock icon, which was labeled as THE HERDS OF NIGHT. Woodlands made up a great deal of the map, and there were valleys cutting through like wrinkles on an old face. The land was populated with numerous creeks, ponds, and lakes. On a few of the bodies of water there were golden rings, marked with text.

THE ELFIN SEA

ROKOKO'S LABYRINTH

ROOM 101

ISLANDS IN SOUP

THE HUTCH

That last ring was centered on a tiny pond, presumably the same pond that Polly had made Alistair dive into, the same one that led to . . .

Alistair pressed his finger to the golden ring and the pages started to flip on their own. He pulled his hand away, as if from snapping teeth, but it took barely a second for the book to stop on the page labeled THE HUTCH.

There it all was. The trails. The village. The platform. The sea of blood. The underground fortress. The tentacles. Golden rings clustered around the tentacles. They were labeled with more ambiguous names. All except for two. One was labeled PLANET POLAR BEAR. Another, THE AMBIT OF CIPHERS.

Alistair pressed the dot next to THE AMBIT OF CIPHERS. Nothing.

"No one's been there and recorded anything," Chip said. "So we don't have any solid data yet. Only rumors."

"What are the rumors?"

"That it's a place where the Whisper keeps the worst of the ciphers. It forms a border around his home. If you make it through, then you make it to him."

Alistair looked back at the map of the Hutch. There was a message written at the top in red ink: *According to swimmer Alistair Cleary, the Mandrake may have dominion over this world. Hadrian may be dead. Until more evidence is presented, consider this map unreliable.*

"We edited that after you went to sleep," Chip explained. "Dot likes to keep things up-to-date."

Along with the golden ring, Alistair saw a red ring labeled THE MANDRAKE. He pressed the red ring and a tab shot up from the page like an illustration in a pop-up book. It displayed the following text:

> The Mandrake is a cipher with hummingbird bones. It can take a few different forms. The best way to identify it is to spot the horseshoe-shaped blue mark behind its ear. Its weakness is blood, but no one has ever managed to get blood on it. Do not trust the Mandrake. Do not attempt to capture the Mandrake unless you are experienced and prepared.

Alistair pressed the red ring again and the tab receded. "These tubes. Hadrian said one led to the Ambit of Ciphers. Was that the only way there?"

Chip shook his head. "If Hadrian was telling the truth—which, who are we kidding, is a gamble—then it may have been the quickest way. But if that means having to go toe-to-toe with the Mandrake, then the better bet has always been to take the long route."

"How long is that?"

Chip picked up the atlas and thumbed the pages like he was cycling through a flip book. "Depends," he said. "If you know what you're doing, it might take two years."

"What?"

Chip closed the atlas. "Not that long, in the grand scheme."

The book was thicker than the heftiest dictionary Alistair

had ever seen. There were probably thousands of pages in it, thousands of worlds. "So what should I do?"

"Sixty-four-thousand-dollar question," Chip said. "As I see it, you've got two options. You can try to do what you've already been doing. You can journey to the Ambit of Ciphers and you can battle through the monsters until you get to the Whisper. Then you can battle him, and if you beat him, maybe you'll find out what happened to your friend."

"Sounds . . . difficult."

"Sure does," Chip said. "But it doesn't mean it's impossible. Actually, I think you have a better shot than anyone. Even better than Polly, who, if I had to guess, has failed in her mission."

"What's my other option?"

"Find your friend's world, add it to our maps, study it. If there's a cipher there, bring that baby to us."

"You don't sound very excited by that option," Alistair said.

"It isn't sexy, but it has potential," Chip said. "Dot's got a theory, actually. She doesn't think we have to look far for the missing daydreamers. She thinks they're still embedded in their worlds."

"Embedded?"

"All the stuff that daydreamers create—you know, landscapes, figments, machines, all of that—it all comes from their minds, right? Those things were once a part of them, like bits of dry skin that flake off."

"Fiona told me something similar once."

"Well, Dot thinks if you can extract the, let's say, *Fiona-ness* from Fiona's world, then you can bring Fiona back."

"Sounds even more difficult."

"Maybe not," Chip said. "Dot's actually made some progress. You see, there are still a bunch of figments on this space station, and she's been running experiments on them. She's learned a lot about the daydreamer who created this place. Even might have conjured . . . well, life."

Chip reached beneath the front of his shirt and pulled out the thin chain of a silver necklace. A cylindrical and clear pendant hung from the chain. In the middle of the pendant, there was a tiny glowing orb, no bigger than a pea.

"What's that?" Alistair asked.

"That's life," Chip said. "Beginnings of it, at least. Dot mixed bits of figments and baked 'em up in a lab with centrifuges and all that. I'm serving as an incubator for the time being, on account of my . . . well . . . Being chubby makes me a good insulator."

As Chip slipped the pendant back beneath his shirt, Alistair asked, "What type of life is it?"

"Daydreamer," Chip said, giving his chest a gentle pat. "The kid who created this place, actually. We're trying a good ol'-fashioned resurrection."

"And it's worked?"

Chip held up crossed fingers. "Three hundredth time's the charm? Seriously, though, we haven't gotten past this stage yet, but getting to this stage is a big honkin' deal."

Ever since Fiona had told him about it, Alistair couldn't shake the image: a pen entering an ear, a pen filling up with sparkling liquid. "What about the soul?" Alistair asked. "Doesn't the Whisper steal their souls? With his pen?"

"What's a soul?"

"Well, a soul is . . . a person's essence . . . a person's story . . . a . . ."

"It's not a trick question," Chip said. "Because I really wonder. I've asked Dot basically the same thing. Even if we do get this little orb to grow arms and legs and all that, will it be anything more than a big old hunk of flesh? Will it be an actual human being with feelings and all that? Dot thinks it will be."

There was another, more recent image that Alistair couldn't shake: Dot typing on her typewriter, her suspicious gaze never retreating from Alistair's face. "She doesn't like me, does she?"

"Dot doesn't like anyone," Chip said. "Don't take it personally. She's stubborn. Hard to convince. That's actually why I wanted to catch you before she wakes up. We discussed things after you went to bed. She thinks you're hiding something from us."

"I'm—"

"And I agree with her," Chip said. "But only on that front. Here's the difference between her and me. She wants to keep you here longer. To study you. Find out what you know. I want to send you out, because I sense something in you. I think you've got the skills to do what has to be done."

"What . . . *has to be done*?" Alistair asked.

"Even if we could resurrect your friend, we may never be able to keep up with all the new daydreamers we're losing. This will keep going on and on and on. Isn't it obvious what has to be done?"

It was. The Whisper had to be defeated. But what did that mean for Charlie? "I'm not sure you realize where I'm from," Alistair said.

Chip shrugged. "I don't give a rat's ass about that. You know how long we've been experimenting and collecting data?"

"A few . . . years?"

Chip shook his head. "If only. Can you imagine how sick of this I am?"

"Very?"

"Very very. You're an anomaly, Alistair, one in a billion. You survived the Mandrake. You found us in a single day. That means something. I'm not going to let you become another of Dot's guinea pigs." Chip pushed the book of maps toward Alistair. "You should take this."

"Won't you need it?" Alistair asked.

Chip waved him off. "We have tons of them. The daydreamer who created this place also made the ink that powers the books and a printing press gadget that reproduces them. When we write in one book, the same thing magically appears in hundreds of other books. So don't worry. We're fully stocked."

Alistair picked the book up. It was surprisingly light, given its size. "So I'm supposed to go to the Ambit of Ciphers?"

"You're supposed to do whatever it is you've been doing," Chip said. "Trust your instincts. I think fate is on your side."

A hilarious notion. For Alistair, the opposite was clearly true. On the walls of the lounge, the four black-and-white movies continued to play. Cowboys and Indians. A heroic dog. Gangsters. Teenagers in love.

1988

---◆---

A FOLDED PIECE OF LOOSE-LEAF HAD EIGHT NAMES WRITTEN on it. There was a ritual to this, but Alistair didn't really get it. It was girl stuff.

"Pick a number," Keri said, her fingertips poised inside an origami fortune-teller, which she held to Alistair's nose like a flower.

"Fine. Six," Alistair grumbled.

"And a color."

"Burnt umber."

"Come on, a real color."

"That is a real color. There's a crayon that color."

"I mean a standard color."

"Okay, whatever. Green."

Keri pursed her lips and tilted her head. "You sure?" she said.

"Just do the stupid thing," Alistair said, turning to the backseat window.

Behind the faint reflection of Keri opening and closing the fortune-teller like the double-jointed jaw of a Venus flytrap, nature swept by in a damp and budding blur. On the stereo, a song heavy on banjos set the mood. They were heading to a campground, a yearly tradition for Memorial Day weekend.

"Crack a window back there, would you?" Alistair's dad said. "We're getting a lot of condensation on the glass." One hand on the wheel and one hand buried in a sleeve, he reached forward to wipe the windshield as Alistair's mom hit the defrost button on the dashboard.

Preferring the filminess, Alistair ignored the request, so Keri latched on to her window crank with the crook of her elbow and rolled it down without taking her fingers out of the fortune-teller. Cool air, oaky and sharp, filled the car.

Keri used the pointy edges of the fortune-teller to nip at Alistair's ear.

"Quit it!" he snapped, and turned with a fist up.

Keri cocked her chin toward their parents in the front seat. Idle threats were nothing new to her. "Pick an animal," she said, pushing the fortune-teller in Alistair's face.

On folded flaps of paper were drawings of a cat, a dog, a fish, and a unicorn. Alistair knew the unicorn was a trick, a silly enticement that he was *supposed* to choose. The cat reminded him a bit too much of Charlie. And the dog? Dogs were great, but he wasn't sure he wanted to know which name would be associated with a dog.

He tapped the picture of the fish.

"Oooo, an underwater breather," Keri said as she pulled one hand out and reached to peel back the flap and reveal the name underneath. "And the girl you shall marry is . . . drum roll please . . ."

"Not doing it," Alistair said, his hands firmly planted on his thighs.

"Fine," Keri said, tapping a few fingertips on the fabric of the seat.

"Just say it!" Alistair barked.

A gust of wind did the talking instead, howling through the car as it snatched the fortune-teller and sucked it out of Keri's open window.

"Pixie farts!" Keri hollered as she went after it, fighting against her seat belt and thrusting a hand out into the spring air.

"Hey now!" Alistair's mom yelped, spinning around to halt the commotion. In the process, her elbow struck a coffee cup resting on the center console, sending it into Alistair's dad's lap. Luckily, it was mostly empty and the scant liquid left inside was cool. It startled him nevertheless.

"Sh—sugar!" he cried, successfully dodging the swear, but jostling the wheel. The car swerved into the other lane.

Alistair saw it before anyone else, or at least he reacted to it first. In the opposite lane, something was barreling down the road, its momentum building. Not another car, though.

"Bear!" Alistair screamed.

Sure enough, a black bear—fur bristling, slobber dripping from its mouth—was hurtling toward them. It showed no signs of slowing.

This time Alistair's dad didn't avoid the swear, but he turned the wheel to avoid the beast. The car swerved back into the correct lane as he eased down on the brake, and the bear galloped past Keri's open window—its breaths thick and rusty, its musk mixing with the leafy scent of the forest and nesting in Alistair's memory. There was madness in its eyes, or maybe just wildness, an instinctual distrust of metallic things on wheels.

"Holy hand grenade, did you see that?" Keri yelled, spinning around to look out the back window. As it reached a curve in the road, the bear bounded off the pavement and escaped into the forest.

"We're . . . all . . . okay?" Alistair's dad asked.

"Okay?" Keri said. "More than okay. That sucker was humungo!"

"I'm fine," Alistair's mom said. "You're fine, Albee? All good?"

It had been years since she'd called him Albee. It was her baby name for him. "I'm cool," he said, trying to sound unfazed, but his body betrayed his words. His head was on a swivel, checking the trees for hidden things.

The car slowed to a stop. Alistair's dad turned down the

stereo. He took a deep breath and eased his hands off the wheel. "So mark that down as our first adventure of the weekend," he said. "I'd say we're off to a rousing start."

Somewhere, either on the road or in the tall wet grass, the ink on the fortune-teller bled through the paper.

CHAPTER 14

———◆———

IT HAD A PULSE. HELD AGAINST ALISTAIR'S CHEST, THE ATLAS throbbed, sending tiny vibrations through his ribs. It was a bit disconcerting. It was a bit comforting. This thing was a fortune-teller too, one of incalculable value.

"You gotta go. Pronto. Before Dot wakes up," Chip said, grabbing Alistair by the shoulders and moving him to the door. But when Chip dialed the code, the door drew open and revealed Dot standing on the other side.

Hands on hips, she said, "Top of the morning."

"Oh . . . hello," Chip responded with a sigh.

When she spotted the book under Alistair's arm, her reply was written all over her wince: *You big dopes.*

"You know I'm right," Chip said. "This is his destiny."

"There's no such thing," she said. "There are probabilities. You don't know who Alistair really is. What he's likely to do. We have to learn that first."

Alistair was sick of them talking about him as if he weren't there, and he saw little point in hiding the truth from them anymore. Their goals were ultimately the same. "If it's not my destiny, then it's my responsibility," he said.

"What in the sam heck is that supposed to mean?" Dot asked.

"I came to Aquavania through Fiona Loomis's portal," Alistair explained. "I stumbled in here, like all swimmers apparently. But I'm pretty sure there was once a portal that was meant for me. I was six. My goldfish died. I buried it in the backyard. My friend Charlie slept over. That night, I heard a voice coming from the water in the goldfish bowl. The bowl disappeared and the water hung there. I ignored it. Charlie obviously didn't. He used my portal."

"Okay . . ." Chip mumbled. "So you're saying there's some swimmer named Charlie out there? So?"

"No," Alistair said, easing open his hands, which had been clenched into fists. "I'm saying that Charlie is the Whisper, that I know the Whisper. I don't know why he is, or how he is, but I know that he is. And I'm going to find him and stop him. It's my responsibility."

It felt good to get that off his chest, but only for a moment. The posture of disgust that possessed Dot's body negated any sense of relief. "You had a portal?" she asked, her voice flirting with anger. "And the person who went through it became the Whisper? You're sure of this?"

Dot's fingers curled, just a little bit. Remembering her

iron grip, Alistair stepped backward and asked, "Why should it matter who the portal was meant for?"

"Unfortunately, in this case, it kinda does," Chip said through his teeth.

Dot tapped her fingers on her hip, along the jumpsuit's white curlicues. She took a step, a slow one, a careful one, and with her eyes locked on Alistair she said, "You *need* to stay." There was more than anger in her voice now, more than insistence. This wasn't a conversation anymore.

Once again, the instinct to run was strong, but where would Alistair go? If he really was in a space station, then there probably weren't lakes or ponds or obvious gateways. That's when he remembered the atlas under his arm. Did he have the time to steal a glance, to scout out an exit?

As he opened it, Dot grabbed one of the white curlicues on her jumpsuit and peeled it off. Flicking her wrist, she snapped it like a whip, and it stretched out and wrapped around Alistair's arms and chest. It had become a lasso, glowing, buzzing, and holding him tight.

"Don't be foolish," Dot said. "You don't know what you're doing."

"You're right." Alistair grimaced as he struggled to free himself. "But I don't know what you're doing either."

"Helping you," Dot replied. "Don't force me to take more drastic measures."

All the while, Chip was standing to the side and mouthing something to Alistair. It looked like *nine, eight, seven* . . .

"I should be free to leave," Alistair said. "I'm a swimmer."

"That's not all you are," Dot said. "We have to run a few more tests."

. . . *one, zero* went Chip's mouth as he peeled off his racing stripe, balled it up, and bounced it off the floor. This time it didn't ricochet around the room. It struck Dot's lasso and cut it in half. The lasso fell limp, like a decapitated snake, and Alistair could move again.

"He's a candidate, Chip!" Dot yelled. "We don't know what he's capable—"

"So you want to hard-boil his brain?" Chip barked back. "Because I know that's what you'll end up doing when all the data come in. And where will that get us?"

"It will keep us here. It will keep us safe."

"No," Chip replied. "It will keep the Whisper safe. I'm done looking. This kid will have to do!"

Like a linebacker, Chip lowered a shoulder and plowed into Alistair, picking him up and pushing him past Dot. Dot fell to the ground as the two boys crashed into the hallway. "Yellow polka-dot egg," Chip whispered into Alistair's ear. "Cow. Chicken. Goat. Goat. Pig. Rabbit."

Then Chip let go of him and skittered on hands and knees back into the room, jumped up, and sealed the door behind him, leaving Alistair alone in the hall. Dot's screams were muffled, but still audible. "Last straw, Chip! We're done! He's not worth it!"

At one end of the hallway was the gallery. At the other end, the unknown. With the atlas tucked under his arm, Alistair hustled into the unknown. Doors flanked him on both sides.

They had porthole-style windows with columns of light blasting out of them. Alistair paused and pressed his face against the window on the first door. Behind it, little green men with antennae worked wrenches and screwdrivers on some elaborate bit of machinery. Alistair pushed on the door, but it didn't move. There was a dial next to it, but he had no idea what the code was.

Yellow polka-dot egg?

Nothing resembling an egg was in sight. He moved on to the next door.

Behind this one there were three cages. In each cage there was an elephantine creature. They were elephantine because they looked like elephants, but they clearly weren't elephants. They had three trunks instead of one and sprouting from their heads were enormous antlers, which they ran back and forth across the bars of the cage like prisoners rattling cups.

Yellow polka-dot egg?

Nothing. He moved on.

Another door, another strange scene. This room was filled with water. It was like looking into an aquarium. Except instead of fish, there were glowing neon discs that spun and swam and bounced off of one another like billiard balls.

Yellow polka-dot egg?

Chip's words still made no sense, until Alistair had passed all the doors. Farther along, nested in the walls, were eggs as big as cars and colored as if for Easter. A blue egg with pink stripes. A solid green one. A tie-dyed egg. A black and white one. An egg with yellow polka dots.

He stopped. It was suddenly dead quiet. He considered knocking on this last egg, like knocking on a door, but he wasn't sure if that might crack it. All Chip had said was *yellow polka-dot egg* and then a bunch of animals. What were the animals again?

Cow. Chicken. Goat. Goat. Pig. Rabbit.

Alistair said the words to himself over and over, like a phone number he wanted to remember. Though he had no idea why he needed to remember them. He'd found the egg, but there weren't any animals around. He would have seen them. He would have heard them. He would have smelled them. The hallway was completely empty.

Except for Dot.

"Alistair! Don't!"

She had gotten past Chip and through the door. Loose-limbed, she rushed toward Alistair like a traveler chasing down a departing train.

Screw it, eggs are meant to be cracked.

He made a fist.

He thrust it forward.

And . . . nothing.

Instead of breaking the shell, it went straight through it. The egg wasn't solid; it was a hologram with a thin force field around it. Sticking his hand through the force field was like sticking his hand out of the open window of a speeding car. There was resistance, but not enough to hold him back.

Cow. Chicken. Goat. Goat. Pig. Rabbit.

Running, fighting, surrendering—all those options were

off the table. The only thing Alistair could think to do was to step inside of the egg and hope his next move would become clear. So that's what he did.

The force field pulled him in, held him up, and cradled him, suspended him in the air as if he were the yolk. There had been no seeing through the eggshell from the outside, but from the inside Alistair could now see out. Not clearly, but enough, like looking through a sheer curtain.

The egg had been hiding something. On a sleek metallic wall behind it, there was a control panel full of buttons. Some were marked with numbers, some with letters, some with pictures, including drawings of animals. A camel. A snake. A little monkey with big ears.

Cow.

He reached through the force field and pressed a button with a cow on it, and like an infant's toy, it emitted a *moooooo*.

"Alistair! Chip was being foolish! You're being foolish!" Dot's voice was getting louder. She was getting closer.

Chicken.

He pressed a button with a chicken on it, and predictably, it responded with a *bock, bock, bugock!*

"You won't survive out there," came Dot's voice, now less a scream and more an admonition. "You need to stay. You'll hurt yourself. You'll hurt others."

Alistair refused to respond, wanting nothing less than to be convinced. His decision involved the buttons, whatever those buttons were.

Goat—neigh.

Goat—neigh.

Pig—oink.

"There's something terribly wrong with you," Dot pleaded. "There's evil in you."

Rabbit—whoosh!

It was instantaneous. Alistair—encased in an egg-shaped capsule, protected by the thin holographic force field—blasted off and out into the dark expanse of space.

November 19, 1989

---◆---

The fishbowl sat on the notebook. The notebook sat on Charlie's dresser. Above Charlie's dresser, mounted on the wall, was a mirror, a big one, big enough that from where he was standing, Alistair could see a reflection of the upper half of his body. The fishbowl, filled with water almost to its cracked rim, was lined up with his torso. In the mirror there was an optical illusion at work. The fishbowl was his heart. It was his stomach. It was his guts, complicated and essential.

He tipped the bowl and pulled the notebook out from underneath it. He examined the cover:

GODS OF NOWHERE

It was the title to a collection of tales, each tale more disturbing than the one that came before it. They told of kids who'd created worlds in Aquavania, kids whose souls had been stolen, kids whose worlds had been captured. There appeared to be no end to it all. There were more souls to steal, more worlds to capture. These tales were a work in progress.

MUCH LIKE
THIS ONE

———•—•———

IN A YEAR IN A DARK AGE

THIS TALE FOLLOWS SOMEONE WHO WASHED UP ONSHORE.

A mother and her son were at the beach, collecting shells to turn into jewelry, when they came upon a girl who was sitting in the sand, arms wrapped around her knees, shivering.

"Hoy!" the mother, whose name was Regina, called out. "Are you hurt, girl?"

The girl turned her head to look at them, but didn't respond.

"Who are you?" the son, whose name was Remus, asked.

Again, the girl didn't respond.

Regina and Remus helped the girl up from the sand and brought her back to their village, because they were generous people. They fed her, clothed her, asked her more questions, and still she gave no answers.

"I do not think she understands us," Regina said.

The rest of the villagers agreed.

There was wildness to the girl, in the way she moved, in

the way she looked at things with her big bulging eyes. Like a wolf or a hawk, she was primal. Her face bore a scar, her long arms swayed when she walked. She reminded them of the savage people who lived inland, the warrior tribes who worshipped trees.

Salam, the village healer, had been captured by one of the warrior tribes when he was a boy, so he knew a bit of their language. He tried to speak to the girl, to figure out who she was, but even when she broke her silence, she used words that no one could understand.

Nevertheless, they accepted her into the village. She turned out to be a skilled fisherwoman. For hours she would stand in the surf, or in the streams that fed into the ocean, and she would spear enough fish to feed multiple families. She contributed more than her share.

They decided to call her Kira, which was the name of an ancestor who once drowned in the sea. Remus, being a young man with young man tendencies, was drawn to Kira and spent as much time with her as possible. He started teaching her their language.

Within a year, she was nearly fluent, and everyone finally came to know her story, which wasn't much of a story at all.

"I know nothing of before," she said. "I must be born from the sea."

This was not an unreasonable assumption. The sea carried strange things ashore—giant beasts and curiously carved bits of wood. Why could it not also birth a fully grown girl?

It was not long before Remus and Kira were married, and

soon after that, they started a family. They lived in a hut on a hill that looked down at the ocean. Their first child's name was Lyra, and she was a rambunctious sort, always slipping away from them to chase a butterfly or colorful bird. Their second child's name was Oric, and he was the opposite, always clinging to his mother and father, for he was painfully shy, afraid of what lay beyond the village.

Lyra died young, which was a tragedy, but it was not uncommon in the village. She had been scrambling over rocks when she came upon a strange sea beast in a tide pool. Crouching to get a closer look, she slipped and cut open her leg on some barnacles, then tumbled into the water and became entangled in the beast's tentacles. The beast was barely alive, foul-stenched and teeming with disease. Lyra managed to free herself and get home, but her leg became infected. The infection spread quickly, and within a few days it had ravaged her body and turned her blood nearly black. There was nothing the healer Salam could do to save her. Her death was fast but ferocious, and her family tied her body to logs and set her adrift at sea, hoping she would reach the afterlife, which they believed lay far beyond the horizon.

Lyra's death stirred something in Oric. Instead of growing more withdrawn, he became braver, as if he were carrying on his sister's legacy. He explored the forests past their village. He even found evidence of the warrior tribes stashed in hollowed-out trees—old spears and clubs that he brought home to show the other boys. He boasted about how when he was older he would defeat the warrior tribes and become their leader. He was bossy and stubborn, cocky and cold.

One night, Kira was putting Oric to bed and he told her, "I have lived for two hundred summers."

It was a strange thing to say, for there had never been anyone in the village who had lived more than seventy summers, and everyone, especially Kira, knew for a fact that Oric had only lived for seven summers.

"Don't be silly," Kira said. "You are a boy."

Oric shook his head. "I go places at night," he said.

"You sleepwalk? Where do you go? To the ocean?"

Oric shook his head. "I go to my own place, a place I built. I have a pet bird there that talks. His name is Potoweet. I have a sea beast that only I command, that can snatch people with its endless arms. I have an underground fortress. I do things I'm not proud of there. I wish I could stop."

"What do you mean?"

Oric hung his head. "I trick people. I scare people. I make them do as I command. If only someone could stop me."

"You should not play at pretend so much," Kira said. "It invades your dreams. All will be fine. You need not feel guilty about things that aren't real. Especially while your father and I are near."

His mother's assurances did little to leach the worry from Oric's eyes, but he didn't say anything more. He kissed his mother on the cheek and settled in for the night.

Kira went to bed a little later, but she couldn't sleep. Oric's words haunted her for reasons she didn't understand.

Worrying about her son was part of it, but there was another part as well. A single word flooded her skull.

Banar. Banar. Banar.

She had no idea where this word originated. The next morning she visited Salam and asked him if he had anything that could banish it from her head. "I have heard this word before," he said. "It is one the warrior tribes use. I cannot remember its meaning. I'm sorry, but I can do nothing for you."

It was only a word, but a word can be a virus, and soon it wasn't simply in her head. It was in the wind, in the songs of birds, in the voices of her family. It became so overwhelming that she left. Didn't explain. Didn't say goodbye. Compelled by a force she had never felt before, Kira simply set off into the forest in search of the warrior tribes.

Countless sunsets passed before she came upon a tribe, and when she did, she wasn't sure she had found the right people. Deep in the woods, at the foot of some mountains, a group of about fifty was living in homes carved out of the cliffsides. When Kira made her presence known, they weren't hostile. Only curious. And when she said the one word from their language that she knew, when she repeated the word that had driven her nearly to madness—"Banar, Banar, Banar"—they led her to a collection of boulders.

Faded paintings decorated the boulders, and the paintings told stories. Men chasing animals. Woman climbing mountains. Gods meting out judgment. On one boulder there was a painting of a turtle with a boy's head.

"Banar," the people said, pointing at the turtle.

There was also a girl in the painting, her face poking out from behind a shrub. Kira pointed at the girl.

"Una," the people said.

Kira started to cry.

The sun slipped behind the trees and the paint glowed in the dark. The tribe returned to their homes, but they let Kira stay among the boulders all night. She studied the stories, gorgeous narratives of the Earth and its inhabitants. When the sun came back up, she left.

Her journey home was excruciating. She found herself emotionally overwhelmed more often than not. Her appetite was virtually nonexistent. She was wasting away, and by the time she stumbled onto the beach near her village, she had barely enough energy to carry on.

The villagers found her and brought her to Salam. His skills at healing were strong, but he wasn't sure he could save her.

"Where have you been?" he asked.

Her voice dry and soft, she said, "Banar was a boy with a turtle shell. He had a sister named Una. She was a liar."

"Ah yes," Salam said. "The stories. Now I remember. That was an old story that went back countless lifetimes. Unfinished, if I recall. It was from the great prophet Cabal. The stories poured from him like a waterfall, even up until the moment they executed him. But they would not let him finish that one."

"I don't understand," Kira said, "because I know the end to that story. The girl, Una, finally realizes her mistakes;

she realizes all the trouble she has caused, and begs Banar to eat her. He agrees, but he only eats her body. He leaves her head so she will always remember what she's done."

"A fitting ending, I suppose," Salam said.

"And how can it go back many lifetimes?" Kira asked. "I am Una. I am sure of it."

"You are delirious," Salam said.

"I am Una," she said again.

"You must rest," Salam said. "Or you won't be with us much longer."

Kira's family came to see her, and her son, Oric, crouched next to her bedside. "Tell me again about this place you created," she whispered.

Oric's eyes narrowed, he placed a hand on his mother's hot cheek, and he said, "I don't know what you mean."

"The place with the bird and the fortress and the sea beast. Where you trick people, where you scare people. You confessed it to me."

"I must have been sharing a dream," Oric said. "A dream I have forgotten."

"How old are you?" she asked.

"Eight summers," Oric said, as if it were the most obvious answer in the world.

"Am I going mad?" Kira asked.

"No," Salam said. "You are sick. I will try to make you better."

He did try, but he did not succeed. She would not eat. She would barely sleep. Her mind was slipping away.

So Salam told her stories. It was the only thing that seemed to give her comfort. He told her all the stories he remembered from his days with the warrior tribe. He told her the stories of their village by the sea. He even made up new stories as best he could.

Something miraculous happened. She got better. The stories restored something in her, giving her the desire to eat, the ability to sleep. Soon she was back to normal health. When her family asked her why she went to visit the warrior tribe, she told them a lie.

"I went looking for new streams to fish and I became lost," she said. "The warrior tribe found me and guided me home."

She didn't tell her family about the *Banar* that was still stuck in her head. She didn't tell them what she had told Salam. She never mentioned the name Una again.

Life rambled on. Oric grew into a man who had dreams and nightmares, like all men do, but he was never again concerned with the place where he did bad things. At night, the village would gather and eat and tell stories, which kept Kira going. As long as she had these stories filling her head, it supplanted the eerie feeling that she had lived another life, that long ago she was a girl named Una.

Kira eventually became a grandmother and time pinched wrinkles into her skin. She was content, but she could feel that her body didn't have much time left in it. Spearing fish wasn't possible anymore, but she could still swim. Every morning she waded out past the waves and floated in the ocean, giving her aching joints some reprieve.

One night, after a round of stories, her body ached so much that she decided to take a moonlit swim. The star-pocked sky was so clear, so vibrant, so inviting that she decided to swim to the horizon.

And she swam out farther and farther, to see what lay beyond the horizon, behind the stars, in the land of her lost memories.

A WHILE LATER

CHAPTER 15

———◆———

ALISTAIR WAS LOST IN A PRAIRIE OF STARS. THE CAPSULE WAS on autopilot, cutting through the dark expanse of space with determination and purpose. Its mission? Unknowable. Alistair was still suspended in the middle of the egg and he could see out, but there was no screen, no computer display, nothing to say, *Your destination is . . .*

An asteroid as big as a house hurtled past, and the egg changed course. A chase was on. It seemed determined to catch the icy hunk.

"Abort mission!" Alistair shouted, not knowing what else to do.

The capsule didn't take orders. The original command of *Cow, Chicken, Goat, Goat, Pig, Rabbit* had sealed the capsule's—and therefore Alistair's—fate. That fate seemed to involve crashing into an asteroid.

Crystals of ice stuck out from the asteroid's surface like

spines on a sea urchin, and as the capsule closed in, Alistair could practically feel them jabbing his skin. He clutched the atlas to his chest and gritted his teeth, because that's what people do in such situations, but when the crystals touched the edge of the force field, they didn't pierce it. They didn't shatter. The ice melted and the water it became clung to the egg, enveloped it in an extra shell, a liquid shell.

So much water, so quickly, gathering like snow on a rolling snowball. Soon the stars were squiggles of light and there was no asteroid to see, only quivering liquid. And soon the weight of the water must have been too great, because the force field imploded and the water collapsed in on Alistair, drenching every inch of his body.

Then he was in a pool.

Not a pond, not a lake, an actual pool. A big one at that, Olympic-size, with lanes sectioned off by buoyed ropes. Banners hung overhead. DISTRICT CHUMPS. STATE CHUMPS. NATIONAL CHUMPS. WORLD CHUMPS. UNIVERSE CHUMPS.

"Kill . . . me . . . now," came a voice, goofy and tuneless. Two dark lines, like lampposts, sprouted from the deck of the pool. "Gawd. A kid who can swim. Like a stinkin' guppy," came the voice again, a boy's voice, but all Alistair could see were those dark lines.

So he swam toward the edge, guiding himself with one arm while holding the atlas with the other. When he had a grip on the concrete, he got a better view. More dark lines, but together they formed a stick figure, a crudely drawn boy in a bathing suit with inflatable swimmies on his flimsy arms.

"Man oh man. Now look what you've done," the stick boy said. "Coach M is gonna see this and he'll be all like, 'Well this kid can swim, so why can't any of you chumps?' And then we're all gonna have to go in there." The boy skittered back and forth like he was excessively caffeinated, until a notion stopped him in his tracks. "Unlesssss . . . you're one of those. Tell me you're one of those?"

Chlorine fumes tickled at his nostrils, and Alistair sneezed and said, "One of what?"

"One of those aliens, one of those dudes or dudettes from another world who pops in and tries to impress us with your skills. Not drowning, for instance. You're all amazing at that. Just so you know, we appreciate that one alien dealing with that bully Tyler, we really, truly do. But usually you make us feel lousy. You *are* one of those, aren't you?"

"I . . . guess so."

"Knew it," the stick boy said. "Well, silver lining is I can tell Coach M that aliens don't count as kids, because I am *so* not getting into that pool. And after that's straightened out, I'd be happy to lead you to one of your wormholes or whatever."

The kid reached down his hand, a scribble of five lines. It didn't seem like something to grab—it seemed like a drawing—and yet Alistair grabbed it, and the stick boy had a firm grip and enough strength to pull him out of the water.

"Is this a school?" Alistair asked.

"Unfortunately," the stick boy said. "I'm Kenny, by the way."

There were bleachers, a scoreboard, and doors marked

EXIT and LOCKERS. It was very similar to the pool back home at Thessaly High School, where Alistair and Charlie took swimming lessons for a few months when they were eight. Only there weren't walking, talking stick boys back home.

"Why are you . . . ?"

"My looks weirding you out, huh?" Kenny said with a nod. "I get it. You aliens aren't used to seeing natural human forms." He spread his stick arms, twirled around. He was three-dimensional, but only barely. What was most disconcerting was the contrast with his surroundings, which appeared entirely real. The boy was a sketch come to life, a kid made of black pipe cleaners who lived in a world of depth, color, and texture.

"Do you mind if I have a moment to myself?" Alistair asked, shaking water off the atlas.

"Actually, I should be going," Kenny said. "We have an assembly in a few. Super secret special guest. Coach M thought he could get me to swim a few laps before it started, but now I'll go tell him, *No can do, Coach, we've got an alien infestation in the pool.*"

With that, Kenny spun around and jogged through a door to one of the locker rooms. Alistair hustled to the bleachers, sat down, and opened the atlas. Along with its other magical qualities, the thing must have been waterproof, because it wasn't soaked. A shake was all that was needed to get it dry.

Alistair wished he could say the same about himself. Water dripped from his soaked clothes as he flipped through the pages, stopping on the one for Quadrant 43. In a dark corner of the paper, he spotted an asteroid tagged with a golden ring and the label SCHOOL FOR INSUFFERABLE LOSERS.

He pressed the golden ring and the pages flipped until he was looking at a map of a school. There was a pool in the center and a maze of hallways and classrooms. There was a red ring in the center of the gym, but it had an *X* over it. Alistair pressed the ring and a tab shot up.

A square-jawed cipher known as Tyler used to terrorize this school of annoying figments, shattering their bodies with Mach 2 dodgeballs and atomic wedgies. A swimmer named Carl tricked Tyler into eating a veggie burger, which stunned him long enough for Carl to tie him up and deliver him to Quadrant 43, where he is currently on display. X-rays reveal he has the bones of a guinea pig.

Alistair surveyed the rest of the map. There were at least ten golden rings. One was in the pool and labeled QUADRANT 43. Another was in a fountain at the front entrance and labeled SCURVYTOWN. *Scurvy* equaled pirates, or so one would assume, and that was bound to be dangerous. In a bathroom on the second floor was a more intriguing ring labeled MAC-ROTOPIA. Macrotopia meant nothing to Alistair, but it sounded like a word he should know. Something scientific, something he might have learned about in science class.

Before he could press that golden ring and give Macrotopia a closer look, a group of kids tumbled into the room. Not stick kids, though. Not like Kenny at all, and not like one another. There was a googly-eyed comic book kid all decked out in primary colors. There was a kid made of dough. A stone kid. A kid that seemed ripped from the canvas of a painting. A kid who looked like a normal kid, like Alistair, but he was much, much larger, three times as big. The only quality these kids shared is that they were all—for lack of a better word—nerdy.

"Kenny was right," said a chubby boy covered in fur like a werewolf. "And this one is even uglier than the others."

"You think he's here for the assembly?" said a bespectacled girl made of a mishmash of doll parts.

A zombified one replied, "Another toilet diver, I bet, probably fishing for floaters." And the crowd rippled with cackles. With all the decomposition, it was hard to judge if this zombie class clown was a boy or a girl. It hardly mattered. Alistair didn't plan to stay long.

Atlas tucked under his arm, he headed for the door marked EXIT. The band of misfits followed, their numbers now in the teens. By the time he was in a locker-lined hallway, the mob had tripled, quadrupled, quintupled, and they were pressing against him as if he were a celebrity on his way to a limo. The fluttering eyes of sighing girls, the respectful nods of rough-and-tumble boys—he craved those things as much as anyone. But he didn't crave this. As the mob pressed into him—pawing, shouting—it felt like a slow form of murder.

"Tell us about the other dimensions!"

"Let us touch your hair!"

"Are you a cannibal?"

Soon their requests and questions were unintelligible yelps, and the only thing that could overpower them was an announcement over the loudspeaker.

"The assembly starts in five minutes. Our special guest today is . . . the Maestro."

Air raid sirens couldn't have done a better job. The kids shut up, and quick. They traded looks of disbelief, and in a frantic but somewhat orderly fashion, they split off from Alistair and streamed away, now yammering instead of yelping, repeating one word with giddy anticipation.

"Maestro. Maestro. Maestro!"

At the tail end of the bunch, a girl shaped like a Weeble —no legs or arms, just a rounded head and torso—rocked back and forth and scooted along as best she could, though her best was painfully slow. Alistair walked alongside and asked, "Who's the Maestro?"

"Motivational speaker of the highest quality," she squeaked. "His stories inspire you to aspire. He's perhaps the greatest person in the universe."

Quite an endorsement, and hard to resist, but once the crowd had filed through a pair of doors marked CAFETORIUM, Alistair was free to do as he pleased. His instinct told him to find another gateway. If he was meant to reach the Ambit of Ciphers, then relying on momentum seemed the logical course of action. It had served him well so far.

And yet, so had learning. The things that Chip and Dot had told him, the things Baxter had told him—heck, even the things Polly and Potoweet had told him—had given him a deeper understanding of Aquavania. It was probably worth sticking around for at least a few minutes to get a taste of what this "Maestro" had to say. By a hair, at that moment, the cafetorium won out.

Alistair was the last one through the doors, and every seat in the place was already filled. The room was a cafeteria and the seats were plastic, utilitarian, the kind you'd find in any school. However, the room was also an auditorium. The lunch tables had been cleared away and there was a small stage on the opposite end from the kitchen.

To remain inconspicuous, Alistair stepped into the kitchen and hid behind a cadre of aproned lunch ladies who were busy cleaning up the day's meal. An odd bunch if there ever was one, each appeared to resemble the food she served. One was shaped like a corncob, another like a green bean. That's to say nothing of the sloppy joe one—too strange to even attempt to describe.

Out among the chairs, the teachers who patrolled the aisles were like the lunch ladies, taking on shapes that seemed to match the subjects they taught—a beaker-shaped chemistry instructor, a protractor-shaped geometry guru. The kids were seated, but their twitching bodies and manic chatter indicated that the atmosphere was poised for a storm. When the lights lowered, the crowd did hush, but every neck craned to get a better view. A boy stepped out from behind a curtain at the back of the stage, and a spotlight moved clumsily to find him.

The harsh light made his face look both giant and ghoulish, but it was the same face he had back home in Thessaly. The Maestro was Charlie Dwyer.

The suit that Charlie wore was made of soft fabric, velvet perhaps, and a dark shade of green. A yellow shirt with ruffled sleeves and a large collar peeked out from underneath. No one seemed to find the outfit ridiculous, though it definitely was ridiculous. They all watched with rapt attention as he paced around the tiny stage, his shoes clacking on the linoleum.

"What a fine afternoon I'm having with a fine crop of young students," Charlie said, winking and waving at the girls in the crowd, who responded with flushed, downturned faces.

For Charlie? Alistair thought, clenching on to the edge of a countertop. *They're blushing for Charlie?*

A crew of gym teachers shaped like balls and rackets surrounded the stage, pacing in circles like security guards. The message was clear: *Don't even think about messing with the Maestro.*

Two thumbs, two pinkies, and a ring finger—that was all that was left of Charlie's hands, but he held them up for all to see their mangled glory. "Last time I was here, I told you about how I lost my fingers when I tried to grab hold of some rockets," he said, his steps matching his voice—buoyant, confident. "Reach for the stars and sometimes you don't even make it to the moon. Sometimes you blow your fingers off."

Laughs arrived on cue. Charlie smirked and went on. "All kidding aside, I told you that story because I wanted you to realize that sometimes when you take a risk, you fail, but that doesn't mean that you shouldn't be out there trying crazy and difficult things. I also told you that story so I can tell you this one."

Charlie pointed to the person running the electronics in the cafetorium, a patchwork man made of audio-visual equipment, a guy with a spotlight for a chest. The guy nodded and the spotlight shifted to a red.

His skin cast in crimson, Charlie asked the crowd, "You've all heard of the one they call the Whisper?"

The crowd booed.

"The Riverman?"

More boos.

"Gryla, Jumbi, lots of names we could use. Terrifying, right?"

Kenny stood from his seat and yelled, "He sent that bully Tyler after us!"

"That's true," Charlie admitted, and he motioned with a pinkie for Kenny to sit, which he did—immediately. "But did you ever ask why he sent that bully Tyler after you?"

"Because he's a double turd burger with extra cheese," yelled the zombified kid.

Charlie smiled and said, "Fair enough. But I think you're missing something. The things you do, you do for two reasons. First reason: You were born to do them. Why do you breathe? Why do you eat? Why do you poop?"

The word *poop* elicited even more laughter in Aquavania than it did back home in Thessaly. Alistair was noticing that these kids loved their toilet humor.

"Second reason," Charlie went on. "You choose to do the things you do. And when you make a choice, you reveal the person you really are. Tell me, by a show of hands, who wants to know who the Whisper really is."

Every hand in the place went up—the hands of the kids, of the teachers, of the lunch ladies. Even Alistair's hand, creeping reluctantly past his head, which he was hiding behind a stack of trays.

"Good," Charlie said. "Because I'm going to tell you his story."

THE MAESTRO'S STORY

A WAYS BACK THERE WAS THIS BOY, A REGULAR OLD KID, LIKE any kid here. He lived in a small, happy community. He had a family and friends and he had a purpose in life. Some people might call that purpose *faith in his creator*, but let's not get too religious. We'll simply call it *devotion*.

One night, this devoted kid was alone, bathing in a pond, when he heard a voice. "I wish I knew the point of this," the voice said. "I need to know why someone so guilty and sad has been given so much power."

The voice came from the pond, so the kid was keen to investigate. He plucked a bamboo reed from the water's edge and used it as a snorkel. He explored the murky depths. He swam around the edges and dove to the bottom. Nothing to be found, not even a frog, but here's the thing: he knew the voice. It was the voice of his creator.

His creator didn't live in the clouds, or in the underworld, or in the confines of his imagination. She lived in a cave, among the people she had created. In other words, the boy was her neighbor.

The boy was a good neighbor. The best, in fact. And he knew he had to help his creator, because she was calling out in distress and, to a person of devotion, that type of call is the most awful sound in the world. So through the forest the boy ran, clutching the bamboo reed, and he ran so fast that by the time he reached the cave, water from the pond still clung to his body.

"Una," he said, for that was his creator's name, "are you all right? Can I help you?"

"You love me, don't you, Banar?" she replied, for that was the boy's name.

"More than anything," Banar said, and before Una could speak, before she could make the most god-awful request she could possibly make, he knew what he had to do. It wasn't something he even thought about. It was like breathing, or eating . . . or pooping. A completely natural reflex.

What she asked of him was this: *Bring about an end. To all of it.*

And that's exactly what he did.

Apologizing as he leaned over, he slipped the bamboo reed into her ear. With his mouth on the other end, he sucked. Gross, right? Actually, no. Because he wasn't sucking out her brains. He was sucking out her soul, and Una's soul—a dense, sparkly, heavenly cocktail—filled the reed.

Boo, you say. Boo! Because this sounds horrific. This sounds unjust. I know. But remember, this is exactly what she wanted, exactly what she needed. And as Una's soul filled that reed, the world in which they lived, the place Una had created, a land called Mahaloo, began to slip away. The color drained out of everything. Out of the plants, the animals, even the people.

Have you ever seen Popsicles melt? It was like that. But instead of Popsicle sticks remaining, it was piles of ash. And what happened to all those swirly and pretty colors? Well, they pooled together and formed a river.

Understandably, Banar gasped and crouched over Una's lifeless body and shook it. "What have I done?" he cried.

But shaking her body was like shaking a seeding dandelion. Poof! It broke apart into tiny pieces, and the pieces drifted into the sky like they never weighed a thing. Fearing her soul might suffer the same fate, Banar quickly plugged the ends of the reed with compressed balls of ash and clutched it to his chest.

Can you imagine what that was like? To have your creator ask such a thing of you? To have to witness all the things you know and love simply disappear or drain away? You'd have trouble believing it, as Banar had trouble believing it.

"Maybe all is not lost," he called out. "Maybe I can get it all back." And he dove into the river with the reed in his mouth, and he swam downstream. It seemed as though his hopes might have been fulfilled, because the river eventually led to . . . Mahaloo. His home. Una's creation.

It wasn't lost! It had moved!

Mahaloo was like an unmoored boat washed up on a

distant shore. Banar climbed out of the water and into a field, where his friends and family were going about their lives—hunting, gathering, all that stuff people must do to survive. But when they saw Banar coming toward them, they didn't welcome him. In fact, they cursed at him.

"You took her from us!" they screamed. "You stole Una!"

Banar wanted to explain, but how could he? Guilty as charged. So with the reed clamped in his teeth, Banar hauled butt, and they chased after him. As they closed in, he monkeyed his way up a tree. It was a tree so tall that no one could see where it ended. Everyone assumed it reached to the top of Mahaloo, but no one knew for sure because no one had climbed it that high. At least not until our buddy Banar did.

Rather than play follow the leader, his people set fire to the tree. Flames crept, grew, and ate away at the bark and branches. Banar was fast enough to outclimb the flames, but when he reached the top, he was met by the sky—gorgeous and tinted green, but empty, except for a small, lumpy cloud no bigger than a pumpkin.

The flames finally caught up, as flames do, and the heat became unbearable. Banar had no choice but to jump. He flexed his legs, clenched his teeth on the reed, and pushed off. His body shot out into the air and collided with the cloud. And you know what?

Instantly, unexpectedly, he was sucked into the sky.

I know. I know. Sounds like one of those wormholes you have in the school, right? But you have to realize, this wasn't in the days when beings moved from world to world. I know

231

you see aliens all the time here, travelers who pop by and charm you with descriptions of magical realms. But for Banar, there was only one realm: Mahaloo. So when he was sucked into the sky and he found himself somewhere new, he was thrown a bit off-kilter, to put it lightly.

This new world consisted of rocks. Yep, rocks, that's about it. A flat plane of rocks with edges that bordered a gray void on every side. There was no one to serve, no one to flee. Definitely no way to get back to Mahaloo. All there was to do was stack.

So that's what he did. Day after day, he stacked rocks. He started by taking rocks from the edges of the plane and bringing them to the center and stacking them in a circle. Then he stacked circles on the circle, until the stacks became a home, a round tower that strained into the void. When he finally moved enough rocks to uncover what was beneath them, he found water. The water rose over what was left of the plane until a moat surrounded the tower. And like a clogged toilet, the water kept coming, spilling over the edges and into the void, creating a circular waterfall that never dried up. Up went the tower, down went the water, but there was no seeing the bottom of the waterfall. Maybe it had no bottom.

From then on, Banar lived in this world alone, in this tower alone, in a room at the top that was so cold that icicles formed from condensed vapor on the ceiling. There were windows in the room that looked out into the void and down to the waterfall. He still had the bamboo reed and he held it close at all times. The ash still plugged the two openings, keeping Una's soul locked away. It was all that he had left of his creator. He couldn't bear to lose it.

Holding it close would never be enough, though. Unplugging the reed, gazing into the sparking liquid, that was the good stuff. That was what he *really* wanted to do, and the temptation eventually overpowered him. This sort of thing rarely goes well, and now was no exception. As soon as he unplugged the reed, it fell from his hand and bounced on the floor. Some, but not all, of the liquid splashed on his body, and the reed flipped up and out a window.

Down the spiral steps of the tower he ran, and when he reached the bottom, it was too late. The reed was floating in the water at the base of the tower. It was empty.

Misery!

Pain!

Tragedy!

It was all too much to bear. He dove into the pool, hoping he would be swept over the waterfall to his death. Yet as he dove, he noticed a strange reflection. It was not Banar diving into the water. It was someone who looked like the night sky, a creature that was the color of nothing and the color of everything.

It was a being of purpose.

Banar's head was suddenly full of new thoughts and ideas, of things only Una could have known, including what he was supposed to do next.

"Come out and play," Banar whispered into the water. "Please come out and play."

What's this? Was he crazy? Not in the slightest. Because his whispers did not fall on deaf ears. Quite the opposite. They traveled through the water, over the waterfall, to far-away places. Kids heard his voice, sneaking out from ponds, and creeks, even puddles. Some kids even followed his invitation. Daydreamers we call them, and they made Aquavania what it is. They built worlds. They played inside the worlds. They lived inside the worlds. And when they grew tired of the worlds, when they were through with it all, they called out for Banar. Because like Una, they needed Banar to do what they didn't have the strength to do.

Bring about an end.

He answered their calls, because that was what he was born to do. But he wasn't known as Banar anymore. Now he had many names.

CHAPTER 16

————◆————

"AGAIN, THIS BOY WAS EXACTLY LIKE ANY OF YOU," CHARLIE
finished by saying. "He was kind and, above all, loyal. He was
born to serve the ones he loved, so that's what he did. The
choices he made were made out of love and survival. Are there
any better reasons than those?"

Kenny was gracious enough to raise his hand, but not patient enough to wait to be called on. "Are you saying that
Banar is the Whisper?" he asked.

"Banar *was* the Whisper," Charlie said. "The first Whisper.
There have been others since. And they have all done what
they were born to do, and they've all made choices out of love
and survival. You might not agree with some of those choices,
but you should at least try to understand them, don't you
think?"

Stunned silence. Obviously nobody had heard this story
before. And the single question that must have been on

everyone's mind was thankfully posed by the girl made of doll parts. "What happened next?"

Charlie chuckled. "You," he said. "You happened next. Where do you think you came from? You wouldn't be here without the Whisper. Because when he called daydreamers to Aquavania, he called your creator. You owe everything to him, because he made it possible for you to exist. And to know that a kid just like any of you can grow up to become the most important person in Aquavania, well . . . that is an encouraging thought, now isn't it? It starts with devotion. It is the result of hard choices. It stems from love. The Whisper is love. That's all there is to it."

Ten minutes before, this comment might have elicited another round of boos, or at least plenty of sniggers, but Charlie's story had them all thinking.

Alistair was tempted to run out of the kitchen yelling, *He's a liar! That's only a part of it, if it's even true! Even if the Whisper helped create worlds, he's destroyed them too.* But Alistair doubted he would fare well with this crowd. They were all clearly devoted to Charlie—or, more accurately, to the Maestro.

On stage, a janitor shaped like a mop used his wooden arms to push a table and chair into place as Charlie held up a book. "Underneath your seats you'll all find copies of my latest tome, which the school kindly bought for each student. It's called *Gods of Nowhere*, and it contains tales similar to Banar's. If you all line up in an orderly fashion, I'll be signing copies."

*　*　*

Alistair was the last one in line, behind a kid who was basically a car with headlights for eyes and a shiny grille for teeth. Alistair didn't have a copy of *Gods of Nowhere*, but he did have his atlas tucked under his arm. Thanks to the car-boy's bulk, Alistair was hidden, at least for the time being, and he was pretty sure Charlie hadn't spotted him yet.

The line moved slowly. Presumably, kids were stopping to chat with Charlie as he graced them with his signature. Giggles coursed through the crowd. Legs twitched and fingers tapped on the covers of books. Even after they had signed copies in hand, most of the kids stuck around, huddled throughout the cafetorium, basking in the moment.

When Alistair finally reached the front, he could hardly control his body. A gagging reflex seemed to command his every muscle. The car-boy beeped, executed a perfect three-point turn, and spun out in excitement. Alistair was standing alone on the stage, face-to-face with his old friend.

Charlie squinted and said, "Well, well, well. Looks like we've come to the end of the—"

And Alistair vomited. Sparkling bits of meat splashed across the linoleum stage, forming a rancid constellation.

"Not the sort of finale I was expecting," Charlie said.

"Where . . . is . . . she?" Alistair asked as he wiped his mouth and stumbled forward.

"Get it together, buddy. People are watching." Charlie leaned forward and placed a hand on Alistair's chest. Alistair's instinct was to recoil, and recoil he did. But as he did, Charlie snatched the atlas from him.

"Where is she?" Alistair said, with more confidence this time. Losing the book meant nothing compared to losing her.

In response, Charlie smiled, opened the atlas, and put his fountain pen on it like he was signing another copy of *Gods of Nowhere*. "To whom should I make this out?" he asked.

"I found you," Alistair said. "I knew I would. Now it's over. Tell me where she is."

"Long name. Not sure I know how to spell it right, but I'll give it my best shot," Charlie said as he finished the inscription and handed the atlas back to Alistair. "I hope you enjoy reading this."

There was something weird about Charlie's skin. It was loose, flabby, like a peach a day past ripe. This was Charlie, and yet it wasn't. Could he be a cipher like Kyle? An imposter? What Alistair would have given for a pair of those X-ray specs. The Maestro sure sounded like Charlie, but what did that prove?

The two boys locked eyes, a good old-fashioned stare-down, until the janitor nudged Alistair out of the way for a moment, sidling in to mop up the vomit, his weathered scowl saying all that needed to be said. Seizing the opportunity, Charlie stood and slithered into the crowd. The kids immediately peppered him with questions, and there was absolutely no way for Alistair to break through their motley ranks.

"I'm afraid I must be leaving, my friends," Charlie announced as he walked backward toward the exit, though he wasn't looking at the clingy, yappy kids. He was looking at Alistair's atlas. He nodded insistently.

Alistair opened it to the cover page. The inscription read: *You're It.*

Again, the Weeble girl was lagging behind, so Alistair picked her brain. "Where are they going?" he asked.

She looked at him as if he were the world's biggest dolt. "The toilet," she said.

1987

THE BATHROOM BY THE GYM, WHERE THE LIGHTS HUMMED
and flickered yellow, was usually empty right after the final
bell. There was never gym class past sixth period, and if you
wanted to participate in illicit activities—selling candy,
sharing dirty magazines—the last stall at three p.m. was
always a good place. Kids in the know referred to it as the
Dungeon.

It was the third week of fifth grade—a Friday afternoon—
and Alistair swung his backpack over his shoulder, closed his
locker, and prepared to call it a day when he learned of the
latest goings-on in the Dungeon. Trevor Weeks, practically
dancing as he moved down the hallway, said, "They got Captain Catpoop in there! Atomic wedgies. Chocolate swirlies.
The whole shebang!"

The hallway presented two roads for Alistair. One
led outside, to where Keri was waiting to walk home.

The other led to the gym, to the bathroom, to the Dungeon.

He hesitated, but he chose.

Ken Wagner, Dan Fritz, and Ryan Chen had Charlie cornered, though it appeared they hadn't done anything to him yet. As Alistair and Trevor burst through the door, they found the trio cracking their knuckles and pounding their fists in their hands, like tough guys in some old movie. Charlie was sitting on the edge of the counter, next to the far sink where the hot water never worked.

"Reinforcements," Charlie remarked with a smile. "But for which side?"

"I'm Switzerland, dudes," Trevor said, showing everyone his empty hands.

Dan stopped cracking his knuckles—a boy like him couldn't be expected to do two things at once—and asked, "Switzerwhat?"

"Neutral," Charlie explained. "So what about you, Alistair? You gonna help me fight these guys?"

Alistair paused, checked the mirror to spy intentions in eyes. These guys were jerks, no doubt about it, but he couldn't really believe they would beat Charlie to a pulp. And yet he didn't want to antagonize them any further.

"What did he do?" Alistair asked.

"Not your concern, Cleary," Ryan said. "We don't have a problem with you."

"Well then, what's your problem with him?" Alistair asked.

"His ugly face," Dan said.

"Nice," Trevor said, licking his finger and tagging the air, as if keeping score.

"Here's the thing, fellas," Charlie said, rocking his feet back and forth like this was no big thing. "Smash my face in and it will become uglier. Then you'll have an even bigger problem with it and you'll have to smash it again. It's a vicious circle, my friends."

Ken shook his head and curled his lip up. "That's *my* problem with you. Your smart ass."

"Actually, my ass is quite dumb," Charlie said. "It's always talking out of turn and making a big stink." He lifted a knee like he was about to let loose, furrowed his brow, and then shook his head. "Sorry, false alarm."

Trevor cracked up, licked his fingers again, and tagged two points in the air for Charlie. Dan sneered and pounded his fist in his palm again. "We doin' this or what?"

Ryan resumed some knuckle-cracking, but there was little left to crack, so he started pulling at his fingers, trying to elicit popping sounds. "You know what my vote is," he said.

Alistair was watching most of this in the mirror—chin down, eyes up—but he still couldn't escape Charlie's gaze. Charlie was sneaking him a signal through the reflection, a message opposite of his bold words. A wrinkle in his brow. A twist in his mouth. *Help. Please help.*

"Excuse me," Alistair said, in a soft, polite tone. And he headed straight for the door.

242

Gasping as he stepped into the hallway, he searched for witnesses. Deserted. There was a fire alarm mounted on the wall, and he went over and opened its panel. The red lever behind the panel almost seemed as though it was vibrating, begging him to pull it. He placed his fingertips on it.

"Fire alarms spray ink on whoever sets them off," Charlie had told him once. "That way people don't pull them as a prank."

His hand shaking, Alistair withdrew. This wasn't a prank, but it wasn't a fire either. Leaving the panel open, he hurried down the hall. His sneakers squeaked on the faux-marble floor, the only sound, echoing like a baby's whimper in a dark hospital.

Keri might still be waiting for me. I'll go home. Pretend I was never there.

Around the corner, a janitor pushed an industrial broom that collected scraps of paper and dust balls as big as fists. The kids called him Lenny, but no one seemed to know if that was actually his name. It sounded like a janitor's name, and he never objected to it. He hardly spoke at all. He communicated in nods, salutes, and sighs.

"There's a toilet . . . by the gym . . . over . . . water over the rim . . . wasn't me," Alistair called out as he passed Lenny, not slowing down at all.

Lenny sighed.

*   *   *

The phone rang at 8:27. Alistair's parents had a rule: no calls after eight thirty. Charlie was well aware of this rule.

"It's you-know-who," Keri said, handing Alistair the phone.

Alistair's dad didn't turn away from the TV, but tapped his watch with a finger.

"I get it," Alistair said, moving out of the room with the mouthpiece pressed to his chest. "I'll only be a few minutes."

When he was out of earshot of his family, Alistair said, "Charlie, I'm—"

"Can you sneak out tonight? Meet me at the clubhouse around eleven?"

"I don't know. I've never snuck out. My parents aren't always asleep by then."

"Twelve, then. Climb out your window. I'll be waiting for you."

Click.

A line of cats moved like a single enormous snake, weaving through the grass soundlessly and into the open door of the clubhouse. Kyle didn't give a damn about the clubhouse anymore. "Have fun with it," he had told Charlie a year before, and that "fun" had amounted to Charlie turning it into a hotel for stray cats.

A cat slid through his legs as Charlie stepped through the clubhouse door and out into his backyard. Alistair kept his distance—he hated that clubhouse—but he could tell that Charlie was carrying something.

"We're swapping," Charlie said as he tossed a balled-up object.

It struck Alistair in the chest, but it didn't hurt. It was soft. It fell into the grass at Alistair's feet. He bent over and picked it up. A T-shirt.

There were bloodstains on the collar, a small rip in the short sleeve. Charlie stepped forward. His bare chest, rippling with small fatty folds, was drenched in moonlight. "Now give me yours," he said.

Alistair was wearing a black rugby jersey. It was expensive—at least that's what he'd been told—and had a hand-stitched fern on the left breast. "It's . . . this is . . . from my uncle," Alistair explained. "He was all the way in New Zealand when he got it."

Charlie blew a little raspberry, which must have stung a bit because his lip was red and swollen, and then he reached out a hand and made a *come here* gesture with his index and middle fingers.

Alistair peeled off the jersey.

"Lenny yelled 'What in tarnation?' when he came in and found those guys busting me up," Charlie said with a little laugh. "*What in tarnation!* Janitor hardly ever speaks, and those are the words he decides to use. I thought only the Looney Tunes talked like that."

Alistair tossed him the jersey. "I sent him in, you know. It's all I could think to do."

"I know," Charlie said, catching it and pressing it to his chest. "That's why we're doing the swap. You think this jersey is big money? That T-shirt I gave you is a limited edition. It's worth even more now because of the blood. You're being rewarded."

Closer inspection revealed that it was a shirt Charlie had made himself, using iron-on decals. White letters on green fabric read POPULAR. Charlie had worn it so much that Alistair no longer saw the joke in it. Now, bloodstained and ripped, it seemed more sad than funny.

"They call me Captain Catpoop," Charlie said as he pulled the rugby over his head.

"I know," Alistair said, trying on his new shirt, which was at least a size too big.

"I'm going to make a T-shirt with 'Captain Catpoop' written on it. If that's what the people want, then that's what they'll get."

The wind rustled leaves on the trees that edged the swamp—a soft, sarcastic round of applause. Alistair hugged himself to stay warm. "I'm so sorry," he said.

Charlie bent over and picked up a cat that was sneaking past. Its coat was ratty and its eyes glowed a ghostly yellow, but as soon as Charlie had it in his arms, it unleashed a delicate purr. "Nothing to be sorry about. Like I said. That's why you get the shirt. You sent in Lenny and he sent the guys scattering. In ten years, that shirt will be a collector's item, something to frame."

The only place Alistair had seen framed T-shirts was at a local restaurant called Hungry Paul's, and those were usually advertising pancakes or a softball team, not really anything worth collecting. "Why will it be a collector's item?" Alistair asked.

"Because I designed it, and people will never forget my designs," Charlie said. He moved his hand down, as if to stroke the cat, but instead, he gave it a pinch. It hissed and Charlie dropped it. It scampered off into the dark swamp behind the clubhouse, and Charlie patted himself on the chest, feeling the fabric of his new shirt, and he purred too, in his own way, a deep, rumbling hum.

CHAPTER 17

———◆——◆———

THE MEMORY MADE ALISTAIR EVEN WOOZIER THAN HE already was, and when he regained his senses, he found himself alone in the cafetorium with the Weeble girl.

"Taking a standing nap?" she asked. "I do those."

"What were you saying again?" he asked. "About where he went?"

"The toilet," she said. "He comes and goes through the crapper. Figured you would know that. That's how all the greats travel."

"Which toilet? Which way?"

The girl couldn't point, so she tried to lean in the right direction, but it sent her body wobbling back and forth. Amusing, but hardly useful, so Alistair consulted his atlas. The gateway to Macrotopia was in a second-floor bathroom. That had to be it.

He gauged a route and followed it through the hallway

and up a flight of stairs. The bathroom was clearly marked by a model toilet hanging from a chain above the door. *Must be fancy,* he thought as he pushed his way in.

Stained sinks, mirrors smudged with fingerprints, urinals with small puddles underneath—it was exactly like a school bathroom back home. There were even a couple of oddballs in the corner, huddled over, trying to spark a cigarette. Only these oddballs were *truly* odd.

They lifted their heads. A lighter hit the floor. They put their hands up like they were being arrested. "Oh, it's only you," a kid that looked like a sock puppet said. "You're too late, alien. The Maestro came and went. The groupies have moved on. But the throne is all yours if you want it."

The other one, who was entirely pixelated, pointed to a stall that was so covered in graffiti that it looked like a printing press had exploded.

Flush, flush, flush yourself, gently down the drain.

Here you stoop, fat and weird, came to poop but disappeared.

Bon voyage, alien!

It was a tiny fraction of the messages—there were much stranger and cruder ones—but the overall point was clear. This stall marked an exit, a gateway.

The toilet that sat in the center of the stall was nothing special. White, porcelain, round. Was he supposed to sit on it? Was he supposed to do what everyone does on a toilet? How could he even attempt such a thing with others watching? As it was, there was no door on the stall.

Alistair turned around and faced the two delinquents. There was nothing to do but shrug.

"Well, get on with it," the pixelated kid said. "If you want the big suck, then step right up."

Alistair checked the toilet, checked the kid. "Step in it?" he asked.

"He's no Maestro," the sock puppet kid said. "That's for damn sure."

Alistair took that as a yes and, bracing himself on the tank, he brought one foot up and placed it in the bowl. His body was still damp from the pool, and he hardly noticed his moccasined foot entering the water.

"Flush, flush, flush," the sock puppet started to chant, not without a fair dose of sarcasm.

Trusting the bowl's sturdiness, Alistair eased the other foot up and in.

"Flush. Flush. Flush." The pixelated kid joined in the chant.

When he felt steady, he straightened his legs, let go of the tank, and stood.

"Flush! Flush! Flush!" Alistair could feel the chant now, pulsing through his ribs. One last time he checked over his shoulder. The two had managed to light their cigarettes, which dangled loosely from their lips. They pumped their fists and blew smoke as they chanted.

The handle was too low to reach with his hand, so Alistair wedged the atlas in an armpit, placed his palms against the wall behind the toilet, and carefully lifted his left foot.

Here we go.

As he pressed the handle down with the tips of his toes, the atlas slipped out, hit the porcelain rim, and fell on the floor.

Flush.

There were days and nights and days and nights. For months the chase went on, Charlie always a step ahead of Alistair.

It started in Macrotopia, a world where everything was large, or maybe it was that Alistair was especially small. Insects and woodland creatures towered over him, and they all spoke in rhyme. He described Charlie Dwyer to them, and a salamander said, "His acquaintance I made in a fair summer glade, though he did not give me his name. I thought it unwise to spar with death flies, but he entered their cave just the same."

The salamander led Alistair through a forest of grass to a hole in the ground full of wasps. Any reluctance Alistair had about entering the hole was overshadowed by the giant gopher that tried to eat him. It was a cipher for sure, and it may have been an out-of-the-frying-pan-into-the-fire situation, but Alistair chose wasp stings over stomach acid and dove headfirst into the hole, landing in a dewdrop that rested on the giant hive.

From the bottom of the wasp hole in Macrotopia, Alistair emerged at the top of a mound of strawberries. He could have sat there, bemoaning the loss of his atlas, but instead he channeled that anger. He slid down the mound of strawberries until he reached a moat of cream that he swam across to a land made of shortcake, where he asked a girl in a bonnet if she saw a boy sneak by, and she giggled and showed him a bathtub cut from peppermint candy, which Alistair sat down in and turned on the tap and transported himself to another world.

For eight days after that, Alistair traveled through a nearly empty desert, sleeping in a tent, drinking mango juice, and eating dried meat sold to him by a camel that asked for payment in a song. He sang "Twinkle, Twinkle, Little Star," which delighted the camel enough to tell him of an oasis many miles in the distance, but not enough to offer Alistair a ride. So Alistair made his way by foot and dove into the oasis's pool at the first chance he got.

A world made exclusively of letters and numerals tested Alistair's mettle, as did the number 666, a cipher that hounded him across a landscape of college-ruled paper, until Alistair realized that if he convinced an *H*, a *2*, and an *O* to huddle together, they would become water and offer him a way to escape.

From world to world he traveled, hoping instinct would guide him. He trusted no one by trusting everyone. Without the atlas, he had no idea where he was going, and whether someone lied to him or not made little difference. His life became one of momentum. Find a gateway. Move on.

He visited a land where babies rode on the backs of whales and cast spells by flapping their oversize ears. He lived in a mountain town for a few days, where mountain men were gruff but welcoming so long as he helped them gut the furry snakes they turned into garments for the rich figments that lived in a glittering city in the valley below. He saw versions of America in the 1950s, China in the 1670s, France in the 1340s, and Africa in a year before years. He steered clear of any obvious ciphers, though there seemed to be one lurking in nearly every world he visited. He chose to run rather than fight, and when he wasn't running, he was describing Charlie Dwyer to locals.

Some knew him as the Maestro. Others knew him by different names: the Chief, Dr. Wondrous, even Captain Catpoop. "He went thattaway," they'd all tell Alistair, pointing to the most treacherous paths imaginable.

The memories, sparked by images and encounters, kept coming, mostly when Alistair slept, but they were less frequent with each day. He remembered other incidents at school and in the neighborhood, other moments with his family, with Charlie.

With Charlie. Almost always with Charlie.

He had no control over them and wished that Fiona were more prominent in them, but beggars can't be choosers and soon he was simply begging to have more memories, *any* memories, to connect him to home. He had longed for home during those first few weeks, but he was missing it less and less. He was forgetting what it was like there.

When it got to the point that he hadn't been visited by a memory in over a week, he worried that he might have no memories at all. *There's evil in you,* Dot had said, and Alistair wondered if that was true, if losing his link to home was punishment, or if it was part of an inevitable transformation into something dark, disconnected, truly lost.

Resting on a puffy batch of cumulonimbus in a land made of clouds, he prayed.

"One more memory. All that I ask. Whoever is in charge. The Whisper, the Riverman, Charlie, whoever. Please."

Sometimes prayers are answered.

1989

FIONA LOOMIS BACK HOME, SIXTH-GRADE ENGLISH CLASS, called to the blackboard.

"Diagram the sentence," Mrs. Delson said.

On the blackboard was written: *The petulant girl ran away from home.* Fiona grumbled something under her breath and picked up the chalk. She held it close to the blackboard for a second, then set it down on the sill. She grabbed the eraser and ran it across the slate, wiping the sentence into oblivion. She walked back to her seat.

"Miss Loomis," Mrs. Delson said, "why would you do that?"

"I don't like that sentence," Fiona said as she sat.

"Well, I hope you like staying after class," Mrs. Delson said.

Later, through the foyer windows, Alistair saw Fiona

standing outside on the basketball courts, clapping two blackboard erasers together. A cloud of chalk dust hung in front of her like a ghost.

CHAPTER 18

THE MEMORY WAS THERE AND GONE IN SECONDS. THE AGONY of the tease jolted Alistair's eyes open. Above him, sitting cross-legged on a small cloud, was Charlie Dwyer.

His thumbs tapped his toes, as if he was excited to see Alistair, or as if he was nervous. It was hard to tell. "Did you enjoy that moment?" Charlie asked.

Alistair lunged, thrusting a hand at Charlie, hoping to grab something, anything. But Charlie was too quick and he flapped his arms twice, causing the cloud he was sitting on to move higher in the sky. Alistair did the same—flapped his arms—but his cloud didn't move.

"I wish I could give you more memories, but I don't have control of that," Charlie said. "It's Aquavania that gives you that. You call it Aquavania, don't you?"

"Is that really you?" Alistair asked, reaching again, trying to touch him, even though he knew he was too far away.

Charlie's skin seemed even saggier than before. In the sunlight, it hardly looked real.

"You know what?" Charlie said. "The figments don't seem to notice when I put this skin on, but a swimmer like you will spot it every time. I guess I don't need it around you."

Grabbing a handful of his own hair, Charlie tugged. One, two, three. Then his skin slipped from his body like a sock from a foot. The body beneath the skin was still shaped liked Charlie, but it was both colorless and faceless. Fiona had described the Riverman as a creature who looked like the spaces between the stars in the night sky, and that's exactly what Charlie looked like. A wraith, a specter. Terrible and wonderful and infinite.

He held the skin up, then tossed it into the breeze, and it flapped away as if it were newspaper. Thin beams of sunlight suddenly became solid and clung to Charlie's body. Tiny luminescent worms undulated on his skin.

"You're . . ."

"This is who I am here," Charlie said. "This is how I look. I often have to wear my Charlie skin so I don't spook the figments. But I'm still Charlie. I'm also the Maestro. And I'm the Riverman. I'm the Whisper."

"So is this it?" Alistair asked.

"What?"

"Is this the Ambit of Ciphers?"

Charlie laughed. "Now that's a silly name. No, this is yet another world. Created by a kid named Boaz. Fiona knew him, actually. Odd boy. Funny hat. He was quite hard to capture.

He and a kid named Rodrigo tried to trick me, and while Rodrigo was an easy one to bag, Boaz was wily. But I always win in the end."

There were many clouds in this world, but otherwise, it was empty. Alistair didn't have to wonder. He knew a cipher must have swept through and done away with whatever lived here.

"How did you find me?" Alistair asked.

Charlie laughed. "I never lost you. Actually, that's not entirely true. The forest in Mahaloo is thick, and you slipped my gaze there for a bit. But when the Mandrake met you, he told me where you were."

There had been that moment when Potoweet had flown away and left Alistair alone on the platform in the Hutch. Alistair figured it was to hide for a few minutes before hitching a ride in his throat, but perhaps there was more to it. Perhaps the monster was checking in with his master. "Was everything he told me a lie?" Alistair asked.

"Who?"

"Potoweet . . . I mean, the Mandrake."

"They're one and the same. I don't remember what he told you, but I can say that his life is a complicated one. When I improved him, he was . . . conflicted."

"Improved him?"

"Undoubtedly," Charlie said. "Swimmers like you are so foolish. These ciphers, as you call them, aren't things I create. They're things that I mold."

"I don't understand."

"When daydreamers create their worlds, they always create the same thing first. A friend. A guide. Some call it a *familiar*, some call it a *daemon*. Doesn't matter. It's an animal that assists them. I take those animals and I help them . . . evolve."

"So . . . Potoweet . . . ?"

"Was once the faithful servant of a boy named Oric, and when Oric left the picture, I molded Potoweet into something better. It's what the bird deserved. Abandoned like that. Living a pointless life. Except for the point on his beak, of course."

Charlie laughed at his own joke.

"Baxter?" Alistair asked.

And Charlie laughed even louder. "Flawless work, don't you think? And fast too. You really believed he was Kyle, didn't you?"

"Why would you do that?"

"To remind you."

"Of what?"

"Of what you did. Of where you are. Of what's back home."

"Is he okay?" Alistair asked. "Kyle? Back home?"

"He was alive when the ambulance picked him up, if that's what you mean. What happens after that, well, is to be determined. The ambulance drove off, then I came to Aquavania, and I called *you* to Aquavania. While we've been here, not even a millisecond has passed at home. Kyle is still on an operating table, I'm sure."

It was the best news Alistair had heard in forever. He

pulled in a glorious breath, but the relief would only last for a moment. "I didn't shoot him on purpose," he said.

"I know," Charlie said. "You meant to shoot *me*."

Denial was pointless. They both knew this was true. "I may be chasing after you," Alistair said, "but all I care about is Fiona. I don't need to hurt you—"

"Hurt *me*! That's funny. That's really funny." Charlie flapped his arms and effortlessly, tauntingly, he made his cloud spin and move through the sky. He was on a magic carpet, a flying saucer. He had complete control.

"All I want to know is where she is," Alistair said.

"Why?"

"Really?"

"Yes. Why?" Charlie began picking at his cloud with his thumb and pinkie, pulling away wispy bits like cotton candy.

"Because you took her," Alistair said.

"And you need her back? She's yours?" Charlie asked as he moved his hands over one of the wispy bits and molded it into the shape of a noose.

"No. She's not mine. But she's also not yours."

"Own up and admit the real reason," Charlie said as he molded another piece of cloud. This time, he made it into the shape of an arrow. "Say what she is to you."

"She's a friend," Alistair replied.

"Say that you—"

"What?"

"Love her."

Alistair paused. He'd said the words before. To himself.

261

At night. Alone. In his room. In his head. But never to her. Never to anyone.

"I . . ."

"Say it," Charlie teased as he molded another wisp of cloud into the shape of a small creature, a beast that looked like a monkey with big eyes.

"I . . . love . . . her," Alistair whispered.

"Horse crap."

Alistair lunged again. Not even close, but he had to try. "Why would you say that?"

"Because it's true," Charlie replied calmly. "Because you don't know anything about her."

"That's a lie. I know her. I love her. I love her!"

Charlie blew on the three little clouds he had molded. The noose, the arrow, and the big-eyed monkey floated down and hung in the air above Alistair. "Tell me," Charlie said. "Do you recognize these things?"

"I . . . I . . ."

"Above Hadrian's head, there were ropes, right? Different colors? There was a purple one with neon green stripes. Fiona's favorite colors."

"So?"

"So, if you'd known that, you would have pulled the purple and neon green one."

"I was . . . It was . . . Choosing which rope to pull wasn't really an option. The Mandrake saw to that."

"The ice huts, then," Charlie said. "There was an arrow

hanging in one. Did you know how much Fiona liked archery? Did you ever bother to find out that she has a bow and arrow in her closet?"

"I don't . . . What? Why would I be in her closet?"

"The control panel?" Charlie barked. "In the Easter egg? With all the buttons and pictures? In Quadrant 43? Did you actually look at that? Did you see the picture of the bush baby? Her friend, her familiar, her guide in Aquavania? Could I have gotten more obvious?"

"You're making no sense," Alistair said.

"Even beyond that. In the school. In Macrotopia. In the desert. Everywhere, I gave you chances to get to Fiona. Symbols that anyone who knew her could figure out. Obvious gateways. Shortcuts to find her."

"That's bull," Alistair said. "I asked people about Fiona. Besides Baxter, no one knew who she was. There was nothing about her in the atlas. There were no shortcuts."

Charlie sprang from his cloud with astonishing speed. Fifteen feet in the air, maybe twenty. And he grabbed two clouds that were floating by and sliced them open with his mangled hands. Rain poured out of them. Purple and green rain from one. Silver and gold rain from the other.

"There were no shortcuts?" Charlie howled as he landed back on his cloud. "I *make* the shortcuts, you moron."

The rain fell on both sides of Alistair. It was so close that he could reach out and touch it if he wanted. But he resisted. "So I didn't find your shortcuts," Alistair said. "So what?"

Charlie's voice softened. "You don't have many memories of her, do you? But you have plenty of me. There's a reason for that. It's not her that you're really after. It's me. It's me that you care about."

"I care about getting her home. That's all."

"When you make a choice, you reveal the person you really are. Over and over, you've chosen me, Alistair. Admit it."

"I've chased you! To find her!"

"I'm giving you one more choice. Touch the purple and green rain, and you'll go to Fiona's world. And I won't bother you there. You can see what she created. You can stay as long as you'd like."

"Is Fiona there? Will I see her there?"

"Have you met any of the creators in any of the worlds you've visited? Do you really think Fiona would still be in her world?"

"I don't know anymore," Alistair said. "Maybe you're tricking me, making me believe one thing while the opposite thing is true. Maybe everything I need to bring Fiona back is there in her world. Dot seemed to think so."

Charlie raised his shoulders and cocked his chin: *Could be.* Then he said, "Touch the silver and gold rain and you get to go to the place you *really* want to go. The Ambit of Ciphers, as you called it. I'll be there. Polly, remember her? She'll be there too. She tricked you, didn't she? Well, you can have your revenge. And we can have fun, me and you. Together. Like we've had fun in the past."

"What about Fiona? Is she there?"

"You can choose me. You can choose her. It shouldn't be a hard choice."

"No, it shouldn't," Alistair said, and he reached out and touched the rain.

CHAPTER 19

RAGING WATERS DRAGGED ALISTAIR DOWNSTREAM. HE battled against the current, nose to the shore. He'd done his share of swimming over the last few months, but this was beyond swimming. This was pure survival. Rocks scraped his legs, and he feared them even more than drowning. A broken neck—that's what would do him in.

Waves flipped and spun him but he struggled on, fighting for the riverbank, where there were things to grab. A wayward root was a perfect handle—it curved out over the water like an elbow. He had one chance and he made sure it counted. Threading his arm through the root, he hooked on and managed to swing his body and plant his feet onshore. It took all of his strength to heft himself to the grassy banks of the river and under an oak tree, and so he lay there for a moment, gathering his breath and gathering his thoughts.

Had he made the right choice? Was this where he needed

to be? Or had something else happened? Had this all been a horrible dream?

"Fiona!" he called out.

The only answer came from the frogs, the crickets, and the cicadas. It was a sound he knew well, a chorus that announced evenings in Thessaly. It was evening here too, the sun low in the distance, over hills and farmland, a vista that was undeniably familiar.

New strength surged through him, new courage, as if granted by the rising moon. Alistair jumped up and scrambled over the banks, through some brush, and onto a paved bike path.

"Fiona!" he called again, more insistently now.

The scramble became a jog, following the path upriver, racing the sunset. After almost a mile, he broke off onto another path that led into a graveyard. He passed a mausoleum with the name BARNES on it, and he wove through the gravestones, reading other names, searching.

The specific grave he sought was exactly where he expected it to be, but he was surprised to see the amount of moss on it. Rotting and broken wooden figurines leaned against the stone. Fiona's grandmother's name was carved into the surface. PHYLLIS LOOMIS.

He ran from the graveyard to the street. Cars crept along slowly, safely. Darkness had arrived and shops were closed for the night, though a diner was buzzing with activity. People were gathering for birthdays, for dates, for meals out.

He ran faster, past the diner, through the center of town,

by a library and a big pine tree, and he kept going, hardly breathing. Moving. Moving. Moving.

Turning left on a street marked SEVEN PINES ROAD, he noticed that a house was painted blue, and that surprised him. He bounded along a stone walkway and opened the door to another house and went inside. His excitement was electric; his desire to holler was irrepressible.

It was all a dream! It's Halloween night and I fell off my bike and into the Oriskanny and I imagined all of this. There is no Aquavania. Charlie is Charlie. Kyle is fine. Fiona is fine.

I'm home!

I'm finally home!

He made a beeline for the kitchen because it was dinnertime and that meant his mom would be at the stove, his dad at the counter cutting veggies for the salad. But the lights were off in the empty kitchen and only the microwave was on.

Pop . . . pop . . . pop, pop, popopopopop!

The smell of popcorn blanketed the space. The microwave beeped, which beckoned a man from his seat in the living room, where the only light was coming from the TV. The man's potbelly cast a shadow on the wall as he walked through the glow and into the darkness at the border of the rooms. He rubbed his brow and mumbled to himself as he looked up at the microwave, which was mounted above the stove. Spotting Alistair in the reflection on the microwave door, he dropped a bottle of beer. The glass didn't break, but the beer spilled across the tile.

"Holy crap," the man said, swinging around.

"Holy crap," Alistair said.

Alistair was looking at himself. The man was looking at himself. Versions of themselves, separated by decades.

"Is she back?" the older Alistair asked.

"I . . . don't . . . You mean Fiona?" the younger Alistair replied.

"Did she create you? To replace me? Once and for all?"

They sat on the back deck, where the uncut grass lapped at the edges. They ate popcorn from a big bowl, and the older Alistair drank a beer while the younger Alistair drank a soda.

"I'm a traveler, a swimmer," the younger told the older. "Have you met anyone like that?"

The older shook his head.

"Ciphers?" the younger asked. "Heard of those?"

"Nope," the older said. "But I don't get out much these days."

"How long has it been since you've seen Fiona?"

"Years." The older Alistair downed the rest of his beer and threw the empty like a tomahawk, overhand, over the yard, and it smashed on a big rock shaped like a frog that sat on the edge of the swamp.

"And she created this place?" the younger asked.

"Who else could've?" He pulled another beer from the six-pack at his side and cracked it open. It hissed like the fuse of a bomb. "If Fiona didn't create you, who did?"

The younger Alistair didn't know how to answer that question, so he asked another of his own. "Do you call this place Thessaly?"

"Of course. Don't really know the names of any other places." The older kept his eyes fixed on the stars. "So are you, like, an alien?"

"In a way," the younger said. "Does that bother you?"

"Who cares," the older said. "As long as I'm not being replaced. You look like I did back when she created me. I figured you were my replacement. I thought it was pretty messed up of her, letting me meet my replacement. But then, she's done some messed-up things. She replaced her parents, you know? Multiple times. Who does that? Your parents are your parents, right?"

"Are *your* parents around?" the younger asked.

"Mom passed a few years back," the older said, and he raised his bottle to the sky. "Dad ran off with Mrs. Loomis number four. Not sure where they ended up."

"Oh." The younger sipped his soda. "Your sister?"

"Got a job. Moved away a long time ago," the older said as he peered over his shoulder at the dark house. "So if you're an alien, what planet are you from?"

"I come from a place very similar to this. It's actually the place that Fiona is from. I'm looking for her. I want to bring her home."

"Bring her wherever you want. Except back here. I don't want her back here. Not after listening to those tapes."

"What tapes?"

* * *

The neighborhood was almost the same as back home. But this was Fiona's impression of it, her perception of it. She had obviously built it from her memory. A house that Alistair always remembered as green was painted blue. Some trees were shorter, some taller. There was also the issue of age. Fiona had created this version of Thessaly and lived in it for twelve years, and according to the older Alistair, she'd been gone for another thirteen. Things had grown. Things had decayed.

"How old are you?" the younger asked.

"Well, I was already twelve when she created me. I guess that makes me thirty-seven. Jesus, that's old, isn't it?" There were moles on his face that the younger Alistair didn't have, wrinkles in his brow, a chin shaded by stubble. He was taller than the younger Alistair, and yet everything was slightly sunken. His hair was cut short, but that didn't hide the fact that it was thinning.

The two stopped in front of Fiona's house. "Do we knock?" the younger asked.

"I have a key," the older said. "Her uncle Dorian and I are pals."

They slipped through the front door and slinked up the stairs that flanked the living room. In the living room, Fiona's uncle Dorian was asleep under a patchwork quilt on the sofa. His body was a round lump. His white hair was tied in a ponytail.

"He waits up every night," the older whispered. "Always expecting her to come home. It's sad, really. He's a good guy, though. Very sweet. I don't have the heart to let him listen to the tapes."

"Where's her dad?"

The older sighed. "She gave up after round five, and I haven't seen one of her dads since. I'm not sure what happened to all those different versions."

Fiona's bedroom was at the top of the stairs. Alistair had been in Fiona's room in Thessaly, but it didn't look like this. The shape was the same, the bones. It had a slanted ceiling and wooden floors, but it had been repainted and redecorated. What were light blue walls back home were dark purple here. White furniture had been supplanted by antique wood.

"I kissed her on her bed once, in the early days," the older said. He ran his hand over tussled sheets on the bed.

"Were you guys like . . . ?" The younger couldn't find the right word. *Dating? Together? Married?*

The older moved over to the window, opening it and letting in a cool breeze. "We weren't like anything," he said. "There was only that one kiss, but it didn't mean squat. Not to her, at least. Besides, I kept getting older. And she did too, but only on the inside. She looked the same on the outside. A kid. It never would have worked out."

The younger went over to the bookshelf and starting perusing the volumes. They were all leather-bound. He recognized a few of the titles, some classics about kids sneaking off to magical places, but one had a name that he knew all too well. "*Sixth Grade for the Outer-Spacers*?" he asked, holding up the book. "By Claire Rastaily?"

"Took you all of ten seconds," the older said. "You must be good with anagrams. I don't think Dorian has ever noticed it, but you knew exactly what it was. Figures."

"What do you mean?"

"Open it," the older said.

The younger lifted the cover to reveal that there wasn't any writing inside. The pages had been carved out. Six cassettes rested in the hollowed-out cavity.

"That book is where Fiona used to hide cigarettes and things like that," the older said. "Kinda funny, actually. Girl was basically a god, but still she'd hide her cigarettes."

The younger lifted the top cassette. There was no label. "What's on them?" he asked.

"Those tapes were buried next to that big rock along the edge of my backyard," the older said. "I dug them up not long after Fiona left. Figured she doesn't need her secret smokes anymore, so I tossed those and hid the tapes in the book. I used to come up here and listen. At first, I was happy to hear her voice. I haven't listened in years, though. They make me angry."

"But what's on them?"

"There's a player hidden under her mattress. She called it Kilgore. Go ahead and take it. Listen if you want. Or chuck it all. Just don't let anyone else know about the tapes. Not the type of things anyone around here should have to think about."

"Are they really bad?"

The older moved to the doorway, and without looking back, he said, "Not all bad for a guy like you. I'm not stupid, you know. I know you're not an alien. And if you're not my replacement, then there's only one person you could be."

"Who?"

"The original."

FIONA'S STORY

TODAY WAS A GOOD DAY. SCRATCH THAT. IT WAS THE BEST DAY.

Nana is gone. Kids are disappearing by the minute. The Riverman is . . . a total prick. But you know what? Today was the best day.

I came to Aquavania this morning and I started over.

I rebuilt Thessaly from the ground up. The neighborhood, the school, the downtown, everything. Even my old tape player, the one I gave to Alistair. Yes, I didn't forget you, Kilgore. Only difference is, this is my Thessaly. With only the people and things I want here.

Funny. It's the first time I've ever created people, but I know my inspiration so well that it wasn't too hard. It's amazing the stuff that's hidden away in the back of your brain and only comes out when you're creating. Voices, smells, the entire skeleton of a friend. I guess we notice more than we realize.

I created Chua, Boaz, Rodrigo, and the rest of the kids

from Aquavania I knew stories about. I introduced them to kids from Thessaly, like Fay-Renee, Kendra, and Alistair. They all seem to get along. Aquavania kids and Solid World kids, living in harmony. Pretty cool.

Alistair was being a bit of a downer. "We're like the real thing, but we're not the real thing," he said. "You created us. You know that this could never really happen?"

Exactly like Alistair in the Solid World. A cynic. He pretends like he's listening really hard and trying to understand, but he's scheming in his head. Trying to find the logic. He means well, but he overthinks things.

Maybe that's the problem. Overthinking. Creating people who are self-aware is a risky kind of magic, isn't it?

I cleared their heads. Yesterday was amazing, but if I'm really starting over, then I should let them start over too. They should have some memories. Good memories, or at least the good ones I'm able to give them. A few bad ones too, so they can recognize the good ones, but I won't overdo it. They should know who their family is and all that stuff. But they won't know who they're supposed to be, where they're supposed to be from. They'll just think they've lived lives like everyone else. They definitely won't know about the Riverman. Beyond that, I won't meddle. I'll let them be whoever they want to be, without fear.

Should it really happen any other way?

I guess I should go to school. Crazy, I know, but that was

my life before, so it's my life now. Maybe I'll get rid of Earth Science. And Social Studies. We'll make our own history.

Mom and Dad are . . . fine so far. Dad made breakfast, which he sometimes did in the Solid World, but not often. Scrambled eggs. I prefer cereal, but I ate the eggs and said that I loved them and he smiled, so that was good.

The sun is shining again. There's no wind. I know it always rains or snows or whatever in the real Thessaly. But today, it's sunny and calm, and I'll let the weather do whatever the weather wants to do.

I'll go for a bike ride and see who's out and about.

A week's gone by and everything is amazing. No one calls Kendra the Wart Woman here, even though she still has her warts. "Love 'em, warts and all" is a saying in the Solid World. It fits here too. I've told everyone that only the smartest people have warts, and everyone believes me. Who knows? Maybe it's true. Kendra *is* smart in the Solid World. Smart here too.

Chua has become the hit of school, which is no surprise. She's friendly and funny and how could you not like her? Of course, Werner is madly in love with her, just like before. And she's madly in love with him, which is the cutest thing. Alistair has been hanging out with Rodrigo and Boaz a little bit, but I'm not sure if they're going to be close friends. That's okay. Not everyone has to be best buddies. They just have to be here.

Nana is dead in the Solid World and I guess I could bring

her back, but it seems weird to do that. It's different with Chua, Rodrigo, and Boaz. First off, I'm not sure that they're dead in the Solid World. Though it seems likely. But mostly, it's because they were kids. They didn't get a chance to live a full life. Nana did, so I let her rest. Uncle Dorian is sad, but he's got a good outlook. It's his words that made me decide once and for all not to bring her back.

"She lived a perfect life," he said when I joined him at the cemetery yesterday.

"How so?" I asked.

"She tried not to hurt people," he said. "And if she did hurt people, without realizing it at first, then she tried to make up for it."

"That's not perfect," I told him. "Perfect is perfect. It's never making a mistake."

He shrugged and said maybe, and we walked home together and he told me stories about when he and my dad were kids and how they tried to build a human slingshot out of two trees, a hammock, and some inner tubes, and even though it's a story I've heard a million times, I laughed again.

Mom came to my room tonight and I could tell she'd had too much to drink already. She sat on the foot of my bed and said that she was sorry for being . . . well, not so much a mom.

"I spent all my momness on Maria and Derek," she explained. "Spent it all up like tickets at a carnival. I didn't mean to. One moment I had lots of tickets . . . but then my pockets were empty. I wish I hadn't been so . . . lazy."

In some ways, it was nice to hear, but mostly it sounded fake. It was like we were in a play.

"You don't have to say that," I told her.

"But I'm . . . I'm supposed to say it," she slurred.

"You're not supposed to say anything," I replied. "You're supposed to live your life. And say what comes to your mind."

She looked around my room, and her face twisted like she was sniffing something gross, and she said, "Okay, then I'd like to go downstairs and sit for a while."

Later, I went downstairs and she was sitting in the kitchen with the lights off and she was doing nothing. Sitting there, hands on her lap. A wine glass was nearby, but she wasn't drinking. Very creepy.

My dad was in the living room watching TV, but when I went in there, the TV was playing rainbow bars. He got up from the sofa and he hugged me, but it was like his arms and chest were made of paper bags, crumpled up inside him like stuffing.

I think I might have to start over with my parents. New versions. Tweaked. Slightly. More for their own good than for mine. I know I said I wasn't going to use my power to interfere with lives, but I'll make this one exception. One do-over. Only for them.

* * *

A month now that I've been here, and life is settling into more of a routine. School is as good as school can be. The teachers focus on the things we all enjoy, and it's a lot of reviewing stuff I already know, but that can be fun. Sometimes after school a bunch of kids meet in the park, and they all ask me questions. They have no idea that I created them, but they can sense that I'm different, that I know things they don't.

Alistair comes by every time and he's often quiet, but when he asks questions, it's things like *What lives out in the void beyond town?* I told him that nothing lives out there, that this is the only world there is. Well, except for maybe other planets, far, far away beyond the stars. This seems to calm his nerves. He's nervous a lot.

Compared to the first try, my new parents are . . . better. They're more lively, more engaged. Dad sings now, in the shower or when he's out mowing the lawn. And Mom dances and plays air guitar when the radio is on. So weird, but that's fine. Better than sitting there like bumps on a log. Like school, my parents are now fun.

Four months have gone by since I started this, and it isn't that I don't love you, Kilgore. It's that I don't have much time to talk to you anymore. Between school and friends and family, life is full in ways it never was before.

It's not always amazing. My friends aren't exactly the same as they were. They look at me cautiously. They speak to me like I'm an adult. The quirky parts of their personalities are amplified, I guess. Which is cool. Except when it isn't. Maybe it's because I didn't know everything I needed to know about them. Maybe they weren't complete when I created them, and the empty spots in their personalities had to be filled in with something. Beats me. I'm in control, but it doesn't mean I understand everything.

Alistair follows me around like a puppy dog, and it's flattering and sweet, but I worry about him. It's like all he cares about is me. I didn't create Charlie Dwyer, or the entire Dwyer family for that matter, because I figured who needs a world with annoying people like the Dwyers in it. Maybe Alistair does. He needs friends, at least. I know that. Trevor Weeks and Mike Cooney are here, and he sits with them at lunch sometimes, but they don't really hang out. And guys like Boaz and Rodrigo don't seem that interested in Alistair anymore. I could *make* everyone like him, but that's not how friendship should be.

He still asks questions at our after-school get-togethers, which Boaz has dubbed "happenings." The toughest question was one about his memories.

"They don't seem real," he said. "I mean, I have images all crammed in my head of being seven, eight, nine years old. But I don't feel them, if you know what I mean."

The other kids nodded, because they definitely knew what he meant, and I said, "What came before is less important than what you do with your lives now."

Those kinds of answers used to get *ooh*s and *ah*s, but these days they only satisfy for a short amount of time, and then people are asking again.

Nearly a year in and I don't worry about the Riverman much anymore. At first I was trying to push him out of my brain, but that never works. Tell someone to not think about unicorns and—you guessed it—they'll think about nothing but unicorns.

I know he's still out there. I know he's probably hunting other kids. But it's up to them to figure out how to do what I did. Right? If you don't get greedy in Aquavania, then you're fine. If you don't wish for the impossible, if you learn to be satisfied, then you're fine.

He can't touch me. He can't do a damn thing to this place. Which means that *I* won.

I invited Alistair up to my room today. He's so, so lonely, and that absolutely kills me. I thought maybe that my friendship was enough for him, but I can tell that he wants more than that. At school, he's always showing up where I show up. He's always lingering around the bike racks after last bell. So I humor him.

Today, in my room, I shared a secret with him. I showed him a hollowed-out book full of cigarettes.

"Only on special occasions," I whispered. "My one true vice."

I could tell it worried him, and I don't know why I did it, but I leaned over and gave him the littlest kiss. It was a lousy kiss.

Actually, that's a lie. The knowing part, at least. I do know why I did it. Same reason I showed him the cigarettes. To make him feel special for a moment. *You're in on a secret, Alistair!* Then to make him realize that the secrets are stupid. Stupid cigarettes. Not much excitement there. Stupid kiss. Lips touching lips. Nothing more. No meaning. No feeling. Nothing.

But I'm pretty sure it backfired. I'm pretty sure he thinks I'm his girlfriend now. If only he were the original. If only he had that spark.

I started dating Rodrigo about two weeks after I kissed Alistair, and in the four months since I've seen less and less of Alistair. He doesn't show up. Doesn't pop in. He stays inside at home and creeps through school with his head down.

I feel bad. I do. But I can't force things here. I have to let life be life. The inevitable is happening, though. It's been over a year and everyone is growing, but I'm staying the same. Rodrigo doesn't seem to notice, but Kendra sure has. She's got boobs now and I'm still as flat as a board.

"When are you coming to sit at the big girls' table?" she joked the other day at lunch. She and Fay-Renee and Chua were all hanging out, laughing at their own private jokes while I was walking by with Rodrigo. I would have sat with them, but Rodrigo likes to have "romantic lunches," which is sweet, but really it's just the two of us sitting alone and sharing chicken nuggets.

My parents love Rodrigo. They think he's the smoothest guy in the world. "He can stay the night if you want," my dad said once. "Or move in. We'd love to have him."

Mom did a little happy dance in agreement.

What? No thank you. God, what a weird thing for him to say. As much as it kills me, I might have to start over with them again. Last time I started over, I told myself no more do-overs, but there have to be exceptions to the rule.

Rodrigo and I are through. It lasted nearly a year, which is pretty good for a first boyfriend. Our differences were more than a few, and as tempted as I was to change him the easy way, I tried the hard way. The hard way is hard.

Dorian hasn't been getting along with Mom and Dad, and that's a problem. Since Derek and Maria decided to leave last year, all we have is the four of us. We have to be a family, and while families can have their differences, there shouldn't be this much shouting. It makes me want to stay outside all the time, which is fine when it's nice, but the winter has found its way in here too.

Not many kids come to the "happenings" anymore. Alistair returned, now that Rodrigo is out of the picture, and I try not to treat him any differently. But while everyone else looks at me with suspicion, he looks at me with such longing that I want to shout, "It's not going to happen! I care about you, but it will never happen."

The sequel is never better than the original. That's what they always say. Is it *always* true? I don't think so. But in Alistair's case, I know it is.

I know the Alistair in Aquavania. I can sense what he will do. He's predictable.

I don't really know the original. And that's what's great about him.

CHAPTER 20

———◦✦◦———

THERE WAS A KNOCK ON THE DOOR TO FIONA'S ROOM. ALISTAIR paused the tape.

"Who's in there?" came Dorian's voice.

"Um, I . . ." Alistair ejected the tape and put it back into the book, which he tucked under one arm. He tucked the tape player under the other.

The door opened and a glassy-eyed, older version of Fiona's uncle Dorian stood in the threshold. "Alistair?" he asked.

"Yes."

"You look so . . ."

"Young?"

Dorian nodded. "I'm dreaming, aren't I?"

"No. I'm real." Alistair stood from Fiona's bed.

"You find the fountain of youth or something?" Dorian reached out as if to touch Alistair's face, but decided against it at the last moment, and his hand withered back.

"The Alistair you know is still here. He went home. I'm a different person. I realize that must seem strange."

Dorian ran a hand across his stubbly face. "I've seen stranger. I've seen things that'll curl your nose hairs. A time-traveling doppelgänger ain't about to throw me for a loop."

"That's not what I am."

"Then what are you?"

"I'm Fiona's friend from her . . . Well, what's important is that I'm here to find her."

"You're looking in the wrong place."

They drove in Dorian's pickup slowly through the neighborhood. "She didn't age," Dorian said, one hand on the wheel, "which weirded people out. And she had magic, control over her mom and dad. My brother and his wife, that is. Fiona was wise beyond her years. Not quite one of us, if you catch my drift."

"I'm not quite one of you either."

"Figured. Don't really care. You're Alistair. That's clear enough."

"And you're not afraid of me. You've seen ciphers around here, haven't you?"

"No clue what you mean."

"Monsters," Alistair said. "Things that'll curl your nose hairs."

"I've been to war. To prison. You want monsters, look there. Around here, there ain't nothin' like that."

"Did Fiona ever tell you about the Riverman?" Alistair asked. "About the Solid World?"

Dorian shook his head. "Fiona asked me to tell her stories. She loved to hear me ramble on. And I was happy to ramble on. She didn't confide much of nothin' in me. And I was cool with that. Her smiles and laughs were enough. I liked her the way she was."

Lights were on in most of the houses in the neighborhood. Dogs sniffed about in yards. The windows on the truck were down and the smell of lighter fluid lingered, remnants of late evening barbecues.

Dorian had told him where they were going, but Alistair hardly saw the point. "Won't it be too dark out there?" Alistair asked.

"Naw," Dorian said. "We're equipped for the dark."

They pulled into a muddy parking lot next to a grassy runway. Lights mounted on short posts drenched everything in pale orange. Dorian cut the engine, jumped down, and retrieved a remote control and a model airplane from the bed of the truck.

"An expensive demo, but seeing is believing," Dorian said.

He led Alistair out into the field, where the grass was mown short. The model was a bright pink biplane with a white lightning stripe down the side. Dorian set it in the grass and used a small device from his pocket to flick the propeller to life. The plane buzzed, vibrated, and waited.

"Why do you play . . . I mean, why do you fly . . . remote control airplanes?" Alistair asked.

Dorian shrugged and poised the remote. "Clears my mind. Never had the eyes to fly in the service. Guess this is the next best thing."

The plane rolled down the runway, hopped twice, and took off, buzzing its way out of the glow of the lights.

"How will you know where it is?" Alistair asked.

"I've flown here so much, I could do it blindfolded," Dorian said. "And the target is easy enough to hit."

"The target?"

The buzzing of the plane was loud, and then suddenly the sound was gone. Dorian set the remote control down and put his hands in the pockets of his jeans. Alistair surveyed the dark sky with a furrowed brow.

"Don't worry," Dorian said. "It ain't gonna crash."

"Where is it?"

Dorian shrugged. "Not long after Fiona left us, I was piloting out here and I noticed this low cloud. Flew the plane into it and *zip zap zoom*. Gone."

"Disappeared?"

"Off the face of the Earth. Haven't seen it since. And that cloud hasn't blown away. Hangs there in fair weather and foul. I've flown close to twenty planes into that thing, and they all suffer the same fate."

"Does anyone else know about this?" Alistair asked.

Dorian shrugged again. "Not sure anyone else would care. Not many people miss her. Me, the other Alistair, maybe a few others. I got an instinct about that cloud, though. I'm guessing it's a crack in our world, and I don't know how she woulda got there, but I'm also guessing that Fiona is on the other side of that crack."

"Have you ever tried to get up to it?"

Dorian chuckled, a phlegmy rumble. "How? With a ladder? It's low, but not that low."

"And nothing weird has ever come out of the cloud?" Alistair asked.

"Not even rain," Dorian said. "You have a lot of questions, don't you?"

"Like I said, I'm trying to find her."

"Build a stairway to heaven, then," Dorian said. "If you think you can do it. I certainly couldn't."

Alistair didn't know whether he could do it. He didn't know if he should even try. But he knew he had to learn at least a little more. "If I were to stay for a few days, where could I sleep?" he asked.

"You're not crashing with . . . other Alistair?"

"That might be a little strange."

"True enough," Dorian said as he put the remote under his arm and moved back toward the truck. "There's room in my house, obviously. The fact that you're a stranger don't mean I'm leaving you out on the street. Not decent."

"Thank you."

"But I'd prefer you not bunk in Fiona's room."

"Of course."

*　*　*

Alistair stayed in a room that was once occupied by Fiona's sister, Maria. The walls were covered in prints of paintings—hay bales and ballet dancers—and posters of heartthrobs—young men with feathery hair and tasseled jackets. The blankets were billowy, and he hid the tape player beneath them. When he was sure Dorian was well out of earshot, he finished listening to the tapes. The recordings had been more infrequent, spread out over twelve years.

Some of it was mundane: "I love tomato sauce, but not tomatoes."

At times, it was a bit cryptic: "Late at night, I use my finger to write poems on the wall. Invisible ones. Free verse or iambic pentameter. Invisible ink, but I know it's there."

Often, melancholy: "Now that Chua, Fay-Renee, Boaz, and all of them have grown up and I still have the body of a kid, we don't talk anymore. Sure, there are new kids. But I don't have anything in common with them."

Mostly they were an account of life in a small town, from the perspective of an observer, an outcast, a freak. People got older, friendships bloomed and faded. People left, though it was never clear exactly where they went. Fiona watched it all and commented. Or didn't. There were gaps, things that Fiona either didn't know or didn't want to tell.

By the time Alistair had gotten to the last entry, he knew infinitely more about Fiona than he had ever known at home. He knew her pet peeves, her guilty pleasures. He knew the things that Charlie said he should know. She did love archery. And purple and neon green. And so much else.

Then he listened to the last entry.

FIONA'S STORY: CODA

TWELVE YEARS. IT GOES SLOW UNTIL IT GOES FAST. AND THEN it's gone, like it never happened. You've been a good friend, Kilgore. A confidant. I sometimes question why I'm making these tapes, though. I've never listened to them, and if people found them, then feelings would get hurt. Which was never my intention.

My intention was to leave evidence, a document of my time here. Because I've decided to go back to the Solid World. If the Solid World can convince me to stay there, then I'll stay there, and these tapes will be history, an account of how things turned out. For someone to find, somewhere down the line.

Things haven't turned out as great as I might have hoped, but they've happened naturally. Most of them, at least. Part of me can be thankful for that. I've created a place where people live, love, and scream at one another sometimes. It's not all about me anymore.

As for them, a few deserve better. The ones like Derek and Maria, who decided that they didn't want to live in this Thessaly, for instance. I guess I gave them a nice place to live, but they still deserve better. My parents. They deserve better too. I never understood them, but maybe that's because I never wanted to.

Most of all, Alistair deserves better. I've been given certain powers, and for so long I used them for selfish things. There has to be a bigger reason for my abilities. If there's something I can do to ease someone's suffering, I should do it. Forget the silly rules I made for myself about not meddling with their lives.

So when I come back from the Solid World, if I come back, I'm going to turn Alistair into someone else. I know the easy thing would be to get rid of him, to box him away like my brother and sister and the others who wanted to get out. But that would be too painful. What I should do is change him, just enough so that I don't mean anything to him anymore, so that he cares about someone else. Enough that he'll still have a life, but he won't remind me of the original Alistair.

All the other originals are important too, but the original Alistair means so much more than he realizes. Not because I love him. Because I *could have* loved him, if I had chosen a different path. If I had opted not to spend my entire childhood here. If I had decided the Solid World was the world worth giving myself to. If. If. If.

It wouldn't feel right to be with the original now, not after all the life I've lived. Maybe someday I can tell him that and he'll understand. Maybe not. For now, I'm going to bury these tapes in the only place they should be buried. The tapes will tell the story of my mistakes.

Then I'll be going to the Solid World, to give it one last try. Maybe I'll come back to Aquavania soon. I kinda think I have to come back. I don't know if I understand how to live in the Solid World anymore.

CHAPTER 21

---◆◆---

MORNING ARRIVED WITH ALISTAIR LYING ON MARIA'S BED, the covers kicked down, the tape player on his stomach. He popped open the deck, pulled the tape out, and yanked at the ribbon. Wincing, he yanked, tore, and kept going until there was a nest of black plastic on the bed.

He did the same thing to the other tapes, his actions more violent with each one. Fiona's voice kept playing in his head.

Not because I love him. Because I could have loved him.

Dot's voice was there too.

There's something terribly wrong with you. There's evil in you.

He didn't know which one to believe, or if to believe both of them. He balled up the ribbon in his fist and hurried from the room, through the hall, and outside. He threw the ribbon in the air and wind caught it and it littered the street like ticker tape.

He jogged the short distance to his house—that is, to the older Alistair's house—and he rang the bell.

"You're still here," the older Alistair said when he opened the door.

"I'm sorry," the younger said.

The older shuffled his feet. "You listened?"

"How did you know where to dig up those tapes?" the younger asked.

The older shrugged. "A memory. A childhood promise. I don't know if Fiona meant for me to find them, or didn't realize what was planted in my brain."

"Did she have a chance to do it? To change you? To make things . . . easier . . . for the both of you?"

The older shrugged again. "I don't know. I still have my memories. I still feel like me. Why don't you ask her? You're the one she could have loved. Did you figure out where she is yet?"

The younger shook his head. "Is there any way I can get a message to everyone? The entire town, I mean."

"Boaz runs the *Sutton Bulletin*. Most everyone reads it. It's a newspaper."

"I know what it is."

The office and printing press for the *Sutton Bulletin* were down a long, lonely road bordered by nothing, by an endless void. From the tapes, Alistair had learned that Fiona had recreated the things she could remember from home, but not much else. Sutton was the next town over from Thessaly, and she didn't know it well. She knew the road and the building, because their class had taken a field trip there when she was in third grade.

The older Alistair drove, and the younger Alistair looked out at the void as they pulled into the lot.

"Anyone ever go out there?" the younger asked.

"When we were kids, Boaz, Rodrigo, and Trevor rode their bikes as far as they could get in a day. They didn't find anything. Sometimes nothing is nothing. That's why they call it Nothingland."

The parking lot was half-full, and the two walked past a variety of rusty and beat-up cars. Inside, the younger Alistair recognized a receptionist who greeted them. She was a thirtysomething version of Kelly Dubois, who was generally considered the prettiest girl in Alistair's class. She was still pretty, but now she looked tired. She barely glanced up when she said, "Morning."

"We're here to see Boaz," the older replied.

Kelly waved them on as she huddled over a mug of fragrant tea. "In the back."

The back was a room of low-walled cubicles with a handful of reporters lazing at cluttered desks, nibbling muffins, chatting quietly. A man, dark-skinned and muscular, stood in the corner, surveying it all like it was his kingdom. This was Boaz, and he looked intimidating, but also a bit silly. He wore a plaid newsboy cap that was barely big enough to cover his shaven head. Spotting the two Alistairs from across the room, he mouthed, *What the hell?*

The younger didn't bother with an introduction. "I've got a story for you," he said.

The story on the front page of the next morning's *Sutton Bulletin* read:

DOPPELGÄNGER HAS A MISSION

Two days ago, a boy who resembles a younger version of our very own Alistair Cleary (and happens to share the same name) arrived in town. He claims to be a friend of Fiona Loomis, the strange girl who never aged and disappeared from our town thirteen years ago. He is searching for her. Any information about Fiona should be brought to Dorian Loomis's home, where this young doppelgänger now resides. He is also willing to answer questions you may have for him about his appearance or his mission. "I have nothing to hide. My sole purpose is to find Fiona," he says.

By the afternoon, the street outside of Dorian's house was clogged with onlookers, but no one bothered to approach the door. So the younger Alistair came out into the yard. The only thing he could think to say was, "I come in peace."

The crowd huddled up and consulted, then sent the mayor as their envoy. The mayor was Werner Schroeder, a handsome German man with an accented voice and a perfectly tailored suit.

"You are welcome in our fair town," he said, and he handed Alistair an oversize novelty key. "We, however, have no information to assist in your search. Best of luck to you."

With that, the crowd dispersed, except for a woman with frizzy brown hair, denim head to toe, and brown tasseled boots. She ambled over and shook Alistair's hand. Her hand was covered in small warts. "The mayor was being too kind," she said. "My name is Kendra Tolliver. I was a friend of Fiona's, at least for a bit."

"Nice to meet you," Alistair said, though he'd met her before, or at least a younger version of her, back home at school.

Kendra ran a finger across her lower lip, which was caked in a thick pink gloss, and she eyed Alistair up and down as she said, "Fiona and I had a chat when we were both kids. She told me a secret. She said that the only reason she'd ever leave town would be if she didn't ever want to come back. Respect her wishes. Let her be."

"But—"

"And she said if anyone suspicious ever showed up in town claiming to be looking for her, then we shouldn't trust that person. You, kid, fit the bill."

Having said her piece, Kendra walked away too, and Dorian came into the yard and placed a hand on Alistair's shoulder. "Prospects aren't looking good," Dorian said.

Staring at the now-empty road, Alistair asked, "Do you have any more of those planes? I'd like to try something."

Using a Sharpie, Alistair wrote a message on a piece of ribbon: *Is Fiona there?*

Dorian then tied the ribbon to the tail of a yellow model airplane. The ribbon fluttered as the airplane hopped down the runway, took off into the damp evening air, flew into the tiny cloud, and disappeared.

They waited. Quietly. Sitting in the grass, looking at the cloud as the sun began to dip. Darkness seeped in, but not so much that they couldn't see when something finally fell from the cloud and landed in the weeds that edged the runway.

They ran over and got down on their hands and knees to search. Dorian was the one who found it: a helmet. A space helmet.

Written across the visor in what might have been red marker, in what might have been blood, was a short but clear message.

You're still It.

NOVEMBER 19, 1989

⎯⎯⎯•◆•⎯⎯⎯

Sitting cross-legged on the floor, Alistair held a controller up. As the hero moved across the TV screen, Alistair moved his arms in the same direction, but it didn't make a difference. This game wasn't motion-activated. All he was supposed to do was push buttons.

"Pathetically amateur" is what Charlie often called Alistair's distracting technique, but he wasn't about to call it that now. Alistair was on the last level, with nothing but the final boss left to defeat, and Charlie didn't want to mess with his head. This was Charlie's best shot at winning a game he couldn't play himself. It had been a month since he'd blown off five of his fingers while messing with bottle rockets. His mangled hands could still press buttons, but not at the speed they once did. Not fast enough to win any video games.

"What do you think happens when we win?" Alistair asked.

"What always happens to winners," Charlie said. "They have to win again. Until they lose."

"Do you have another game to play after this one?" Alistair asked.

"Sure. And we can always get another one after that."

"Not really," Alistair said. "There are only so many video games in the world. A few thousand maybe? What if a person won them all?"

Charlie had been lazing on the sofa, but the idea brought him to his feet. He stood in the middle of the room, smacking his lips, considering such a delicious question. "Then I guess you hang up your hat and call it a day. Let someone else have a turn."

"Like you're doing right now?" Alistair asked, wielding the controller that for the last few years had rested firmly in Charlie's hands. Until, of course, those fireworks put an end to that.

"Maybe," Charlie said. Though this was hardly the end of Charlie's turn.

BUT PERHAPS *THIS* WAS THE BEGINNING

———— ✦ ————

IN THE YEAR 1983

———◆———

THIS TALE FEATURES TWO FRIENDS AND A JAR.

It started on a day hissing with heat. A helicopter carrying Polly Dobson hovered over a dusty expanse, preparing to land.

"This was all forest once," the pilot explained. "But that was hundreds of years back. Farmers cleared the trees. Worked the soil. Then let it go fallow after too many droughts. Now, it's hardly good enough for goats."

But there were goats there just the same, pulling at the weeds and brush with their brown teeth and scattering when the helicopter finally touched down. Polly and her mom hopped out as soon as the helicopter's blades stopped spinning.

"We're really going to live in this dump?" Polly asked.

"I've heard the camp is very nice," said her mom, a broad-shouldered woman with a streak of white in her blond hair and a masculine name: Carter. "And there's a village nearby with a market and beautiful stone huts. See those mountains in the distance? With snow icing the top? Those are pretty, right?"

"Woo-hoo. Stone huts. Mountains you won't ever let me climb. Better than Disneyland."

Her mom harrumphed, but she couldn't be surprised. Even when she was a baby, Polly was an eye-roller. Now, at twelve, she was a fountain of sarcasm.

A jeep pulled up, coughing like it had tuberculosis. "You two must be the Dobsons, then," said the woman who was driving. Her body was heavy, to match her accent, and she wore a floral-print dress. A tiny girl in overalls sat next to her.

"And you must be . . . ?" Carter asked as she pulled a flattened cowboy hat from her shoulder bag, flicked it to life, and deposited it on her head.

"Delia," the woman said. "Your driver. Your cook. Your mama, if you need one."

"Already got one too many mamas, thank you very much," Polly said, and it made Carter frown and Delia squint, but it made the little girl in overalls laugh.

"The gigglebox here is Henrietta Bowerbird Monroe," Delia said as she helped the helicopter pilot load bags onto the jeep. "My youngest. Don't believe a word she says. A scatterbrain and a stargazer, that one."

Henrietta flashed Polly a crooked smile, and Polly liked her immediately. Polly could do with some scatterbrained stargazing.

The camp was about a mile away, set in the shade next to

a creek. It was basically the most fabulous tree house Polly had ever seen, with platforms adhered to the thick trunks of willow trees, with spiral staircases and rope ladders and hatches and slides and pulleys and thatched roofs. It had been built in the 1950s by some ornithologists who had come to study the unique birdlife, but had only recently been restored to its former glory.

"Now do you want Disneyland?" Carter asked.

"No stinkin' way!" Polly hollered. "Why didn't you tell me about this?"

"Your old mom still has a few surprises up her sleeve for you."

Polly hugged Carter around the shoulders, vaulted from the jeep, and bulldozed toward the camp. And Henrietta, legs no bigger than a pair of drumsticks, scurried after her.

All the kids back home in Tucson asked Polly if her mom was Indiana Jones. Carter did little to dispel this notion, what with the cowboy hat and all, but Polly always said, "Archaeologists sit in the dirt with a brush for hours on end. Or in a dingy office with a microscope. Bore! Ing!"

And yet, her mom's newest project wasn't boring at all. A few months before, a villager had uncovered some interesting stones while digging a well. They turned out to be fragments of boulders that had been shattered and buried. Which wouldn't be of much interest, except for the fact that they were covered in faded pigment, in ancient drawings. They depicted animals like frogs and turtles, as well as people who looked like hunters and shamans. The drawings told stories, at least they seemed to.

Carter knew a fair bit about geology and cave paintings, so they called her in to assist with the dig. It was the opportunity of a lifetime, and she figured it was worth pulling Polly out of seventh grade for at least a year.

"You get the best education from traveling," Carter told her. "From experiencing other people and their lives."

As much as she enjoyed contradicting her mother, Polly couldn't argue with this. Henrietta Bowerbird Monroe alone was worth a year of schooling. She was a wonderfully strange girl who skittered through life fueled on chatter. She was tiny, but her voice was raspy and rumbly, like some jazz singer. She and Polly became fast friends.

Delia wasn't exaggerating. Henrietta's brain was all over the place. She'd go from reciting random trivia about polar bears to doing birdcalls to giving names to constellations to asking Polly what it was like to be from America where everybody drinks whiskey and owns a gun.

"You've seen too many Westerns," Polly said.

"I haven't seen nearly enough!" Henrietta replied.

Every Friday, the archaeologists would host movie night at the camp and invite the villagers to come sit around a TV and VCR that they plugged into a generator and set on a tree stump. The movies were mostly Westerns, because that's what made up the majority of lead archaeologist Fred Tsonga's collection, but no one ever objected. Henrietta, in particular, adored them. Sitting as close to the screen as possible, she'd cheer both the heroes and the villains, because, as she always told Polly, "There wouldn't be much of a story without both of them."

And there wouldn't be much of *this* story without Polly and Henrietta, though their relationship was hardly antagonistic. They were, in fact, inseparable. Whenever her mom was off at the dig, a few miles from the camp, Polly was with Henrietta. They were either studying together with the camp's tutor, an often-frazzled Scottish woman named Sophie Campbell, or they were exploring the village and eating meals cooked by Delia in Henrietta's cozy stone hut.

Polly had friends back home in Tucson, but none like Henrietta. The girl's imagination was astounding—she spoke of ideas, landscapes, and creatures the types of which not even novelists could conceive. And yet, there was nothing selfish about her constant yammering. She focused on things that would fascinate Polly—dastardly boy-kings, giant cockroaches who excelled at poetry—and Polly was never homesick because Henrietta was tireless in her effort to entertain and comfort her.

Henrietta had other friends as well, a few kids from the village, but none like Polly. That's because Polly never underestimated or patronized Henrietta, who was twelve years old but not much bigger than a kindergartner. In fact, Polly looked up to her, metaphorically at least. There was wisdom behind the motormouth, and Polly was the only one who seemed to notice.

In quieter moments, they confided in each other.

"I have icky thoughts sometimes," Henrietta often said.

"We all do," Polly always assured her, petting her hair.

And every evening, before Polly returned to the camp and Henrietta to her stone hut, they'd hug and whisper the same thing in each other's ears.

"Forever or until. Forever or until."

The *forever* probably wasn't possible. They weren't naïve. They knew that. The *until* was more likely. What it meant was, they were there for each other, at least until Polly stepped back into that helicopter in a year or so.

Or until one fateful evening.

It was an evening like any other. They were hugging good night, as they always did, but Henrietta hugged longer than normal this time. And she didn't say what they always said. Instead, she whispered, "Can I tell you a story?"

"Can you!" Polly yelped, because she always wanted to hear a story from Henrietta. Sure, Henrietta was frequently off on some wild tangent or another, but she rarely possessed the attention span to stay on one narrative for very long, to get to the end of anything.

"It's a sad story," Henrietta said.

"That's okay," Polly said. "The world needs tearjerkers too. Write it down and sell it to Hollywood. It'll be better than those Westerns, I bet."

"No, no, no." Henrietta wagged a finger. "This is a secret

story. One that only best friends should share. You are my best friend, aren't you?"

Polly put out a pinkie and Henrietta did the same and they hooked them together, which was as good as a handshake. "This place would suck eggs without you," Polly said.

Suck eggs was enough to make Henrietta smile, and the pinkie lock was enough to give her the courage to finally say something she had been keeping to herself.

"There once was a girl named Henrietta," she said. "And she lived in a little village that wasn't like the big city at all. A small, small place, not too far from the sea or the mountains, but far away from anywhere else."

"Henrietta like you?" Polly asked. "A place like this place?"

With a coy twist in her mouth, not quite a smile, she kept on with the story. "When Henrietta was very little, her papa passed away. An icy thing fell from the sky, knocked him on the head, and ended his life as fast as can be. People said the thing was a chunk of hail, but Henrietta's mama was convinced it was from outer space. The family burned her papa's body and put his ashes in the creek."

"Oh, Henrietta, I knew he wasn't with you anymore—" Polly started to say, but Henrietta wasn't going to be interrupted.

"She was supposed to let the ashes stay in the creek, but Henrietta loved her papa so much that when no one was watching, she scooped up some of the water in a jar and she ran upstream. She hid the jar in a red bush, and at night she would visit it and talk to the water. 'I miss you,' she would say to the water. 'I love you.'"

"Oh Henrietta," Polly said again, because she could relate. Polly's father wasn't dead, but he was gone. He had left when Polly was barely six, divorced Carter, and remarried a hairdresser who had little interest in raising a rambunctious young girl.

Henrietta's voice inched a few octaves lower as she said, "But this is not the saddest part of the story. You see, one day the water talked back. 'Come and meet me,' it said. Then the glass of the jar disappeared. Poof. There was only water now. Magic water. Floating in the air. Henrietta touched it."

Polly wanted to say something like, *Disappearing glass? As if!* but Henrietta seemed so invested in her tale, so confident in her telling, so doggone serious, that Polly knew better than to interrupt. She owed her friend many things, most of all her attention.

"When Henrietta touched the water, her body felt like there were little fishies swimming in it," she went on. "And with a body full of little fishies, she made a journey. The creek went poof now too, and Henrietta magically arrived in a round room with stone walls, high up in a tower, where it was so chilly that there were icicles on the ceiling. She'd never seen icicles before. And she'd never seen anything like the monster that was standing before her. That's right, a monster. It had no face and no color, but it had arms, legs, and a body. And it had a voice. 'You heard my call,' the monster whispered.

"Henrietta said, 'Papa, is that you?' even though it didn't sound like her papa's voice.

"And the monster said, 'Many years ago, I was standing where you are standing. And I was afraid. But I had no reason to be. I was meant to be here *then* as you are meant to be here *now*.'

"Henrietta took a step back and said, 'You don't know where I'm meant to be!'

"The monster held out a pen. It was a fountain pen, like the one the doctor who sometimes visited Henrietta's village used. 'Place this in my ear,' the monster said. 'Suck on the other end.'

"And Henrietta said, 'No thank you, sir. That's disgusting.'

"The monster chuckled and whispered, 'The pen will fill up, and all you have to do is pour the ink on yourself. Then everything will be clear.'

"Henrietta said, 'I will do nothing of the sort. I came here to see my papa, and what's clear is that you *are not* my papa.'

"The monster whispered, 'Please. I need this.'

"Henrietta crossed her arms and turned away and said, 'I don't care what you need.'

"And the monster didn't say anything else. When Henrietta looked for a way to escape, she heard a whimper, then she heard something crash to the ground. When she turned, the monster was lying down with the pen in its ear. The pen was filling up with the shiniest ink she'd ever seen.

"Every little fear Henrietta had was suddenly gone. All she wanted was that beautiful pen. She grabbed it from the ground. You must understand, Henrietta wasn't the type of kid who did whatever people told her to do, especially nasty monsters. She did what she wanted to do. But what she wanted to do, what she wanted more than anything, was to pour that ink on her body.

"So she held the pen up high and dripped the ink on her head. And she changed. Her mind filled up like a cup. With memories and thoughts and visions of magical places. Henrietta was still Henrietta, but now she was also the monster."

Polly couldn't resist interrupting at this point. "Wait! What? Hold up. She became a monster?"

Henrietta wagged a finger. "She looked like a monster—no face, no color—but she wasn't a monster. She was an angel. Doing what all the other angels before her did. Doing what she was supposed to do, what she wanted to do."

"And what's that?" Polly asked.

"Helping people who needed help. Folks who called out for her to end things. And that's what she did. Until she made a mistake."

"A mistake?"

"She helped a girl who didn't need her help. A girl who lived in a space station deep in the stars. A scientist."

"I don't understand," Polly said.

Henrietta's voice sped up, each word becoming more hurried than the one before it. "Henrietta took this girl away when this girl didn't ask to be taken away. She poured this girl's soul on her body because she wanted to know all the things the girl knew, outer space things, things that might explain why her papa died. This was wrong, wrong, wrong, and Henrietta knew it. What she should have done was pour the girl's soul in the waterfall and set her free. Because now she was Henrietta, she was the monster, but she was also the girl!"

"Took her away?" Polly asked. "A waterfall? The girl's soul? A space station? What are you talking about?"

Henrietta didn't explain. She simply started to cry. Polly had never seen Henrietta cry, and she froze. She didn't reach out to touch her friend. She didn't offer condolences. She was so confused.

Without another word, Henrietta sprinted away into the darkness. When Polly finally broke out of her daze, she followed, but wasn't sure where Henrietta had gone. Polly headed to the village and the hut, but didn't find her. She went back to the camp, but she wasn't there either.

That's when Polly recalled something from Henrietta's story: the red bush where she hid the jar. There was a small red bush about a mile upstream from the camp. Polly had always thought it strange, but she never looked at it close-up. She figured it was full of thorns like so many bushes in this scrubby wilderness.

Polly jogged upstream as fast as she could. She reached the bush within ten minutes, and sure enough, there was Henrietta. She was sitting cross-legged on the banks of the creek. She had a jar of water resting in her lap.

"Why did you tell me that story?" Polly asked. "What did it mean?"

Her face bombed out, ruined, Henrietta said, "Because it's time for someone else. I've been doing this too long. I need to find a replacement. Someone good. Someone better than me."

Raising the jar in her hands, Henrietta closed her eyes and began whispering into its opening. Moments later, the glass disappeared, and there was a cylinder of water floating in the air.

"Henrietta?" Polly asked. "What are you doing? What have you done?"

"Forever," Henrietta said as she closed her hands on the cylinder of water.

And she disappeared.

SIX YEARS (OR EONS) LATER (DEPENDING ON HOW YOU LOOK AT IT)

———•—•—

CHAPTER 22

———— ·—·—· ————

IT WOULD TAKE A WHILE. IF HE HAD TO GUESS, ALISTAIR WOULD have said that the cloud was at least three hundred feet off the ground. There were no ladders that tall around, no trees. Even the memorial tree downtown, which always seemed so towering to Alistair, was only seventy feet high.

To reach the cloud would take effort and time. Effort was hard to come by. No one, except for Dorian, was interested in helping him, not even the older Alistair, who dismissed the idea as a suicide mission.

"So you travel through this cloud to another world where some dude is waiting for you, and he's a friend of yours who's, like, a great puppet master or something, right?" the older asked. "And he's the one who captured Fiona, and lots of other kids, including some girl named Polly who's, like, the toughest girl in the universe? And what do you plan to do when you get there? How are you gonna defeat such a character?"

The conversation took place two days after the helmet had rained from the cloud. Alistair had gone to Boaz the day before and asked him to publish another story in the paper. *Meet us at the model airplane runway tomorrow at ten a.m. and help us find Fiona* was the gist of it. When tomorrow became today and the hour was closer to one in the afternoon, only three people stood on the grass runway: two Alistairs and a Dorian. To pass the time, to gain their trust, Alistair had told them about Charlie.

"I don't know exactly what I'm going to do when I see him," the younger said. "But I need to get there, because that's where he'll be waiting. This is a game to him. Everything is a game. And he wants to challenge me. And if I win, then maybe he'll let me know where Fiona is, where Chua is, where all of them are."

"He gave you a chance, though, right?" Dorian asked. "When you were in the world of clouds? You could have touched the silver and gold rain, right? Gone chin-to-chin with him? So why didn't you? Why'd you come here? Did you really think you'd find her here?"

Alistair kicked at the ground and said, "I was hoping that maybe this place held what I needed to bring her back."

"What do you mean?" Dorian asked.

"Nothing," Alistair said with a sigh. "A stupid theory that some kids had. The more I think about it, the more impossible it seems. And the more I think about it, the more I realize the real reason I came here. Charlie was right; I don't know Fiona. Not really. But I needed to know her. I needed to see the place where she spent twelve years. The place she thought was better than home."

"If this is better than your home," the older said, "then I feel sorry for you. Count me out." And he abandoned them for the air-conditioning and solitude of his car.

"Well, you still got me," Dorian said. "So how we gonna do it?"

"Too high for a ladder. A stairway that high would need to be insanely long."

"A tower?" Dorian asked.

"Is there enough material to build one? Can we even afford material?"

"Maybe not anything from town. But we could dig up some dirt and make it out of that. If we dig around here, we'll end up with trenches and holes in our way, but there's a whole mess of dirt out there in Nothingland. No one will ever charge us for that. A few holes out there won't get in anyone's way."

This is how the younger Alistair's days went.

He would wake and meet Dorian downstairs—he lived with Dorian still, in Maria's old room, for the simple reason that there wasn't anywhere else to live. The two would then drive into Nothingland, where they kept a barely functional backhoe and a rusty dump truck Dorian borrowed from a contractor who occasionally employed him to do light carpentry.

Dorian would run the backhoe, digging up chunks of the ground, which was soft and a bit sticky, like clay. Alistair would oversee his progress and direct him to the dump truck, which they'd fill to the brim.

Next they'd drive the dump truck to the runway and deposit the mounds of earth. The rest of the morning would be spent shoveling the earth and molding it into walls.

They'd break for lunch, followed by an afternoon of drawing plans. It was a work in progress, a trial by fire, and neither of them knew what they were doing.

After two weeks, they had a ten-foot-tall, leaning tower of mud.

"This ain't gonna happen," Dorian said.

"You're right," Alistair said. "How about a mountain, then? The digging is the easy part, and there's more ground than anyone knows what to do with out there in Nothingland. Let's pile it up until we can't pile it anymore."

Two weeks later, they had a mountain twenty feet high. A good start. But out in Nothingland, they struck something, and the digging stopped for the moment. Dorian climbed down from the backhoe to see what it could be. He unearthed a book.

"The Life . . . of . . . Rodrigo . . . Hermanez," Dorian said, wiping dirt from the cover.

Alistair scrambled down into the hole and reached for the book, saying, "Gimme that."

It seemed like a game to Dorian, who chuckled as he pulled the book away. "Whoa, cowboy, I wanna have a look-see first."

"I'm not sure you do," Alistair said.

"Rodrigo Hermanez was born way down in Argentina," Dorian read aloud, "on a dairy farm where he milked cows, chased chickens, and all that agricultural stuff."

"See?" Alistair said, reaching again. "It's nonsense. Rodrigo was born and raised in Thessaly. You all know that."

Pulling the book away again, Dorian said, "Who wrote this thing, anyhow?" He wiped more dirt from the cover to reveal the author's name.

Fiona Loomis.

In a booth at the local diner called the Skylark, flanked on both sides by his two small children—Doria and Felix—Rodrigo Hermanez read about his life, or a version of his life, one he didn't recognize.

Alistair had pleaded with Dorian not to show Rodrigo the book, but Dorian had asserted that "a man deserves to know what others might be saying about him." And since a man deserves such things, Dorian had called Rodrigo and invited him to the Skylark, where he handed him this curious biography.

Closing the book after reading the first few pages, Rodrigo said, "When did Fiona write this?"

"Before," Alistair explained.

"Before what?" Dorian asked.

Alistair put a hand over his face, like he was watching an awful scene in a movie—teeth being pulled, eyes being poked. "Before . . . she . . . created . . . you," he said.

Rodrigo pushed the book across the table and pulled his kids, who were fiddling with straws, closer to his ribs. "Fiona was a girl, a weird girl, a smart girl, some even called her a magical girl. But still a girl," he said, and he placed a hand over each of his kids' outer ears. "I dated her, so I should know."

Alistair took a sip of an iced tea and said, "This is not something I wanted to tell people. But it's the truth. I've had enough lies for a lifetime. People deserve the truth."

"People?" Dorian asked.

"You, him, all of this," Alistair said as he spread his arms out. "Everything is something she made up. And that book? It's about one of the original people who inspired it."

Dorian picked the book up and examined all sides of it, as if it were dangerous, as if it were infested. "There are more books like this?" Dorian asked.

"Yes," Alistair said.

"How do you know these things?" Rodrigo asked. "What if this is her making up stories about me? Because she's a fan? Because she loves me so much?"

Alistair sighed and said, "I know these things because she told me. Before she created this place, she spent a year out in Nothingland writing books about people. Some of the people she only knew stories about. Some of the people she loved. But she was trying to get to know them *all* better. She was trying to make sure they were never forgotten."

"Books about everyone?"

"No," Alistair said. "Some people."

"Were those books buried too?" Dorian asked, shaking the biography. "Like this one?"

At the counters, in the booths, there were folks Alistair recognized, others he didn't. Some he wasn't sure about. "I wish we hadn't dug out there," he said. "I should have known better. These aren't things she wanted people to read."

"If you write it, you want people to read it," Rodrigo said. "Especially if you bury it."

"And people deserve to read it," Dorian said.

It started slowly. A few people went out to Nothingland with shovels. They didn't get very far. Digging a hole with a shovel isn't easy, even when the ground is soft like clay.

"I think we oughta hold off on the mountain for a bit," Dorian said one morning as they drove to Nothingland. "Use the backhoe to help folks find more of these books."

"I'm pretty sure there isn't a book about you down there," Alistair said.

"I don't care about that," Dorian said. "I care about finding Fiona, maybe even more than you. And maybe the secret ain't in that cloud. Charlie is a bit of a con man, right? Maybe he's trying to distract us from what's down below by making us look up into the sky. You yourself said this place might have what you need to bring her back."

There was no arguing with Dorian. His mind was suddenly set. And the mountain was put on hold. Now it was solely about digging for books. Rather than moving the earth to the runway, it was placed along the borders of Nothingland.

When word spread, thanks to Boaz writing stories in the *Sutton Bulletin* with titles like "It's Only Your Life Buried Out There," bulldozers, excavators, and every truck in town showed up. A wall of dirt rose around the edge of Nothingland, and more books were found.

Chua Ling approached Alistair in the grocery store one day with the story of her life in her hand. "I don't care what's true and what's fiction," she said. "Why'd she write this?"

"Because she loved Chua," Alistair said as he filled his cart with the only thing he knew how to cook—microwavable egg rolls. "Because she missed Chua."

"But I'm Chua!" she said, storming away. "*I'm* Chua!"

There were other encounters like this. At the Skylark, on the sidewalk, in the library. Alistair was treated as Fiona's representative. People had little interest in him other than as a target for their frustrations. Some of them wanted to hear about Fiona's life before, so he told her story as best he could. It rarely helped. It frustrated some. Perplexed many. Saddened the handful who really missed her—Dorian especially.

One thing became apparent. No one was going to help him with the mountain, because they all sure as heck wanted to know what she had written about them before seeing her again. Most actually didn't care where she was, or how she got there. Her opinions were all that mattered, not her safety.

Alistair kept working on the mountain alone. All the

machinery in town was dedicated to Nothingland digs, and he didn't have access to a car. So he made do by hooking a trailer to a bicycle and ferrying loads of earth to the runway. It was slow, solitary work, but he didn't know of any other options.

It went on for a few weeks like this. Alistair lived with Dorian, though they stayed out of each other's way. Dorian still concentrated on the digs, but he was kind enough to pay Alistair a small amount of cash for doing chores around the house, which kept him fed and going. Back in the Solid World, Alistair had never trusted Dorian Loomis, but here, he owed his life to him. Dorian was one of the only people he could trust, maybe even more than he could trust himself.

The younger Alistair hardly saw the older Alistair, except for the afternoon he popped by the runway. "A mountain out of a molehill," the older said, marveling at the now thirty-foot mound.

"You're welcome to help," the younger said.

The older brushed him off. "I'm past wanting that. And I'm past wanting whatever it is they all want. Out there in Nothingland."

"What does that mean?"

"They'll end up like me," the older said as he walked away. "That's why I never told them about the tapes. My advice: build faster. Get the hell out of here while you can."

The others did end up like the older Alistair. The ones who found their own stories were bitter at first. Angry. Confused.

329

But eventually, they became sad. Withdrawn. They quit their jobs. They hardly left their houses. No one could prove that these books were the truth, but they felt like the truth. Which was enough.

The ones who didn't find their own stories kept digging. They became obsessed, until their machinery broke down and couldn't be fixed anymore. They were left with shovels, so some of them gave up. Then those ones became sad. Withdrawn. They burrowed at home.

A strange thing happened to Alistair. He stopped noticing. Days and weeks and months rolled by, and he kept building the mountain and thought about little else. Memories of the Solid World didn't visit him at all anymore. He had no contact with others except for the occasional small talk with Dorian at the house.

"How's the digging going?"

"Fine," Dorian replied. "Found other things out there. Mattresses. Clothes. And another book yesterday. *Story of Diana Kluszewski*. I'm piecing things together, bit by bit. There are things in common about these kids, you know. No one else cares, but I'm pretty sure the key to what happened to Fiona is in these stories. How 'bout you? How high are you these days?"

"A hundred and fifty feet, I'd guess. Two times as high as the highest trees, which are seventy-five feet or so."

"Halfway there. Not bad."

Halfway wasn't really halfway. The higher the mountain got, the amount of dirt needed to get it higher increased exponentially. But by this point, that was fine. Alistair was on autopilot. Building. Building. Building.

Years passed. People died. Dorian slowly became a withered old man. The older Alistair's gut grew larger, and he acquired a hunch and lost most of his hair. Chua divorced Werner and married Mike Cooney, then divorced him. Rodrigo's kids grew up and had kids of their own. Mostly, the town limped along, barely surviving.

The younger Alistair didn't age, of course, which only made everyone all the more suspicious of him. They gave him a wide berth. When he wasn't building, Alistair was eating, sleeping, occasionally reading or watching television. Book and TV selections were scant, limited to things Fiona had read or seen in the Solid World, but they worked as distractions. They taught him new vocabulary, seasoned his perspectives on things.

Twenty-five years. That's how long it took to reach higher than any natural formation or building or anything else in town. Whether he was three hundred feet high or higher, Alistair didn't know for sure. All he knew was that it was still about twenty feet to the cloud.

Dorian didn't have the strength to dig anymore, but he had a shovel-wielding skeleton crew that had moved on from Nothingland and were now digging in the town. They chopped down the memorial tree and dug under that. They tore apart houses that were left abandoned after the owners passed away and they dug. All the cars and trucks available fell into disrepair, forcing them to do everything by hand. It was almost inhuman, the obsession. Alistair had to remind himself it's because they *weren't* human. They were figments.

It was a blustery afternoon when Alistair had a rare visitor. Dorian hobbled, aided by a cane, to the base of the mountain. Under his arm, he had a dirty green metal box, an Army ammo can.

He placed the can on Alistair's trailer and unlatched it. "Tell me that you know what this is," he said. "I realize it's my old ammo can, but what's inside has got me flummoxed."

Alistair nibbled at his dirty knuckle and sighed.

"Come on, buddy, what did I dig up here?" Dorian pleaded. "Seriously and truly, tell me. You know I can't see so well anymore, even with this." Dorian handed Alistair a magnifying glass and opened the ammo can.

Inside was a tiny world, like a diorama. An island in an ocean, with little creatures scurrying around it. Alistair held the magnifying glass close. Even though it was hard to make out, he was pretty sure he saw people on the island too. Which caused him to flinch.

"It's nothing," he told Dorian. "Something Fiona created a very long time ago. Something she wanted to forget about."

"But what is it?"

Alistair closed the ammo can and picked it up. "It's nothing," he said. "The past. Meant to stay buried."

"Well, let me have it back," Dorian said. "It might hold some clues."

"No," Alistair said, and he started walking up the slope of the mountain. "I can't do that."

Dorian was too feeble to follow. "Why?" he asked.

"I don't know," Alistair called back, still climbing.

But he did know. As he climbed higher and higher, he looked out onto what used to be a home for Fiona. A place she built, a place she loved, a place that was gone. It was a landscape of destruction and decay now. Walls and piles of dirt, holes, rubble, flattened homes. All that was truly left of what she had created was tucked under Alistair's arm.

When he reached the top, he sat down and, though he had the urge to cry, he didn't cry. He sat there, cradling the box.

As the sun was setting, he had another visitor. The older Alistair appeared over a crest of dirt, huffing and hacking. He flopped his girth down next to the younger and ran a hand over his brow, using sweat to flatten the few thin patches of hair he had left.

"So what's in the box?" the older asked.

"Where Fiona used to live," the younger said. "The first place she created. A tropical paradise with a bush baby named Toby and all sorts of beautiful creatures. She shrunk it down because she decided it was silly and didn't want to think about it anymore. But she didn't want it destroyed. You can see there are tiny people living there now. Fiona talked about giving people a nice place to live, about boxing them up. I think this is where she sent the ones who decided to leave town. The ones who got jobs or ran off. The people you never saw again. Her brother. Her sister. Your dad. Your sister."

"Can I have a look?" the older asked.

The younger opened the ammo can and handed it over. As the older took it and examined the tiny island inside, the younger said, "Someone asked me a riddle once. She said, 'Let's pretend you have this magic lamp and there's a genie inside. The genie grants you three wishes. He says that one wish will come true. One wish will not come true. And one wish will backfire. It will cause the opposite to happen. Only you don't know what will happen with each wish. So what are your three wishes?'"

Still entranced by the box, the older said, "I'm not clever enough for those things."

"Neither am I," the younger said. "But give it a try anyway."

"Well," the older said, "I guess I'd wish for a ton of confidence. I'd wish for a woman to love me. And I'd wish for something like what's in this box. A paradise."

"But one of the wishes will backfire," the younger said.

"But I get one of them, right? All I need is one of them to come true. And then maybe that one wish will lead me to get the other two on my own."

"That answer," the younger said, "is supposed to tell me what type of person you are. I'm not sure why."

"It's the best answer I could think up, is all."

"I'd wish the same wish three times," the younger said.

"Wouldn't they cancel one another out?"

"That's what I used to think," the younger said. "But not if I wished to die. Death is final. As soon as the one wish for death comes true, then what happens with the other wishes doesn't matter, does it?"

The older closed the ammo can. "Well, that's morbid," he said. "So what type of person does that make you?"

"I don't know," the younger said. "But it kinda feels like I've become a cipher."

His words opened something up. The cloud let loose with snow, shining in silver and gold. And right before the snow-flakes touched his skin, the younger Alistair slipped into a memory, his first memory in twenty-five years.

1986

———— ·————·•————· ————

THE RABBIT WAS A BIRTHDAY GIFT. CHARLIE WAS TURNING
nine, and it was something he asked for, so it was something
he got.

"You feed it. You clean the cage. You make sure its water
bowl is full," his dad said, handing over a white furball with
a pink bow around its neck.

Still chewing his cake, Charlie took in the armful of rabbit and cried, "So awesome!"

The party attendance might have seemed abysmal—there
was Kyle and Alistair, of course, as well as Keri, out of
politeness—but it turned out that they were the only people
Charlie wanted to be there. They all sat, along with Charlie's parents, at a picnic table clad with a striped nylon tablecloth in the Dwyers' backyard. The cake, shaped like a tower,
was vanilla with chocolate frosting.

"So rabbits are basically like cats, but they hop, right?"

Keri asked as she dipped a finger in the icing and brought it to her mouth.

Charlie's mom winced and pulled the cake out of Keri's reach, while Charlie hugged the rabbit tighter and said, "No, genius. Rabbits aren't anything like cats. They're lagomorphs, for one. Lagomorphs and cats are sworn enemies."

"Keep him away from all those strays you feed," Kyle said.

"Duh," Charlie replied.

"He's a girl," Charlie's dad said.

"Huh?" almost everyone at the table replied.

"The rabbit is a female," he said. "At least that's what the vet told me."

"I will name her Una," Charlie announced. "It means the first of her kind."

For the next few weeks, the rabbit named Una lived in a cage made of wood and chicken wire that Charlie's father attached to Kyle's clubhouse. Una was safe from cats, as well as coyotes, which were actually the bigger concern.

Every day, Charlie would give Una vegetables and food pellets and he would let her hop through the grass as he scrubbed her cage. He had always adored cats, as far back as Alistair could remember, but he had only recently started mentioning rabbits. And yet his passion for Una seemed genuine, even if she was a sworn enemy of his beloved felines.

Alistair came upon Una's lifeless body early on a Sunday morning. Charlie was on a trip with his parents to visit a boarding school for the young and unique. Kyle had been left alone for the night and was therefore in charge of watching Una. "Can you check up on her?" Charlie had asked Alistair the day before. "I don't trust him. He's fifteen and he hardly knows how to bathe himself."

The white fur around Una's eyes was stained with blood. Frost lined the uneaten vegetables scattered throughout the cage. Alistair poked at Una with a stick, and the body yielded, but didn't react.

He sprinted to the front door of the Dwyers' house and slapped the bell. A red-eyed Kyle answered after the third insistent ring.

"Jesus, man," Kyle said. "Where's the fire?"

"I think Una's dead," Alistair said between wheezing breaths.

Kyle leaned against the door and closed his eyes. "Not possible," he mumbled. "Josie came over and we took care of that last night."

"I don't know," Alistair said. "She's bloody. She's not moving. Did you feed her?"

"Sure."

"Did you let her out in the grass and wash her cage?"

"Of course," Kyle said as he wiped his face with his hand and opened his eyes. "Well, I didn't let her out, but I hosed the whole thing down pretty good."

"You hosed it down while she was still in it?"

"Sure," Kyle said. "That's what you do with animals. I've seen them do that with elephants at the zoo."

"I think she froze to death," Alistair said. "Or had a heart attack, or something. Oh my god, what do we tell Charlie?"

"Lemme see her."

Alistair led him out back, where Kyle stumbled and had to brace himself against the clubhouse as he said, "Oh man, oh man, oh man."

Wrapping his fingers around the chicken wire at the front of the cage, Alistair gave it a gentle tug and said, "I was thinking, and this isn't what we have to do, but what if we ripped a hole in the wire? And we buried the rabbit in the swamp? Pretend like a coyote got her."

Kyle pounded a fist against the clubhouse three times, and then took three deep breaths. "If we do that," he said, "no one can ever know."

"I'm not stupid."

Kyle put a hand on Alistair's shoulder and squeezed it hard. "No one. Ever."

"I get it."

"Come with me."

Kyle led the way into the clubhouse, where he pointed at a crawl space below the floorboards. "At the bottom," he said.

Alistair reached down and pulled out a stop sign and placed it on the floor. "Is that the sign that went missing from Cheshire and—" Alistair started to say, but cut himself short.

Kyle glared at him and said, "Underneath that."

Alistair reached down and pulled out a shovel. It clanged as he dropped it on the sign. He looked up and Kyle said, "Let's get to it."

That evening, when Charlie returned home with stories about how boarding school was for snots and morons, Kyle and Alistair invited him to the backyard and showed him the hole in the wire.

"I doubt she suffered," Kyle said.

Charlie didn't gasp or cry. He simply stared at the hole, at the bloodstained cage. Then he turned away. "Circle of life," he said. "That's what she gets for being a stupid lagomorph."

"You're not upset?" Alistair asked.

Charlie patted Alistair on the cheek like he was a little kid and he said, "Don't you think I knew this would happen?"

There was another big gift that Charlie got for his birthday that year: a Nintendo. Leaving Kyle and Alistair standing in the yard, he went inside and turned it on.

Kyle kicked the clubhouse. "I've been done with this baby crap for years," he said. "You and Charlie can have it."

"What?"

"The clubhouse."

"What about the stop sign?" Alistair asked. "It's illegal to have that, right?"

Kyle rolled his eyes. "I'll chuck it out in the swamp if that makes you feel better."

"Someone could've crashed because you stole that," Alistair said. "Someone could've died."

"And that rabbit could've lived if you'd checked up on it

last night. *Could've* is a helluva lot different from *did*. We never speak of that rabbit again, understand?" Kyle said.

The air was even chillier than the night before. Shivering in a T-shirt, his silence as good as a yes, Alistair checked the sky for constellations he might know—Orion, the hunter, was a favorite. Summer was still a few weeks off, but the stars were absolute marvels that night. They went on forever.

CHAPTER 23

ICICLES DRIPPED WATER ON ALISTAIR'S FACE. HE WAS NO longer on the mountain. The memory had come and gone. The snow from the cloud had coated his skin and transported him somewhere new. On his back looking up, it might have seemed as though he were in a world of icicles, until that colorless head appeared over him and Charlie's voice filled the room.

"Twenty-five years," he said. "I have to admit, I never imagined it would take this long."

Alistair felt no need to lunge for him. He'd lost that desire somewhere along the way. He rolled over to his side and sat up. He was in a round room made of stone. There were arched windows on the walls. The ceiling was crawling with icicles.

"This is where you live?" Alistair asked.

"Shhh," Charlie whispered as he tiptoed backward across the room, as if from a sleeping baby. "Listen."

Drips on the stone floor. Muffled growls. The sound of rushing water below. And voices.

I need to go home and never come back.

I need courage.

I need to have the life I once had.

I need my mom to be healthy.

"Constant," Charlie said. "Forever and ever. *This* is where I live. Amid all this pathetic begging."

"Who are they?" Alistair asked.

"I think you refer to them as daydreamers," Charlie said, wielding the fountain pen, tapping its tip playfully on his chin. "As long as I can be what they need, or pretend to be what they need, I can go to their worlds and shut them up. Which is what *I* need. Sometimes some of them are friends and I have to take out the whole bunch as fast as possible. I don't want fearmongering, after all."

Alistair climbed to his feet. Charlie, his body lithe and colorless, was a few yards out of his reach. "So I'm supposed to touch you, right?" he asked. "Is that the idea?"

"What?" Charlie asked, and then a realization birthed a grin. "Oh, poor you. You think this is a game of tag. You misunderstood."

"You clearly said I was *It*. You were baiting me."

Charlie moved over to a window and sat on its stone sill. Placing the pen behind his ear and holding the edge, he rocked back and forth, his body dipping outside with each cycle. "You are most certainly *It*, but it's not about tagging me. You could never catch me unless I let you catch me."

343

"So is that what you're letting me do?" Cold water dripped on Alistair's head and his body seized up, but he didn't take a step. For years on the mountain, he had thought about this moment, and yet he had never decided what he was going to do. Punch Charlie? Choke Charlie? Scream at him until his vocal cords bled?

"I'm letting you realize that *I'm* the one who molded you," Charlie said. "Not Fiona. She may have been able to create things, but I help things evolve. Her creations were no match for what you became. *You*, Alistair, are my masterpiece."

"So being *It* was being your toy? Your cipher?" Alistair asked, barely opening his mouth, the words leaking out like gasoline fumes from a car wreck.

"No," Charlie said. "You were never a cipher. You destroyed Fiona's world, that's true. But you're bigger than a cipher. Better. You're *It*. Only you've refused to acknowledge you've always been *It*, that you were born to be *It*."

Alistair rubbed his eyes with his thumb and forefinger, and through measured breaths he said, "You told a story at that school about being born to do things and making choices. You capture all these worlds and then you choose to destroy them. What . . . in the hell . . . is the point?"

Charlie kept rocking, dipping farther and farther out the window. "You said it yourself to that penguin all those years ago," Charlie said with a chuckle. "I do it for fun."

Alistair shook his head quickly, tightly. "No. No. I'm older now. I know it's not that simple."

"Sometimes it is."

"What happened to her? Where is she?"

"You want me to tell you a story about it?"

"Yes."

"You *need* me to tell you a story about it?"

"Yes!"

Charlie chuckled and said, "It's better to show than to tell." And he let go of the sill and fell backward out of the window. There, then gone—like a firefly, like a memory.

Faster than he'd ever moved, Alistair sprinted to the window, but the floor was icy and he started to slide. He couldn't slow down and he struck the sill with his hip and toppled through the window as well.

The storm in his gut that came from falling was something he hadn't felt in ages. It had been the ultimate in terror before, but now it was the ultimate in relief, the hurricane that flattens everything—the fear, the doubt, everything. Fluttering through the cold void, looking down at a shimmering pool and a bottomless waterfall, he knew he had gotten as far as he was going to get in Aquavania.

During his years building the mountain, he had looked up the words *ambit* and *cipher* in a dictionary. An ambit was the outer limits of something, the boundary. A cipher was a nonentity, an empty vessel. That was where he was: the edge, the end. That was who he was: a nobody, a guy who would die here, whose body would probably end up in Fiona's basement without any explanation, no one to ever tell his story.

Flipping over changed all that. Alistair's body somersaulted, gifting him an upside-down view of what was behind him. The tower was made of stone, but you would have only known that from the inside. Every square inch of the outside, except for the windows at the top, was infested with ciphers. Creatures perched, or clung, or dangled, or simply stood there horizontally, defying gravity, their claws, tentacles, spikes, and wings sticking into the void.

A giant hand shot out from the madness and snatched Alistair before his back could crash into the water. It pulled him toward the tower as fast as he had been falling from it. The storm in his gut shifted to terror again, because this clearly wasn't over. Limbs swung and jaws snapped. Roars and hisses that had been muffled by the sound of the waterfall were now too close to ignore. Thick saliva pummeled his face, and fur stuck to the saliva. At first, he could see the individual ciphers, but in a blink, he was in the thick of them. No faces, no shapes. A stew of monster, dense and repugnant.

So he didn't realize it when the giant hand pulled him through the pile of monsters and set him down on a pile of monster parts. It took Charlie's voice to clue him in.

"You have your mountain, and I have mine," he said.

The hand had brought Alistair back inside the tower, into a room markedly bigger and significantly warmer than the one at the top. There was no floor, at least not one Alistair could see. Like a dragon on his gold, he was standing on Charlie's massive treasure, only this treasure consisted of legs, arms, heads, teeth, and every other animal body part imaginable. Charlie was there too, of course, but standing between him and Alistair there was someone else.

Polly Dobson.

Alistair could only recognize her face and the tattered remains of the space suit that clung to her torso. The rest of her body was deformed. Most notably, her arms and hands were enormous, bigger than King Kong's, big enough to snatch two boys out of a void and pull them back into a tower and set them on a peak of grotesqueries.

"The familiars, the daemons, whatever you want to call them," Charlie went on, "you know, those little animal guides like Baxter the penguin and Potoweet the hummingbird? They make the very best ciphers. It's because it's in their nature to be subservient. Swimmers, on the other hand—I rarely ever make ciphers out of them. Too ornery, too independent. Best to suck out their souls and be done with them. For Polly, I made an exception."

Polly didn't speak. She was hunched over, breaths straining out of her like curdled milk through a tight spout.

Breathing wasn't easy for Alistair either, but he managed to ask, "How long has she been here?"

"As long as you've been out there. She came for revenge. Isn't that sweet? Turns out her friend Henrietta was the Whisper before me. For a long time, I thought the Whisper before me was a boy, because of the raspy voice and the crush it had on some girl named Polly in the Solid World. But there are always surprises, even when you have access to all the information."

There was nowhere safe for Alistair to look. Every sight turned his stomach. "She's been your . . . zombie?" he asked.

"She's been my experiment. I've made her into thousands of ciphers. She's been a model, a drawing board, a department store mannequin. You remember that Kyle cipher I sent after you? Well, I tested the design on her first."

Charlie walked over to Polly and started waving his hands in front of her chest. A tornado of body parts erupted from the mountain and swirled around her, and when it subsided, the spitting image of Kyle was standing in her place.

"Didn't want to lose my favorite test dummy, obviously," Charlie went on. "So I sent a penguin sacrifice to that space station instead."

If he had a pair of those X-ray specs, Alistair might've been able to see Polly's bones beneath the skin, just as he'd seen Baxter's bones. "You're sick," Alistair said.

"No," Charlie said with a laugh. "*This* is sick." He waved his hands again, over and under each other—exactly like that night when he waved his hands above the bullet wound in his brother's stomach. The tornado of body parts spun around, and when they calmed, there was a giant rabbit with bleeding eyes standing between the two boys.

"Stop it!" Alistair screamed.

"Come on," Charlie said. "I'm only having fun. This girl has no problem with revenge. So have your revenge on her. Don't you remember how she left you high and dry on Hadrian's pedestal? Tell me what to turn her into and I'll do it. I've collected every body part imaginable from the worlds I watch over. Your imagination is the only limit, Alistair. Whatever you want. Remember, you've become who you are because of me, but I've also become who I am because of you. We owe each other everything."

"Fiona," Alistair snapped. "You were supposed to tell me what happened to her."

Charlie clucked his tongue and said, "Show, don't tell." Then he moved his mangled hands in front of the bloody-eyed rabbit—in front of Polly—and the tornado sprouted and collapsed, and a version of Fiona was now standing there.

Sad-eyed and low-shouldered, she was in a purple dress and a neon green coat. Most of the details were right—the crooked nose, the hair so black it almost didn't exist, the thin and awkward limbs—and yet this wasn't Fiona. It had been twenty-five years since Alistair had seen her, since he'd even been able to picture her, but with one look at this imposter, the real Fiona invited herself back into his head.

"That is not her!" Alistair shouted.

Charlie ignored him, turned to the Fiona cipher, and said, "Exactly as we rehearsed."

The Fiona cipher nodded limply as Charlie waved his hands again. This time the tornado of body parts didn't surround her. Instead, legs, arms, and other appendages interlocked, twisted, and bound together to form the shapes of bookshelves, a dresser, a headboard, and a mattress. They became a bedroom, the most colorful, alive, and yet macabre bedroom imaginable. They became the set of a play, and Charlie and the Fiona cipher were center stage.

"I am a silly girl who would rather live a pretend version of life than a real version of life," the Fiona cipher droned.

"That's not fair!" Alistair shouted.

Charlie wagged a finger at him. *Settle down,* that finger said. *We will not tolerate hecklers.*

"To bed with me, but first I will make a wish," the Fiona cipher said. "I need to see the Riverman."

Charlie's head perked up and he stepped forward, spinning his hands theatrically. "You rang?" he said.

"The last time I encountered you, you informed me that you spared my soul because you wanted me to give you Alistair. Well, I will not do it. I simply will not," the Fiona cipher responded, her performance more mechanical and pitiful with every badly scripted word.

Charlie's performance was the opposite. It was high-stepping and enthusiastic. Hammy. "Because you have a crush on him?" he sang.

The Fiona cipher laid her body down on the maniac bed, arms draped back, eyes closed. "Because he needs to see the world for what it really is. He needs to see what you are capable of. Before he can really live his life, he needs to realize who you really are."

"Who I am?" Charlie said with a snort. "I am a substitute, a temp, a seat filler. All I am is what Alistair was supposed to be. Which is this!"

A jolt. Charlie leapt onto the bed and plunged the fountain pen into the Fiona cipher's ear. His lips were on the pen before Alistair could stop him, and he was sucking out another soul. Polly's soul.

Standing on the pile of body parts was like standing on a heap of junk, but running on it was like running on quicksand. Alistair tried to kick off, but his feet sank, and soon he was knee-deep in the bits and pieces.

In seconds, the pen was full of sparkling liquid and Fiona's features fell away. The face and body looked like Polly's for a moment, and then it wasn't a face and body at all. It split apart into thousands of tiny bits, like snowflakes, which flurried and evaporated into the air.

Holding the pen aloft, Charlie announced, "There's a way this story could have ended. I could have poured Fiona's soul into my waterfall, and she could have returned to the Solid World without any memories of Aquavania. Her part in the process would be over. She would have contributed her creations to the mix and moved on."

Alistair strained, but he only sank deeper into the body ball-crawl. "Please. I get it. You don't have to do this anymore. Put Polly's soul into the waterfall. Let her go home."

"Show, don't tell," Charlie said again. "And I need to *show* you what I did to Fiona."

The ink dripped leisurely, like the rubber cement Alistair had poured into that wasp hole back when they were both so little. If Alistair could have moved, he might have stopped Charlie. A big, and impossible, if.

The drops finally reached their destination, and when they touched Charlie's colorless skin, his body shimmered for a moment and he howled, "You don't realize how good it feels! To know everything that someone else knows. To feel all the things that someone else feels. To become someone else."

More struggling. Frantic and pointless, because Alistair only sank deeper—beaks, gills, hooves, poking at his ribs. "You are not Fiona! You could never be her!"

"I *am* Fiona. And I am Polly. I am Chua, I am Boaz, I am every soul that hasn't been sent back to the Solid World. You asked me once where Fiona was and I told you I didn't know. I wasn't lying. Because that's like asking a guy where his soul lives."

Even without struggling, Alistair sank deeper. His chin rubbed against dinosaur heads, eagle talons, leopard tails. "Then show some kindness and let them go," he whimpered. "What if you throw yourself into the waterfall? Will they all be released?"

"Possibly, but then I'd be released too, and who would take my place?" Charlie asked. "There always has to be a Whisper."

"Does there?"

Charlie moved closer and crouched down, his head inches away from Alistair's. "Of course. And if you weren't ready before, then I think I've molded you enough that you're ready now."

"No. Please, no."

"I forgive you, Alistair," Charlie whispered.

"What? That's doesn't make—"

"For all of it. For not having the courage to tell the truth so many, many times. For not having the courage to do what has to be done."

With that, Charlie took the pen and he plunged it into his own ear, and that wonderfully horrible body of his collapsed. It spilled over everything, a stain on a paisley pile.

The tip of the pen remained lodged in his ear, and the other end was tantalizingly close to Alistair's head. Strain his neck forward a bit and Alistair could get it in his mouth. "Charlie," he said softly. "Are you . . . ?"

No response.

Alistair had stopped sinking. Like a shipwreck survivor, his head poked up at the surface. Outside, he could hear the yelps and howls of the ciphers, the rush of the waterfall, but those sounds weren't overwhelming. He had the luxury of thought for a moment, the chance for contemplation.

And yet he didn't take that chance. Instead, he used his tongue to pull the pen to his mouth and he treated it like a straw, sucking, yanking at Charlie's soul, or whatever his soul had become. It was instinct, it was anger, it was twenty-five years of not knowing what to do.

When sparkling liquid filled the pen, Charlie disintegrated exactly as Polly had disintegrated, like ash caught in a breeze and melding with the sky. And all those other body parts—the horns, the fins, the trunks—took to the air too, but they didn't break apart. They streamed out of the windows like clouds of bats, so fast that Alistair didn't realize he was sitting on a stone floor until the pile was gone and he was alone. Except for the pen, still poised between his teeth.

He dashed straight to a window and poked his head out to see that the ciphers were gone. Where to, it wasn't clear. There was the void and there was the tower, and at the base, there was the pool and the bottomless waterfall. That was it. Nothing else.

Pen now clutched to his chest, Alistair located some stairs along the edge of the room and he hurried down them until he reached the bottom and the entranceway of the tower. The roar of the waterfall was nearly deafening now, but somehow voices found their way to him. They were the voices of day-dreamers.

I need to say goodbye to my creations.

I need my friends to forgive me for the thing I did.

I need love.

I need an end. I need the end.

Alistair stood in the arched entrance, at the edge of the pool. He gazed at his reflection, the face of a boy, a kid not even thirteen years old. The reflection wasn't quite a lie, but it was an illusion. That boy didn't exist anymore. He'd hardly existed when he had washed up in Mahaloo so long ago.

Alistair knew what he had to do. There was only one place his story could lead. He lifted the pen and, rather than looking at it, he watched the reflection. As the ink stretched and yearned and finally touched the skin of his face, the face disappeared.

In its place, many faces flashed in the reflection. For a

moment, there was a girl with a scar on her cheek, followed by a boy, who looked similar to the girl, as if he could be her brother. Then there was a procession of visages. Boys and girls, different shades and shapes. Werner, Chua, Rodrigo, Boaz, and Polly.

Among them was Fiona. Fiona, her dark eyes staring up from the water, her crooked nose perfectly crooked. Fiona, not a fake one, the one from home, the one from his memories. She mouthed something.

I'm here. We're all here. You can bring us back.

Finally, there was Charlie. The real Charlie, the kid Charlie, not the monster Charlie. He didn't mouth anything, but he looked up with jealousy and admiration, with anger and love.

And when Charlie's face was gone, when all the faces were gone, there was one clear, unchanging reflection. There in the pool was the Riverman. There was the Whisper.

November 19 and 20, 1989

————— ·❖· —————

A whisper is a story with many endings. Joyful, tragic, inevitable—it depends on who's listening. There are whispers in the water, but only some of the time. There also must be silence.

It was dead quiet in Fiona Loomis's basement when Alistair stood with his hand on the boiler, which was tall and round again, complete. After all he'd been through, he was back where he began.

Climbing the stairs, he tried to find himself, his own memories, within the maelstrom of his mind. A boy's face in the water—that was his anchor. A boy's face looking up at him.

In Fiona's room, he loaded a tape into her tape player, pressed Record, and started to talk, because he needed to talk. He needed to remember who he was, who he had been before. When he finished talking, it was the next day, but the sun hadn't risen yet.

So he crept out of the Loomises' back door and snuck all the way home through the darkness of neighbors' lawns. In the swamp behind his house, next to a rock that looked like a frog, by the light of police cars moving up and down the street, he buried the tape recorder with the tape still in it. Then he walked around to the front yard and sat down in the grass. He looked up at the stars.

That's where his parents found him. That's where the police, flashlights head-high and angled down, joined them. Among the barrage of questions, the one they all kept asking was, "Where's Charlie? Where's Charlie?"

They might as well have been asking him where his soul was. Alistair didn't make a sound.

Acknowledgments

Second volumes in trilogies are notoriously tricky things. They often feel like they're, for lack of a better term, *all middle*. When I wrote **The Whisper**, however, I focused on the new. My daughter, Hannah, arrived in the world as I was trying to figure out how to make a crazy, unwieldy sequel come together, and her beautiful, babbling presence inspired me to treat it as an origin story—not just of the Riverman and Aquavania, but also of Alistair and Charlie's relationship and of Fiona's reluctant journey into adulthood. I wanted to show why the first volume was told the way it was told, and I wanted readers to anticipate the third volume with a fresh perspective on events. If I achieved that goal, I certainly didn't do it alone. The following people guided and encouraged me along the way:

Joy Peskin was the first person who read **The Whisper**, and she infused it with her brilliance and a healthy dose of

confidence and clarity, which is what all books need. Therefore, in my humble opinion, she should edit all books. I'm not
sure she has the time, though. Maybe with Angie Chen's help
she can do it. Actually, together, they definitely can.

Michael Bourret, the man I'm honored to call my agent, continued to trust me, advise me, and keep me sane through the
entire publishing process. Why? It's because he's a sorcerer.
Everyone at Dystel & Goderich, including Lauren Abramo,
dabbles in sorcery, actually. How else would they understand
these byzantine contracts and represent such an awe-
inspiring group of authors?

Beth Clark had an even trickier job designing this book
than she did with the first volume, considering all the multiple narratives and their unique appearances. Did she pull
it off? Come on! Of course she did.

Yelena Bryksenkova created yet another stunning cover
that I'm sure people will tell me is stunning, when they really should be telling her. Now they have no excuse. Tell her:
yelenabryksenkova.com

Mary Van Akin has been an advocate like no other. She's
tireless and talented and you better watch out, because she
will make you read this book. Perhaps she already did, by
handing you the copy you're holding right now. If so, thank
her and the rest of the gang at Macmillan Kids for me.

Kate Hurley and Karla Reganold have taught me a lot
about writing with their essential copyedits. I would look like
a fool without them. I really wood (sic).

Some other authors read **The Riverman** and said some

amazingly kind things about it. Jack Gantos was the first, and I'm still flabbergasted that his words graced the cover of volume one. Following in his sizable wake were Kurtis Scaletta, Laurel Snyder, Nova Ren Suma, Bryan Bliss, Steve Brezenoff, Kelly Barnhill, Kim Baker, Stephanie Kuehn, Kate Milford, Robin Wasserman, Jeff Kay, Laura Marx Fitzgerald, Stephanie Bodeen, Dan Poblocki, and many others I'm sure I'm forgetting. I hope they read this book too. And I hope you read their books, because they are better books than this one.

All the bloggers, librarians, teachers, journalists, booksellers, festival organizers, and fans who have reached out to me and helped me share my stories, I don't know what I'd do without you. Probably pursue a career in break dancing, which would be unwise.

Thank you to my family. To Jim, Gwenn, Pete, and the extended Wells and Evans clans. To all the Amundsens and Starmers out there. To Tim, Toril, Dave, Jacob, and Will, because this is a story of siblings and kids. And to Mom and Dad, the finest and most caring creators I know.

Finally, Cate and Hannah, you inspire me every day, and I love you dearly. Now put down this book and let's go get into some more adventures together!

GOFISH

AARON STARMER

What did you want to be when you grew up?
A movie director or a soccer player. Preferably both. Maybe I'd make a soccer movie.

When did you realize you wanted to be a writer?
Very early on, probably in first grade when my teacher let the class write and perform our own play. I proposed that we write a play called *The Magic Leopard,* and everyone agreed. Coincidentally (wink, wink), I just happened to have a leopard costume left over from Halloween that fit me perfectly. So I got to play the lead!

What's your most embarrassing childhood memory?
An "accident" in first grade. We'll just leave it at that.

What's your favorite childhood memory?
Exploring the forests near my home, building forts, and making movies on camcorders with my friends.

As a young person, who did you look up to most?
My parents. They've always been kind, clever, and encouraging, which I hope I can be with my daughter.

What was your favorite thing about school?
Class discussions. I loved to talk about books and if they had any deeper or hidden meanings. I still love that.

What were your hobbies as a kid? What are your hobbies now?
As a kid, I liked making up songs and stories (big surprise). These days, I like to take a break from stories by cooking, jogging, and doing outdoorsy things like kayaking and skiing.

Did you play sports as a kid?
I was a big soccer player when I was young and then picked up lacrosse when I was older. I played lacrosse all the way through college.

What was your first job, and what was your "worst" job?
My first job was as a soccer referee but it only lasted a few games. My worst job was as a liquor store clerk, a combination of boring and depressing.

What book is on your nightstand now?
Code Name Verity by Elizabeth Wein. Lovely novel.

How did you celebrate publishing your first book?
By writing another!

Where do you write your books?
I write them at home, at the library, or in a café, depending on where and when I can find a quiet spot for a few hours.

What sparked your imagination for The Riverman Trilogy?
I wanted to write a story about what would happen if a girl like Alice (from *Alice in Wonderland*) came home. What would her friends think of her story? Would they believe her or would they think she was going crazy?

Did you have any girls next door growing up?
No, and I'm glad I didn't! There were plenty of girls I had crushes on, but they all lived in other neighborhoods. If they had lived nearby, it would have been torture because I was so shy, and even though I'd see them constantly, I probably never would have had the guts to talk to them.

What got you interested in fantasy/magical realism?
I'm not sure. I've always liked stories that are very realistic but then the reality twists or bends in a way that challenges the characters.

How did you pick the names Alistair and Fiona?
I'm not entirely sure where the names come from, but I know the idea of "staring" is important for Alistair. When you stare at something, you look at it intensely, but you don't necessarily understand it. The name Fiona might have originated from an e-mail newsletter I often receive from the Scottish tourism board. It always says it comes from someone named Fiona. Scotland reminds me of a medieval fantasyland, and I think the name Fiona will now always have a fantasy connotation to me.

What challenges do you face in the writing process, and how do you overcome them?
The hardest part is making the story emotionally believable, logically believable, and entertaining all at the same

time. I'm not sure I accomplished that, but I hope I came close.

Which of your characters is most like you?
I guess Alistair is most like me, though I'm sure there are bits of Charlie in my personality. I'd like to say I'm like Fiona, but I'm not sure I'm that brave.

What makes you laugh out loud?
My daughter laughing.

What do you do on a rainy day?
Read a book, go to the movies, and cook. Ideally all three.

What's your idea of fun?
Exploring a foreign landscape or city, then sitting down for a great meal with family and friends.

What is your favorite word?
Orangutan. I just like saying it. And they seem like a nice bunch of primates.

If you could live in any fictional world, what would it be?
Anyplace without talking animals. Talking animals kind of freak me out.

What's your favorite song?
It changes all the time, but while writing *The Riverman*, I'd say "Thirteen" by Big Star was the most influential.

Who is your favorite fictional character?
Cool Hand Luke!

What was your favorite book when you were a kid? Do you have a favorite book now?
As a kid, it was probably *George's Marvelous Medicine*, one of the more obscure (and pitch-dark) Roald Dahl books. These days, it's Truman Capote's *In Cold Blood*, which is a master class in writing. Precise, poetic, and powerful.

What's your favorite TV show or movie?
It's hard to beat *Breaking Bad* for TV: a perfect TV show. And though I don't think it's my favorite, the one movie that always makes me smile is Richard Linklater's *Dazed and Confused*. It came out my senior year of high school so it probably hit me at just the right time.

If you were stranded on a desert island, who would you want for company?
My wife and daughter, of course. Don't be cruel. Don't make me choose! The island is big enough for all three of us, isn't it?

If you could travel anywhere in the world, where would you go and what would you do?
I've always wanted to hike the Inca Trail to Machu Picchu.

If you could travel in time, where would you go and what would you do?
I'd go see the dinosaurs. And I'd probably do a lot of running and screaming.

What's the best advice you have ever received about writing?
Don't ever be satisfied with something that's "good enough." If it's only "good enough," then it's not good enough.

What advice do you wish someone had given you when you were younger?

Slow down. Be patient. Everyone has a different timeline for writing. It's not a race.

Do you ever get writer's block? What do you do to get back on track?

All the time. Only cure is to keep writing. I sit down and force myself to do it.

What do you want readers to remember about your books?

That, as readers, they were surprised and they were emotionally involved in my stories.

What would you do if you ever stopped writing?

I doubt I'll stop, but if I do, I hope I find a new creative outlet. Maybe renovating an old house. Maybe gardening. Maybe painting.

If you were a superhero, what would your superpower be?

I'd have to agree with Fiona in *The Whisper*: stopping time.

Do you have any strange or funny habits? Did you when you were a kid?

Whenever I'm anxious about something, for example, if someone is late to meet me somewhere, I become obsessed with counting things. Birds, cars, etc. Alistair does the same thing in *The Riverman*.

What do you consider to be your greatest accomplishment?
Each time I finish a book, it's a bigger accomplishment than I ever thought I could manage when I was younger. I started and gave up on writing at least half a dozen books before I ever finished my first one.

What do you wish you could do better?
Sing. And play an instrument. Any instrument. At all.

What would your readers be most surprised to learn about you?
That my best subject in school was always math. I only got average grades in English because I've always been a slow reader. But I was never that interested in math. Maybe because there are right and wrong answers and I like answers (and characters) that fall somewhere in between.

FIRST FIONA LOOMIS,

then Charlie Dwyer. How did these kids go missing?
Who really shot Kyle Dwyer? What does Alistair know,
and why won't he tell anyone about it? Keri Cleary
and the rest of the world want to know. But will they
believe what Alistair has to say?

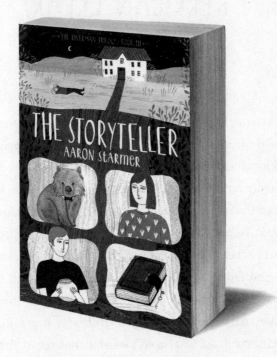

Read on for an excerpt of

►—·» THE STORYTELLER «·—◄

THE CHRONICLES OF KERRIGAN CLEARY

———— ·◆· ————

SOMETIMES I'M A SISTER WHO GIVES ADVICE AND TEASES AND all of that, and sometimes I'm just a girl who wonders how the kid who sleeps in the next room could ever be related to her. Only natural, right? We all love our brothers, in spite of the fact that none of us has a clue what's really in their hearts.

Even before Fiona Loomis took off, or got killed, or who knows . . . before this neighborhood was all sirens, search parties, and ladies standing by their windows at all hours . . . weeks before someone shot Kyle Dwyer in the stomach, my brother, Alistair, had changed. Puberty: it got him and it got him good. At least that's what I thought at first. That's not what I think now. Because when they found him in our front yard, looking up at the stars, that wasn't the boy I knew, and that wasn't even the one I didn't know yet. That was someone from outer space.

Here's what we can say so far: Kyle Dwyer will live. For

now. He's in a coma, so he isn't talking. Can't tell us who shot him. My money is on Charlie because, well, he's Charlie, and Charlie has always been a bit off. But Charlie is nowhere to be found, and the police bagged up Alistair's wet and bloody clothes. They say Alistair is the one who made the 911 call.

"It's not how it looks," Alistair told me two nights ago as he stood in our hallway, dripping wet and terrified. "Just make sure they know it's not how it looks."

I didn't make sure "they" knew anything. I love the kid, but he has to speak for himself. He has to start talking. He put a padlock on his mouth, though. Swallowed the key. Mom and Dad think he's still in shock. It's only been a couple of days, so they may be right. A psychologist tried to get him to open up and will try again. The police gave it a try too. Nothing doing. Not enough evidence to arrest him, I guess, but they can't help but think this has something to do with Fiona Loomis.

Everyone thinks that.

The town prays for Kyle Dwyer. A sentence I thought I'd never write.

The town misses Charlie Dwyer. Another sentence that tests the laws of logic.

The town is sure my brother shot someone in the gut. Ding, ding, ding! That's three in a row.

Oh, the town. Forgot to tell you about that. The town is Thessaly, up here in the forehead of New York State, where no one notices us until a couple of kids go *poof*.

Oh, and me. I'm Kerrigan Cleary. Keri to friends. I'll admit,

Keri Cleary is a bit of a tongue twister. *Keri Cleary carried cherries for cheery chipmunks.* Say that ten times fast. What can I do, though? It's the name I got and I can't get another.

Oh, and one more thing. I haven't even told you the date yet, which I guess is pretty much necessary for this sort of . . . endeavor. I hesitate to call this a diary, even though that's what it is. Hopefully it becomes more than that. A place to confess. A place to tell stories. Truth and fiction.

Anyway, I'm writing this on:

TUESDAY, 11/21/1989
EVENING

Which is two days after Kyle was shot and Charlie disappeared. A day after they found my brother sitting in our yard, looking up at the stars. Hours after I started thinking up a story about a wombat.

Yes, a wombat.

That's yet another thing. There are no wombats here in Thessaly, at least that I know of. Most of my neighbors probably don't even have a clue what a wombat is. For the record, it's a marsupial, which means it has a pouch like a kangaroo or koala, and lives in Australia. It looks a bit like a woodchuck, but it isn't related. Not even close.

How much wom could a wombat bat if a wombat could bat wom?

Dumb joke. Forget it.

The story is the important thing. In it, this brother and

sister find a wombat on the side of the road, and the wombat has a sign around her neck that reads: PERFECTLY FINE WOMBAT. This is the type of story where kids believe signs like that, so they take her home and make her their pet.

I don't think I'm ready to write any of it down yet, but I do have a pretty good idea how it'll end. In a waterfall. Images and ideas have been crashing into me like a meteor shower for the last day, and the image of a waterfall is the clearest. The story starts with a brother and a sister on a road. It ends with a wombat and a waterfall. That's what I've got so far.

I've never thought of myself as a writer. Don't get me wrong, I've written stories before. For school. A few times for fun. But this is the first time I've really felt like I needed to do it. I'm finding out that if you have the ending from the get-go, then you're in good shape. Problem is, I rarely have the ending from the get-go.

Here, for instance, is a different story, a shorter story, one about endings that doesn't really have an ending. I don't care. That won't stop me from writing it.

THE ENDING

———— ✦ ————

Justine Barlow was a runner. She wore sweat suits. She drank Gatorade. Every morning, when her cuckoo clock cheeped six times, she got up, got out of the house, clipped a Walkman to her waistband, stretched against a tree, hopped in place a few times, and then set off into her neighborhood.

It cleared her head. It kept her heart healthy, which was important because hers was a good heart. She gave money to the homeless, even when they weren't begging. She said "Good morning" to people and meant it.

Why not? Mornings *were* good. Cold mornings, rainy ones. It didn't matter. They were new beginnings. Justine had recently graduated from college, was living on her own for the first time, and had her entire life ahead of her. "Each day is a blank page," she told people. "A fresh thing to write on. Have fun with it."

Running was hard work, but it was fun too. The

sounds—the barks, beeps, and buzzes—always entertained and they were never the same, even if her route was, a four-mile loop that passed by the school and the reservoir, through the center of town and back home past the rickety old houses on Palmer Street. The images were always different too. The trees that went from green to brown to white to pink to green, depending on the season. The babies who went from slings to strollers to feet to bikes. Change. Beauty. Life. All that crap.

And death. That came later.

It started with one baby bird, clear-feathered and dead on the sidewalk beneath an oak tree. *Poor little thing must have fallen from her nest,* Justine thought. She even considered burying it, giving it a proper funeral, but she knew that wasn't how nature was supposed to work. A stray cat or raccoon would eat it and poop it out, and then the poop would become dirt and plants would grow from the poop and other birds would eat the plants. This was called the circle of life.

So the next morning, when she saw two dead birds on the sidewalk, she thought, *Poor little things,* and she ran on.

The next morning she saw four. *Poor little things.* The cats and raccoons were going to be plump as can be.

It kept doubling, though. Eight the next day. Then sixteen. Thirty-two. Sixty-four dead birds by the end of the week, all along the same running route.

Justine was disturbed. "Have you noticed a lot of dead birds lately?" she asked her friend Laura.

"Always see some in the spring," Laura said. "It's a shame. The world is a tough place."

"How many have you seen this spring?" Justine asked.

"I don't know. Normal amount, I guess. I haven't counted."

Justine had been counting. She had started by keeping tabs in her head, but now she put little check marks in a pocket notebook as she ran.

One hundred and twenty-eight baby birds the next day. Two hundred and fifty-six the next.

Was this an omen of something worse to come? How could other people not be noticing? She asked around. "What's with the birds?"

People would reply by looking into the cloudless sky and shrugging.

The birds weren't imaginary. They were flesh and blood. Cold flesh and cold blood, that is. Justine knew because she poked them with her finger. There weren't enough cats and raccoons to possibly eat them all, so she started scooping the bodies up in plastic grocery bags like little logs of dog poop. Or at least that's what it looked like to her neighbors.

"You probably have yourself one of those Great Danes," a postman joked as Justine jogged past with two sagging plastic bags.

Strange thing to say, Justine thought. *If that's the case, then where's the dog? I don't just run around scooping poop. No sir. This is death. Something serious is afoot.*

"Aren't you worried?" Justine asked him. It wasn't the type of question she normally posed. For her entire life up until that point, she believed in a world without worry.

"Worried about what?" the postman asked.

"All the death."

He too looked up at the sky, but he kissed his fingers. "Our time comes when our time comes," he said, and returned to his route.

Justine returned to her route, but she couldn't run anymore. Too many birds to pick up. When she made it home, she buried them all in a hole in her backyard as a suspicious neighbor boy watched from a perch in a tree house.

"It'll be okay," she assured him, but he didn't respond. Maybe it was the wobble in her voice, the tone that said it would, in fact, not *be okay*, that it was actually going to be pretty damn horrible.

Because Justine could do the math: 512; 1,024; 2,048; 4,096; 8,192. That was just one more week's worth if it kept doubling, and she was sure it would. It meant in two more weeks there would be a billion dead birds. A month after that? She couldn't fathom such a number. Enough to cover the entire earth, she suspected. It seemed biblical. Beyond biblical.

She locked herself in the house. She started making phone calls. The police, senators' offices, her parents.

"What will we do to stop it?" she asked.

They all laughed her off. "You're too sensitive," her father said. "Heck, your mother's cat alone probably kills one hundred birds a year. These things have a way of balancing themselves out."

Two weeks before, she would have agreed. Two weeks

before, she wouldn't have boarded up her windows. But that's what she did now.

The next day, the birds started showing up in her house. In the toilet, down the chimney, in the air-conditioning ducts. The numbers held true. She ticked them off in her notebook and filled the bathtub with the bodies.

There would be no more running. Mornings weren't *good* anymore. There was only the inevitable sunrise and the inevitable double dose of dead baby birds. Within a few days the bathroom was full. Justine didn't dare look out her windows. Not because she feared seeing more dead birds outside, but because she feared seeing none.

She was the problem. *She* was the cause of all this. They followed *her*. Was this punishment for her positivity? Or was she simply going crazy? Whatever the case, she couldn't face the world anymore. Each day was definitely not a blank page. It was a black page. And it didn't matter what you wrote on it; it would always be black.

Within five more days, the birds filled the house. There was nowhere to stand, to eat, to sleep. Justine huddled in the corner, surrounded by the stinking mess.

I can't do it, she thought. *I can't go on like this.*